COLD COGNITION

K.A.

Suite 300 - 990 Fort St
Victoria, BC, V8V 3K2
Canada

www.friesenpress.com

First Edition — 2016

ISBN
978-1-4602-8923-5 (Hardcover)
978-1-4602-8924-2 (Paperback)
978-1-4602-8925-9 (eBook)

1. FICTION, SCIENCE FICTION, APOCALYPTIC & POST-APOCALYPTIC

Distributed to the trade by The Ingram Book Company

Dearest Danielle Renata Ruth Schafer,

First of all, let me say that you have a very long name. Second of all, let me say thank you for being my life-long best friend and always supporting my crazy dreams and ideas. You are the best and I love you very much! We still have many more crazy-marvelous-unforgettable adventures ahead of us! Te amo ♡

KA

Thank you to the amazing photographer & artist,
Hannah Lacrampe, for allowing her incredible artwork to grace the front cover.

Also, thank you to my wonderful parents who forced me to
learn how to read and write – hopefully they don't regret it…

Chapter One

"Thank you again! That was quite an amazing experience!" the enthusiastic elderly man said as he shook my hand.

"The pleasure is mine! I'm glad that you had so much fun!" I had to yell to be heard over the group of eighty-something howling sled dogs behind me.

"I will definitely recommend this company to anyone who is wanting to go dog sledding," the man said, still smiling.

"Thank you so much sir! That would be awesome! Enjoy the rest of your trip."

The man thanked me once more before turning away, heading to the shuttle that would take him back down the mountain into town.

"Hey, Teslin!" I turned towards the voice yelling my name. It was Namao, my boss. She was about five metres from me, in the midst of trying to untangle some of the extra rowdy sled dogs.

"What's up?" I yelled back.

"That was the last tour of the day. So if you take your team and mine down to the yard, you can call it a day. It's above minus twenty today so you should go out and enjoy the beautiful weather!"

I laughed at her apparent sarcasm, "Aww, thanks Namao, you're a doll! It is such a nice day out, isn't it? I think I may have to do some sun tanning to take advantage of this heat!"

Namao smiled and shook her head. "Don't forget to put on sunscreen, Teslin Grove," she said in a serious tone of voice, using my full name for dramatic effect.

"Okay, mom," I said with the sweetest smile that I could muster. This made Namao laugh, "Get out of here girl! Before the sun goes down! Have a great weekend and say hello to your parents for me."

"Will do. See you on Monday! Thanks, Namao."

I then immediately changed my focus to the fifteen huskies in front of me that I needed to load into the truck. Three years ago this task would have made me very anxious, but now I was a seasoned pro. After three winters of working with the same sled dog company, you learn a few things.

"Alright Paloma, let's start with you." I unhooked the blue-eyed husky from the sled and walked her over to the nearby truck.

"Up you go," I said as I boosted her up into one of the metal cages on the back of the large truck. She yelped with excitement, knowing that she would receive a treat for this 'oh-so-difficult' task that she never wanted to do. All the other staff were always so amazed at how well Paloma listened to me (as she was infamous for being a difficult and sassy princess). Little did they know, I had been secretly feeding her bits of beef jerky to get her to obey me. It cost about five bucks a week to keep up this rouse, but I liked being called the Dog Whisperer too much to stop. After I had Paloma safely secured in her cage, I continued the process with the fourteen other dogs without a hitch. I was just about to jump into the driver's seat, when two arms embraced me from behind and pulled me tightly against their body. Then a seductive voice whispered in my ear:

"Those snow pants make your butt look so good."

I instantly recognized the voice.

"Get off me you weirdo! Were you not at the sexual harassment workshop on Tuesday? I could sue you for this!"

I freed myself from the embrace and felt proud of myself for so quickly remembering about the sexual harassment presentation that we actually did just have, and being able to reference it already. I turned to face my harasser. A just over six-foot tall, handsome in every way of the definition, young man stood in front of me. He had a look on his face as if he truly believed that he was God's gift to women. I personally despised these kind of guys – the ones who look at women as mainly sex objects and nothing else. In most situations, I would have never given this guy the time of day, but unfortunately, we had grown up together in our beloved town of Canmore, Alberta. And if I was to be completely honest, I would have to say that he had been one of my best friends since kindergarten.

Dawson cocked his head and pretended to be in deep thought in response to my threat. Then he ran his fingers through his light brown hair before he spoke.

"You know I do recall some kind of presentation on that topic. But I mostly recall getting it on with the sexy fox giving the workshop." He smiled coyly, waiting for my reaction.

"I'm sure she was probably just furthering her research on how easy it is to sleep with 22-year-old boys," I replied calmly. I hated giving him the satisfaction of reacting to his male chauvinistic comments.

"Well in that case, I am pretty sure I gave her a whole lot of new material to use. Stuff that she never knew was even possible until she met me." He ended his outrageous statement with a wink and a conceited grin.

"Oh really?" I said, raising my left eyebrow at him.

"Yeah. Want a private demonstration?" He then proceeded to send a smoldering look in my direction.

"Nah. I don't want herpes today, thank you very much. Maybe another time." I replied sassily, leaning up against the truck so I could angle my body in a way that didn't require straining my neck to look up at the narcissistic giant.

"Oh Teslin, come on! You know you want to!" he said playfully, winking his dark blue eye at me yet again.

"There is a lot of things that I want from you Dawson, but your body is not one of them." I responded in a faux-serious tone. Dawson moved closer to me and put one hand on the truck above the left side of my head, and placed his other hand gently on my right cheek.

"What do you want from me, Teslin? You know that I would do anything for you."

If I had not known him as well as I did, I would have definitely been fooled by his seemingly genuine concern for me - he was a charming little devil after all. Surely I would have thought that his sweet, warm eyes were true. However, unfortunately for him, I knew better. That being said, I absolutely loved to play around with his head and pretend that I had a hint of feelings for him (I considered my actions as well-deserved payback in the interest of all the poor girls he had swindled in the past). I took in a deep breath before I spoke:

"Dawson, this is hard for me to say..." I paused for dramatic effect. "But I've been thinking about it for a while now, and I can't go another day without asking you something."

I looked deeply into his eyes and placed my hand on the back of his neck, softly pulling him toward me. I made sure we were almost nose to nose before I slowly tilted my head upwards, and then moved my lips toward his right ear, brushing his own lips as I passed by. Then I whispered into his ear, drawing out each word in a painfully slow and alluring manner.

"Can you please stop leaving your garbage in my car? It annoys the hell out of me."

I held it together for about a second after I said this, and then I couldn't contain myself anymore; I burst out laughing and so did he. He pushed out of our close embrace, still laughing, and pulled my bright blue toque over my eyes. I was now completely blind as I felt myself being lifted up and turned upside down.

"Teslin, when are you going to accept the fact that you are going to be my future wife?" Dawson jokingly asked while continuing to hold me upside down.

"The day that you stop leaving your crap in my car and clean up after your dishes, I solemnly swear that I will be your life-long wife." Dawson flipped me back over and put me down. I pulled my toque off of my eyes so that I could once again see my surroundings.

"Aww... then you'll never get to be my wife," he said pouting.

"Suck it up, princess. Life's not fair." I retorted. He laughed and started walking towards his exhausted team of sled dogs.

"See you tonight at Devon's birthday party, right?" he yelled over his shoulder.

"Yeah, I will be there around 7:30 to help set up for the party," I yelled back, climbing into the truck.

"Okay sounds good. I'll be there around nine."

"Sounds good, princess!" I said loudly, and then quickly shut the driver's door before he had time to reply.

I laughed to myself as I drove down the winding mountain road. Dawson may be a real douchebag with the ladies, but he always had a charming way of getting me to smile. He had been there for me through every bad exam, break-up, and just plain horrible days. He always knew how to make me laugh. Both Devon and him had been my best friends even before I knew what a best friend was. As I started to think about all of the things that I needed to bring to Devon's party, my thoughts were interrupted by the beautiful mountains surrounding me (I had been fortunate enough to travel Europe for six months after I graduated high school, and I had indeed experienced the beauty of so many countries. But even so, no cathedral, sculpture, building, nor any piece of art, would ever come close to the beauty of my Canadian Rocky Mountains). I was now inspired to examine the mountains more closely as I drove past them. Covered in a thick blanket of glistening white snow, they stood so powerful and yet so graceful at the same time. Words were simply not enough to describe such magnificence. I felt very lucky to be one of the few people living amongst such natural beauty. In all honestly, I never wanted to live anywhere else. The extreme cold weather was just the price I had to pay in order to wake up to these towering unique works of art every day. After about twenty minutes on the winding road, I finally arrived at the bottom of the mountain.

"Only five more minutes of driving, then twenty minutes to put the dogs away, and then I am free to paaaaarty!" I said out loud to myself, syncing the words to the rhythm of the song I was currently listening to. Yes, it is true. I was one of those weird people who liked to talk to themselves out loud. It actually really helped me organize my thoughts. Or at least that's how I justified it when someone caught me talking to myself. Perhaps I was a bit insane, I'm positive most people are. But this was not what I needed to be pondering about right now (figuring out if I was mentally stable or not), what I needed to be thinking about was the fastest way possible to unload the group of howling huskies in the back of my truck. My psychological self-assessment would have to wait.

****

About forty minutes later, I opened up the door to my home and was greeted by the wonderful smell of mother's cooking.

"Hey, mom! I'm home!" I yelled from the door, beginning to take off my many layers of winter clothing.

"Hello my darling! How was work?" I heard my mother's voice coming from the kitchen. But before I had the chance to reply, I was attacked by a large bundle of black and white fur.

"Nikita!" I screeched in between slobbery kisses. "Calm down! It's like you haven't seen me in years! I just saw you this morning, silly dog!" I pushed the overly-excited Siberian husky down to the ground. She sat down obediently, but whined in disagreement. Her piercing blue eyes looked at me as if she was in pure torture for being unable to touch me.

"Okay, come here you fluffy butt!"

And I commenced the daily butt massage ritual at the front door.

"Come in here, Teslin. I need help with supper, please. Your father is not coming home for dinner. He's very busy at work apparently, so it will just be the two of us again."

My mother's voice sounded a bit stressed and annoyed. I'm guessing because of the fact that my father had been spending all of his free time in the laboratory for the past month and a half. He had always spent much of his time at the lab, but lately he wouldn't even call or text to tell us if he would be missing supper. Not only that, but on the rare chance he did bless us with his presence, he was entirely secretive about the research he was doing in his lab. This was not like him at all. My father had always been a great parent to my older brother Rimbey and I. He was never afraid to tell us how much he loved us (his dramatized proclamations of devotion consistently occurred in front of our friends when we were easily embarrassed teenagers). Family dinners were especially sacred to him. So much so, that he was absolutely heartbroken last year, when Rimbey moved away to the city of Edmonton. The realization that family dinners would never be the same, was almost too much for his heart to take. As a result, he now cherished our small family dinners even more. Needless to say, it was very odd behaviour for my father to miss our family dinners for so many consecutive days. He must be working on something extremely important if he had no time for his precious family. This was probably true, as my father, Doctor David Grove, was a well-renowned brain surgeon in many parts of the world. He had lived in many countries around the world because of his talent. In fact, it was while he was mentoring at a hospital in the

Ukraine when he met my mother, Katya. She was a doctor in the pediatric ward at the same hospital. The attraction between the two of them was undeniable. Consequently, the two fell in love and then travelled the world together. After a few years of jumping around from country to country, they finally decided that Canmore, Alberta was their favourite place to live. And it was here, in my home town, that they settled down and began a family.

I was very close with my Father. I could tell him anything. Even with his busy career, he always found a way to put aside Sunday mornings just for us. These mornings were a special time for the two of us to talk about everything and anything. In the summers we would hike up the mountain trails as we talked, and in the winter (as it was now, and for most of the year…) we would always go to my favourite café, which was owned by our dear family friend, Mrs. Rundle.

Come to think of it, it had been about a month since our last Sunday morning together. I guess I hadn't taken his constant rain checks as hard as my mother had, because I saw it as an opportunity to sleep in on Sunday mornings (something I rarely got to do as a result of our weekly father-daughter dates). I racked my brain, trying to think of our last morning at the café, and what was said. I suppose my father was acting a bit strange that day if I remembered correctly. He was really focusing on all the violence going on in the world:

"The world has become a place where violence is becoming the norm, and peace has become a rarity. Teslin, I don't know if you care to remember, but ten years ago terrorist attacks were still making the headlines, and causing worldwide panic. Yet since the leaders of the world really did nothing to stop these attacks, the supporters of violence and chaos only grew. Nowadays these acts of violence are simply reported like the weather, because they are that common and frequent. It has now gotten to the point where the violent extremists hold the power of the world, while the well-meaning leaders of the world have their hands tied behind their back; unable to reason with the unreasonable, because the terrorists do not want money or power, but simply chaos and blood. How did it come to this?"

He put his hands in his head. Wanting to try to console him and attempt to answer his question at the same time, I held his hands in mine as I spoke softly:

"Well, in a way it kind of makes sense – of how things got so out-of-hand. Governments are filled with politicians who have very strong yet very different opinions. This is supposed to be a good thing, in the way that it represents more voices from a nation's diverse population. However, when it comes to making a decision, this is when a myriad of opinions become a problem. Because while the good people of the world take their time, struggling to make the best decision for their country, it only gives the extremists more time to recruit and grow stronger. This is because they have no quarrel amongst themselves on the most important things. They know what they are fighting for. While the goals of nations are constantly changing, theirs never does. Like you said, they want chaos and violence."

I took a second to catch my breath, feeling a bit surprised at the morbid turn our conversation had taken. My father was looking at me with strange eyes, as if he was prompting me to continue speaking but not wanting to use the words to tell me. Thinking that this was what he wanted, I continued speaking, but with a more positive tone.

"I think that the world could find a way to overcome the violence, if everyone had the same goal. If everyone came together with the legitimate goal of attaining peace, and not just talking about it but actually taking action, then maybe this would be the motivation the world needed to end the attacks. You know, give people a purpose to fight for. I suppose fighting for peace is a bit of an oxymoron, but I don't see any other option. Kind words of friendship and promise don't work on those with hearts filled with hate and anger. The only way to stop a person with an evil heart, is to end their heartbeat completely." I sighed loudly, disheartened by the sad reality of our planet's situation. "Ugh. I don't know how to solve the problems of the world, dad. It's too early in the morning. Can we please talk about something else?" I asked, rubbing my tired eyes.

My father smiled at me. The kind of smile that he used when he was very proud of me (though I hardly knew why he would be so proud of me at this moment).

"Teslin, you are so wise for your age. If only everyone could think as logically as you, then the world would not be such a dark place. Now we don't have to talk about this topic any further, but before we change the subject, I just have one question to ask you."

"What question is that?"

He looked deep into my eyes before he answered, "If there was something, someway to change the minds of the violent people in this world, would you be open to trying it? If you were given the opportunity to make a world full of peaceful people… would you do it?"

My father looked so serious as he continued staring into my eyes. I felt as if he actually knew of a way to make such a world, but that's impossible.

"Yes, of course, dad. If there was anyway to have world peace you know that I would do it. It's a silly wish to think it could ever happen, but if it could, then yes, I would do anything in my power to make it possible."

"I'm very glad to hear that, Teslin." Then he smiled again, but this time with a curious twinkle in his eyes that I didn't quite understand.

The voice of my mother loudly requesting my presence in the kitchen brought me back to reality.

"I'm coming, mom! Just give me one sec," I yelled as I finished Nikita's intensive body rub and hung up my snow gear. I walked into the cozy kitchen with Nikita following closely behind me. My mother was taking out a pan of delicious smelling food from the oven as I came into the kitchen.

"Mmmm. It smells so good! My mouth is watering!"

My mother smiled. "It is your Baba's secret recipe that makes it smell so good," she said in her heavy Ukrainian accent as she put the pan on top of the stove.

"Well Baba sure knows how to make some great food!" I said as I took out the dishes from the cabinet and set the table. We dished out the appetizing pedaheh, holopchi and nalysnyky, and then started to eat.

"So what are your plans this evening my darling?" my mother asked me in between bites.

"We're celebrating Devon's birthday tonight! The whole gang is coming out, so it should be a lot of fun!" I said a bit too enthusiastically (already starting to feel the much awaited freedom of the weekend).

"Don't have too much fun. And don't drink too much either." My mom gave me her usual warning look that I hadn't taken seriously since I was seventeen.

"Okay, mother," I said mockingly.

She stifled a smile, but then her face turned serious. "Teslin, I am worried about your father. He really hasn't been at home at all for over a month. And when he does come home, he is different. He doesn't laugh or joke like he normally does. He just talks very seriously if he talks at all. He's never acted this way before and I don't know what to do."

My mother's face was full of concern, and her voice even held a hint of fear. I had never seen my mother afraid of anything, therefore, I was taken aback at the realization of my mother being frightened for my father's well-being. But I decided to ignore this unsettling notion for the moment, and instead, lighten up the mood for her sake:

"Mom! Dad is getting really old. Maybe he's having a delayed mid-life crisis or going through male menopause or something. So he's probably just adjusting to the lower levels of testosterone in his body. He'll be back to normal in about a week." I said all this in a very know-it-all manner, like I knew exactly what I was talking about. My mother let out a weak chuckle in response,

"I really hope you are right dear. That it is just nothing." Her voice didn't sound scared anymore. Now it just sounded tired from lack of sleep. Probably from staying up all night worrying about dad.

"My darling, don't let me ruin your night. Go! Have fun with your strange friends and tell Devon I say Happy Birthday." She smiled. I could tell that she was trying very hard to be positive and happy for my own benefit. Walking over to her side of the table, I gave her a big hug and a kiss on the cheek,

"Don't worry about dad so much. I'm sure he will be fine."

"Thank you my love."

"Anything for you, mama!"

"Okay, okay! Go already! Go see your friends!"

"Okay! Thanks, mom! I'll be back super late so don't wait up. I love you!"

And with that I ran upstairs to prepare myself for the crazy night ahead.

It didn't take me long to get dressed, as I had already planned my outfit this morning in my head as I was driving to work. Eight hours later, I finally got to see how the emerald coloured dress looked in real-life, as I observed my reflection in the floor-length mirror of my room. It was indeed my favourite dress. I loved it so much not only for the rich green colour, but also for the fact that it magnified my barely-there curves by about a thousand! Not only that, but the daring high slit on the left side made me feel, dare I say it, a little bit sexy (a feeling that I normally didn't feel on a day-to-day basis due to my less than glamorous job). As I put on my makeup I examined my face in the mirror. I definitely inherited my mother's Slavic features. This was obvious from my sharp cheekbones and round chin. Yet at the same time, I also inherited by father's cute little nose and his bright green eyes (he was of Irish decent). My hair, which I always kept at shoulder length, was thick and wild like my father's, but kept the dark brown colour of my mother's. To say the least, I was quite a mix of the two. My parents had always been very amused by my interesting genetic composition. They said it was a result of their genes being so strong that they refused to mix, so instead they compromised on which features they could have of me. I guess I turned out alright. I mean, I was no supermodel, but I was not unfortunate looking either. To be honest, physical appearances were never that important to me. Especially since I grew up in a family that held intellectual abilities to the highest of importance, while an aesthetically pleasing physical appearance was just an added bonus, but not something to honour. I usually thought about this topic on the rare occasion that I actually wore makeup. Only important social events, like a best friend's birthday, merited war paint. Needless to say, my makeup creativity skills were definitely lacking, so it took no time at all to finish getting ready. Taking one last satisfied look in the mirror, I grabbed my bag full of party supplies and ran out the door into the warm taxi that was waiting for me.

****

I arrived at Devon's house a bit later than I had hoped, about an hour later (I blame this on being Ukrainian). Fortunately, she was quick to forgive my tardiness as she was in such a gleeful mood.

I was greeted with one of her infamous big hugs accompanied by squeals of excitement.

"Oh my god! Teslin, you have no idea how excited I am for tonight! Literally all the best people we know are coming! And on top of the two kegs that we have, the hot tub is finally fixed so we can have a hot tub party as well! Can you believe it?!"

I could not handle her insane energy and I burst out laughing, giving her another big hug. Her energy was contagious, so I couldn't help but play along,

"Devon, this is going to be the best party ever. I mean, I'm talking about going down in the history of this town!"

Devon practically screamed in elation, "I know! Maybe we will even be on the news for the craziest party ever?! Then we will get invited to some big talk show, so the world can meet the best party creators of the world! Wouldn't that be so amazing?!"

I had to shake my head and laugh at her. I loved this girl's imagination. It made even the most boring school lectures actually quite interesting.

"Holy crap, Devon! We are going to be famous!"

She squealed again in delight and appeared a bit starry-eyed (no doubt dreaming about living the life of a famous party planner). But only for a second; she then quickly turned her mind to the current task at hand.

"Okay," she said in her boss-like tone while smoothing down her wild, long, blonde hair. "I already cleaned the house and stocked up the bar, but if you could set up the snack table that would be awesome. I am going on a hunt to find those damn ping pong balls so we can play beer pong later tonight. Sounds good?" she asked me. Although I knew it was more of a rhetorical question.

"Whatever you say birthday girl!" I answered with enthusiasm.

"Fantastic!" she exclaimed with a huge smile. "And thank you again for helping me set up. I really appreciate it." She gave me another big hug.

"No worries, girl. Just think of it as part of your amazing birthday gift."

"What? You got me a gift too?! You didn't have to do that!"

I raised my eyebrows at her sarcastically. Then we burst out laughing, because we both knew how ridiculous her last statement was. Everyone knew that Devon absolutely loved gifts. You could even buy her a cheap keychain from Tijuana and she would be happy. Just the fact that someone was thinking of her enough to buy her a gift, made her ecstatic.

"Okay, enough with the chit-chat. Get to work! We have to make this place best-party-ever worthy in 2 hours! Let's do this," I said with my best game face on. Devon clapped her hands together in delight, and then promptly bounced off in search of the always aloof ping pong balls.

As I began setting up the snack table, I paused to think of all the things Devon and I had accomplished together as best friends. We graduated high school together, we completed four years of on-line university together, and now we were taking a year off to work and save up money so that we could travel the world together for a few months the following year. This was something that we had always planned since we were sixteen: to travel the world and go on crazy adventures together. We really hadn't decided where we were going yet. We only knew that we wanted to have a life-inspiring experience before we had to find stable jobs and start acting like adults (if this was even possible). I honestly couldn't believe how fast the time flew by. It seemed like only yesterday that we were nine years old and running through the mountain trails, pretending we were Pocahontas. I had so many fond memories with this girl. She was a troublemaker. She would always get us into some kind of mess, and I would always have to cleverly get us out of it. But then again, sometimes my sassy nature would get us into even more trouble. I was just thinking about the time we tried to convince the backstage security at a Justin Timberlake concert that we were the hired back-up dancers so we could get backstage (we even wore dance costumes, stage makeup and fake passes), when a loud voice startled me.

"Oh. My. God. She's finally lost it! So this is why you don't want me, you're secretly in love with carrots!"

I suddenly became aware of my surroundings and realized that while my mind had been lost in a wave of memories, the rest of my body had been in a frozen position, with my arms holding a bag of carrots out in front of my face. From an outsider's perspective it probably appeared as if I had been fixedly staring at the bag of carrots for an embarrassingly long amount of time; hence the comment from none other than Dawson, whom currently stood across the table from me. His arms crossed and eyebrows raised. I defensively said the first thing that came to my mind,

"No one ever gives carrots the love that they deserve. I am just thanking these carrots for all the wonderful healthy nutrition that they provide us on behalf of all the billions of ungrateful people who forget." I then gave the bag of carrots a loving embrace. "I've carried this burden alone for quite some time, but maybe now I have someone to share this honour with. Come here, and let us show our love and appreciation for the carrots together," I extended my hand towards Dawson in a welcoming manner.

"Honey, there's only room enough for one of us on that crazy train, and you're already a preferred first class member," he replied, still looking a bit amused and weirded out about my carrot rant.

"Very well then, you may now be blessed to witness the sacred appreciation ritual of the carrots." I then began to hum a mesmerizing tune accompanied by beautiful lyrics from the Elvish language (or what I considered to be the Elvish language), as I held the bag of carrots in front of my face and gazed at them fondly. I was just about to change to a higher key register, when Devon walked into the dining room. She paused to look at me and then turned to Dawson.

"Do I even want to know?" she directed her question towards him.

"Not unless you want a twenty-minute-long explanation about the rare carrot loving ritual," he replied while keeping his gaze on me.

"Hmmm, maybe not today," she replied quickly.

"Suit yourself," I said in a mock-hurt voice. Finished with the ritual, I delicately placed the carrots down into a large glass bowl on the table.

Devon rolled her eyes, "Well I must have done something right to have such weird friends." She threw her hands up dramatically. "Come here you weirdos! Group hug!"

We all laughed, and Dawson and I did as we were told.

Once we were all in a big group hug Devon started to get a bit emotional, "You know guys, we are all 22 now. We have been friends for so long, and I can honestly say that you two will always be my best friends. No matter where we end up in life, I will always love you guys!" she hugged us even tighter.

"Devon, you haven't even started drinking yet! Hold the emotional stuff until we are all drunk and will cry with you too," Dawson piped in annoyingly. Why did he always have to ruin a good moment?

"You're such an ass! Why are you so scared of your emotions? You can tell people you love them when you're sober too, you know?" I retorted. I was used to his phobia of emotions, but that didn't mean I ever let him get away with saying comments like this. I also liked to hear his responses after I confronted him on the topic. What people do to cover up their true feelings always intrigued me. Really anything people did amused me, which is probably why I chose to study psychology as I found human behaviour fascinating.

"Of course you can, Teslin. But it's way more entertaining when you're drunk, isn't it?" he then smiled his irritating but effective Cheshire cat smile in my direction.

"Whatever, Dawson. Hey, weren't you not supposed to be here until later?" I said changing the topic. I wasn't going to continue arguing with him on Devon's birthday.

"Did you really think that I would leave my best friends to get ready for the best party ever without me?!" he made a shocked face.

"Oh Dawson, I knew you cared about us!" Devon practically sang out with joy. "Since you are going to help us, do you want to move the furniture around to give it a more open and welcoming party look?" she asked in her sweetest voice.

But before he could reply I interrupted, "He can't even match his own socks and you want to leave him in charge of the interior designing?" I asked in disbelief. Dawson playfully punched me in the arm.

"Have a little faith in me will you, Teslin? Devon believes in me. Don't you, Devon?" He held Devon affectionately and gave her a kiss on the cheek, making her blush.

"Once you actually start throwing your garbage IN the garbage can, I will start to become more open to the idea that you can do other things as well," I replied sassily.

This comment resulted in all three of us laughing, as we knew this was my absolute biggest pet peeve about Dawson. He would always throw his garbage from halfway across a room, usually miss the garbage can, then say: "Aww, maybe next time", and continue on his merry way without ever picking up the garbage and putting it in the can. I had confronted him about this disgusting habit many times, but he would always reply the same way: "I can't pick up the garbage after I missed the bin! That would be cheating!" He is such a logical individual, I know.

"Okay ladies, I say we start the night out right with a tequila shot!" Dawson's loud voice brought me back to reality, and out of my daydream of him actually picking up his damn garbage.

"Yeah, I love tequila!" Devon cried out as she ran to grab the tequila and shot glasses. She came back in less than thirty seconds (obviously over excited for the night ahead of us).

"To best friends and to the best party ever!" Devon exclaimed, raising her shot glass in the air.

"Cheers!" we all said in unison, clinking our glasses together and then downing the tequila.

That was the first of many shots that night.

****

In the recently upgraded medical laboratory in the town of Canmore, Dr. David Grove and his colleagues sat around the conference table discussing the results of the latest 223 mass surgeries. All but a miniscule fifteen surgeries were a success. This was encouraging news, as it meant that the amount of successful operations had been continuing to increase with every new batch of human subjects.

In the beginning, switching to human subjects had been problematic. Not only because the original surgery was not effective on the human brain, but also because no one wanted to volunteer. Even when substantial monetary compensation was offered, people were still appalled at the idea of having their minds altered. This was only a small hitch in the plan, however, as there are other ways to come about human subjects. They may not be particularly ethical options, but Dr. Grove and his team had decided that these risks were worth it, as the results would eventually strengthen the human race in the near future.

This being said, they had to be extremely careful and secretive on how they extracted test subjects from their normal lives. In the past years, the team of scientists working under Dr. Grove had picked individuals that would not be missed if they suddenly disappeared. When the team required more specific individuals to operate on, they would strategically fill a plane full of people possessing these desired traits (telling the unsuspecting people they had won a vacation, or by setting up a business trip, or a family reunion, etc.), and fly them to the underground laboratory (which had increasingly grown larger with every year). Meanwhile, the rest of the world would be under the impression that the plane had mysteriously vanished over the ocean. The team preferred the missing plane scenario, but sometimes they also took advantage of natural disasters, terrorist attacks, and wars as distractions to cover their mass collection of human subjects.

Today, however, the team's deadline was almost at a close. They were currently taking in the largest amount of human subjects than ever before. It was crucial that Dr. Grove's team cleverly chose people who would be gone for two weeks or more on vacation or for work. This way the team could easily continue to keep in contact with the abducted person's friends and family through social media (keeping the world unaware of their disappearance). Yet even so, they only had a short time limit to work with until mass missing person searches came to the attention of the media and the authorities. Well aware of this imminent threat to the Movement, Dr. Grove and his team had been rapidly cumulating their very own army. The assembling of soldiers had been virtually flawless. Each of the four thousand five hundred and ninety-five chosen individuals had undergone a brain surgery, also known as the Cold Surgery. The surgery lasted about five to ten minutes, and was performed while the subjects were awake with a mild anesthetic applied to the scalp area (this was so no pain was felt during the initial drilling through the skin). As a result of the neurosurgeons being highly skilled, they knew exactly which connections to sever in order to complete the surgery successfully. After the main connections to the frontal cortex were cut, the subject was taken to be conditioned.

During the conditioning stage, a team of neurologists would show the subject pictures and videos of emotional situations, and ask the subject to explain how they felt about these images. If the subject replied in a logical manner with no hint of emotions present, the surgery was a complete success. However, if there was still an emotional response to any of the tests, or in general if the subject was still afraid of being strapped to a white chair and the fact that they just had a brain surgery against their will, either shock therapy or more severing of connections had to be done until the neurosurgeons and neurologists were satisfied with the results (normally the surgeries were performed during regular work hours, but now due to the rapidly approaching deadline, the surgeries were continued throughout the day and night. As there was not a single second that could be lost.)

After the Cold Surgery was recognized as a success, the new recruits were then taken through an orientation that explained to them the reasoning behind their apparent abduction and subsequent brain surgery. They were escorted to a large, white, underground lecture hall, which had the capacity to seat over five hundred people. The newly operated on members were then instructed to sit and watch a video that was played on the large theatre screen. They all listened obediently and without a fuss.

The star of this orientation-like-video was the creator of the Cold Surgery himself, Dr. Joshua Lacombe. Dr. Lacombe's image appeared on the dominating screen. He sat peacefully on a large white sofa, looking absolutely pristine in an all-black suit with not a hair out of place. His facial expression looked almost emotionless, if it wasn't for the hint of smugness that hid behind his icy blue eyes. He looked directly into the camera and spoke in a strong, ominous voice:

"Welcome to the Cold Cognition Movement Headquarters. This is now your temporary home. You may be a bit confused as to why you are here, and also why your brain is functioning so differently and yet so clearly. You should be afraid, being in an unknown place, and with strangers who just operated on your brain without your consent. But you aren't, are you? Instead, you have attempted to use the clues around you to discover where you are, realizing that you do not know the way out of this facility, and then registering that we are not a direct threat to you. Therefore, you have decided that it is in your best interest to follow our orders until you can make a more knowledgeable and accurate assumption on what is going on here. Congratulations, you have chosen the most logical decision. This means that the Cold Surgery has worked, and you are cured. Now let me explain in detail the nature of the surgery that you have just undergone:

"My intensive research on emotions in the brain has led me to find a vital connection in the processing of emotions. This connection passes information from all the emotional centres of the brain – including the amygdala, the cingulate gyrus, the thalamus, etc. – onto the prefrontal cortex where your thoughts and responses to these emotions are processed. By severing this connection, emotions will no longer affect your decision-making, as they will no longer be present in your prefrontal cortex. Emotions will still exist in your brain, however, without this connection they are no longer processed in your frontal lobe, and therefore, do not influence your decisions or behaviour. We have freed you from the burden of emotions and given you the greatest gift of all: pure, logical reasoning. You now only possess what is referred to as "cold cognition". By stripping you of your emotions, we are also removing hate, anger, and fear from your mind; changing you into a completely rational being. You are now a part of an international movement that will change the world forever.

The Cold Cognition Movement was created for the sole purpose of establishing a world of peace, equality, and intelligence. Unfortunately, this objective is almost impossible to attain in the current state of the earth. In order to change the world, we must first change the people. How can we change the people, you ask?

The answer is simple, the Cold Surgery. You have all personally experienced how successful the surgery is at creating logical minds. Now it is time to show the rest of the world…

On January 11th, at 00:00 hours, all forms of communications, electricity, and water services will be cut-off from the town of Canmore – which will be blamed on the impending snow storm. We will then have a small time period to collect every inhabitant of this town and the surrounding area, ultimately performing the Cold Surgery on each individual. Some of you, those with the required skills, will be assigned to performing these mass surgeries, while others will be on the ground collecting the citizens, or posted at other equally important assignments such as in our computer, educational, food, clothing, or weapon facilities. Once your mission is successful, the Headquarters' Commander, Dr. Grove, will report to me and I will authorize the Movement in the 64 other locations around the globe. By this time, our Movement will be discovered by the rest of the world and we will most likely be met by opposing forces. Many people will resist the Cold Cognition Movement, because they fear change, regardless of the beneficial outcome. They will fight back. Nevertheless, we will, of course, triumph over the illogical resistance. Sacrifices will have to be made. But this resistance will be a blessing, as it will be necessary to significantly cut down the world population to provide equal amounts of food, water, shelter and opportunity to everyone. This may seem like a harsh course of action, but these sacrifices must be made if we want our dream to be realized.

Our Earth is dying. It cannot sustain our wasteful and harmful race much longer. A change needs to happen. This change is to transform ourselves into advanced logical beings, and rid the world of all lesser beings. Only then can we ensure that the Earth will survive and support our future peaceful race.

You have been chosen to be a part of this world-changing Movement. Together we will create a better and peaceful world with a race of purely logical beings. You will now be assigned to an important position according to your skillset, and there you will work until we have completed the mission. I thank you in advance for your hard work and dedication. And once again, welcome to the Cold Cognition Movement."

Once the video finished, the chosen individuals were assigned to an appropriate position based on their skillset and level of intelligence. All of the new recruits obeyed and did not once question their new life. Neither did they question the Cold Cognition Movement. This was because they now possessed entirely rational minds, and the Cold Cognition Movement was a purely logical solution to save the world. Emotions were no longer welcomed in their decision-making process, and as a result, this was the most logical plan of action. Because in all truthfulness, the world was dying, and the human race was only getting worse. There was so much hate, fear, anger, deceit, greed, and simply so many horrid people in the world, that a peaceful Earth could never be possible in its current state. It was just not plausible to change the minds of the entire human race through good deeds or words of compassion. No. The only way to successfully change a world full of appalling humans, is to physically alter their state of being. In other words, physically modify their brain. The Cold Surgery was the cure that the world had been waiting for.

****

At 23:59 on January 10th, the White Soldiers were lined up and waiting; ready to collect the citizens of the snow-covered town. Unaware of the horror about to begin, the town was quiet and peaceful. Only the sound of the heavy snowflakes hitting the ground could be heard. The omniscient mountains surrounding the town stood silent and observant, knowing the secrets of the underground Movement, and patiently waiting to see the outcome. These peaceful giants had witnessed the lives of countless inhabitants since the very beginning of the planet. Yet no creature had ever fascinated the giants as much as the humans did. They were the most intelligent beings on the Earth, yet the most problematic. Mainly because they were all so very different. Some were loving, joyous, caring and nurturing, while others were hateful, destructive, greedy and murderous. They were creatures of an extreme nature; while one human may show compassion to a complete stranger, another may kill their own brother for any trivial reason. This is something that the mountains never quite understood. Even the most vicious and wild animals had a valid reason for why they would kill their own: either to show dominance, for food, when fighting over a mate, taking out a sick or injured member, or when competing for resources. And indeed the humans did kill for these reasons as well, but also for senseless reasons. For instance, if they did not like the look of certain humans, or they didn't approve of the way they thought or how they acted, this was a good enough reason to kill them. The peaceful mountains had witnessed innumerable conflicts and wars between the humans over the years, but something about this newest venture of the humans seemed different. Because this time, they were different. They no longer had the very thing that made them human: their emotions. Their ability to feel joy, excitement, happiness and love was gone. Their humanity was gone. And now, with three seconds till midnight, even the mighty Rocky Mountains felt afraid for the future of the Earth.

The clock struck midnight, and the White Soldiers silently marched into the town.

****

SIX YEARS EARLIER

Chapter Two

Dr. Joshua Lacombe cleared his throat and straightened his posture. He took another long look in the mirror before finally coming to the decision that he did indeed look quite dapper. And in all honesty, many people would have to agree with him. For Joshua was a 'tall glass of water' in the words of most elderly women in his posh neighbourhood. Taller than the average man, he was blessed with his mother's high cheek bones and blue eyes, while his dark hair and tan skin were compliments of his father. He was the only child born to an upper class family that were loved and admired by everyone they bothered to meet. Mrs. Lacombe was one of the top corporate lawyers in the country, while his father was a highly in demand plastic surgeon. Not to be outdone by his successful parents, Joshua found his passion for science at a young age, and pursued that passion until he became the most successful neuroscientist specializing in neuropsychology in the world.

At the age of 32, Joshua had spent the majority of his life dedicated to researching the human brain, focusing on the intricacy of emotion. There was very little else that held such importance to him as his research did. It came first before everything. Including his family, his few friends, and his latest girlfriend. Nearly all people would pity the man for spending the majority of his life in a laboratory, but oddly enough it was where he felt the most at home. It was one of the few places he could completely clear his mind and direct all energy into his very important research. The white spacious laboratory had become his sanctuary over the years. While inside his white-walled haven, he felt so alive and energized; free to hypothesize, experiment and theorize for hours on end. As a result, Joshua felt little desire for human contact as no human could provide him with the equal satisfaction that his sanctuary gave. Of course, he still enjoyed his time with his friends and female company, but over the years he had come to realize that he did not have the desire or time to develop good relationships. Instead, he put in the minimal effort required to retain somewhat friendly relations.

All of Joshua's friends had at least one PhD behind their name. This was not because he couldn't bear to associate with someone lacking doctoral status, but simply because science was the only thing he felt was worth talking about. He rarely succeeded in continuing a conversation with topics such as daily life, art, the legal system, or politics. Mainly because there was so much emotion attached to these topics – something he couldn't stand as it always affected a person's better judgment. Joshua had always thought that emotion was humankind's biggest flaw. People seem to always be swayed into illogical decisions when emotions were involved. They were never able to register and analyze the cold hard facts if emotions were running high. He truly believed that humans would never have peace, equality, or world-wide intelligence and progress, as emotions would always prevent them to do so. Around the dinner table with his colleagues, this was his favourite topic:

"I mean think about it, every war that ever started was based on emotion. Either anger, fear, hate, love, you name it. If humans could remove emotion from their thoughts and therefore, think logically, there would never be another war. As it never makes logical sense to go to war. War costs money, lives and resources. Not even war against a nation for prized land would be a logical decision. It would make more sense to establish ties between countries by trade agreements or leasing land, as this strengthens the economy and benefits both parties. I can give you thousands of other examples of where emotions have failed humanity, but the bottom line is: I strongly believe that the human race would be better off without emotion at all!"

His friends would always laugh at his usual rant, and then give a reply along the lines of:

"My dear friend, humans would cease to be humans without emotions! They would be more like computers or robots. Seriously Joshua, why would you want that? If all people were able to think logically then we would all be out of jobs!"

"But think of all the benefits it would have!" Joshua always retorted. "No more racism, sexism, prejudice or war. All of these problems would be a thing of the past! Then we could focus on more important things, like strengthening the world economy and advances in the medical field."

"Yes, I can see the benefits of such a phenomenon, but why put so much energy into an idea that is highly improbable? The human brain is still a rather large mystery to us. And furthermore, it is such an interconnected entity that it would be close to impossible to remove emotion from the brain without also removing something integral as well."

"Very well. You may have your opinions, but I think that with our technology it is more plausible than you believe."

"Only time will tell my friend."

This was the usual ending to Joshua's repeated topic. Afterwards, the group would go on enjoying their wine and dinner whilst dissecting scientific theories and recently published studies.

Yet even in the presence of his highly educated friends, Joshua observed how emotions also influenced their thoughts in the form of biasness, greed and stubbornness. He had been a firsthand observer of an unlawful, emotionally-based decision that proceeded to change his preconceived ideas about the scientific community.

From a young boy he had always thought that the worlds of science and mathematics were the most black-and-white places you could find in the universe, as there is only one right answer. One number plus another will always produce one exact answer. A true experiment has only one result that can be repeated thousands of times over with the same results. Joshua kept this view about science until his first year in graduate school, where he had the honour of working alongside one of the world's best neuroscientist at that time. This professor was Joshua's hero, and he believed in everything the man did. But one day, his perfect fairy-tale view of the pristine science world shattered into millions of jagged pieces, severely wounding his respect for all scientists.

This occurred when Joshua discovered that the professor was skewing lab results so he could continue to receive grant money for his research. In the beginning, Joshua understood this act of deception, as he believed that the research was indeed promising. However, in time he realized that in actuality it was a failed research project. Simply because the professor had spent the last seven years working on this research, did he continue to prolong it out of pride. This was the first time that Joshua observed that even one of the top scientists in the world could let emotions influence them. No one was immune to emotions. And as far as Joshua was concerned, this was the biggest defect in human beings.

Emotions were dangerous; especially fear and hate. The fear of change, success, failure, the unknown, fear and hate of each other. How much better off would the world be if people were no longer scared of change? Would racism be a thing of the past if hate was no longer an option? These are the questions that Joshua wondered about on a daily basis. A future without emotion seemed like the ideal answer to the many problems of the current human race.

For instance, throughout history, wars and murders have been a direct cause of hate and fear, even greed. All violent deaths and fights are fueled by emotions. One can convince a man to do anything by using their emotions against them, even to kill another human being for no other reason other than hatred or fear. Because it never appeals to logic to pursue a war, there is too much to lose. Countless lives are sacrificed, finances are stretched thin on supplies and food, and so much land and architecture is destroyed. Therefore, it appeared to Joshua that wars could potentially be stopped through decisions completely void of emotions. Especially when it came to war over religious views.

Religion was something that the science community had mixed feelings about. While some of Joshua's colleagues believed in God, others believed that only week-minded, brain-washed people were religious since they refused to see the truth of science. Not partial to either opinion, Joshua sat somewhere in the middle of these two sides. For he could see that both sides, religious or not, both believed strongly in something, even if that something was nothing. Joshua would always wonder what people would believe in if there was no emotion to influence their ideas. Would believing that God created this earth be more logical than an earth created by pure chance and evolution, or vice versa? Or would a new and more truthful theory be formed, once emotions were no longer a factor. Because like it or not, every decision a human makes happens to be also influenced by their emotions. Humans are not machines or computers after all. They are imperfect creatures. Selfish and immensely flawed - at least this is what Joshua thought. And since Dr. Joshua Lacombe was in fact the world's top scientist in the area of emotion in the human brain, he thought he did indeed know best.

He had spent the last five years working furiously on a research project that he knew would 'change the world for the better'. At least that's what he told people to justify all the time he neglected to see them because of the project. Nevertheless, it was today, that he would be sharing his latest ground-breaking research on the human brain. Today he had the world's most elite scientists, psychologists, doctors and investors, all together in one room to hear about his 'world-changing' discovery. And it was on this day that the beginnings of something indescribable began. For little did they know, everyone in that room was about to witness the spark that led to a domino of inconceivable events.

****

A rapid knock on his door signalled that they were ready for him. Dr. Joshua Lacombe ignored the knock, and instead took another look in the mirror, straightening his tie as he observed himself in the floor length mirror of his private suite. Calmness and absolute confidence danced around his aesthetically pleasing face. With his hand, he ran his fingers through his dark hair until it fell exactly the way he liked it. His icy blue eyes then travelled down to his body, which wore a fitted, all-black suit. He smoothed down the front of his suit jacket and then gave it a tug, so it fell perfectly on his toned torso. Happy with his appearance, he took one last look in the mirror before turning on his heels and walking towards the dark wooden door. Upon opening the door, he encountered a young woman who was dressed in a fitted purple dress suit, wearing a headset and carrying a clipboard full of papers. She was speaking into the headset and appeared to be terribly stressed. Since she was looking down at her clipboard and was so engulfed in her important conversation, she did not even notice that Joshua had opened the door.

"Good afternoon," Joshua spoke in a cold tone, as he did not like to be ignored (even if it was for a second).

"Oh!" the startled woman looked up, surprised to see Joshua standing in the doorway looking at her with a slightly unimpressed look. She opened her mouth to speak but no words came out. Because not only was she a bit startled, but now she was taken aback by the dashing good looks of the man standing in front of her. Joshua gave her two seconds to recover, and when she had not yet spoken he broke the silence:

"Are they ready for me?" he asked in low and irritated voice. The young woman blushed and fumbled with her headset, before she recovered enough to respond.

"Yes, Dr. Lacombe, we are ready. Please follow me."

And with that she turned around and began walking away at a brisk pace, too embarrassed to look back to see if the handsome doctor was even following her.

Joshua smiled to himself in amusement as he closed the door and began following the frazzled woman (he was used to this kind of reaction from women, which many men would use to their advantage, but Joshua was more interested in his science projects than seducing women). He easily caught up to the quick pace of the woman, thanks to the help of his long legs. Every move he made, was made with grace and purpose. Walking was no exception to this rule. He came to his firmness and confidence all by himself, but his gracefulness was a result of his mother forcing him to take ballroom dance classes with her for many years.

His mother loved to dance, it was her passion. It was the only place where she could completely let go and forget about her stressful job. And since Joshua's father refused to dance on account of being born with a disorder that made him incapable of dancing (his father was the drama queen of the family), Joshua was forced to take his place and dance with his mother. Yes, Mrs. Lacombe forced her poor son to dance with her from the tender age of eleven until Joshua's first year of university, in which he finally convinced his mother that he no longer had time for dance class. She reluctantly had to agree, as she knew how dedicated her son was to his academic career. But the truth was, Joshua secretly enjoyed all those years dancing with his mother. Of course, he would never in a million years admit this to her. Instead, he preferred to tell her how evil she was for torturing him every time they went to class. Although there was a time where he truly believed the dance classes were torture, he quickly realized that he loved every single second of the dance class, because that was another second he got to spend with his beautiful mother. Being one of the top attorneys in the city meant that free time was a very sparse thing for Mrs. Lacombe. As a result, sometimes this once-a-week dance class was the only time he received his mother's undivided attention.

Therefore, as he now walked through the dim lit hallways of the conference centre and into the dark backstage briefing area, he held himself with exquisite poise. As this was ingrained in his muscle memory from years of ballroom dance.

The woman in the purple dress suit, now fully recovered from her earlier embarrassment, turned around to face Joshua.

"Excuse me sir, I have to attend to another guest. Please wait here and Miss Springfield will be with you in a moment to give you further instructions."

Joshua nodded his head in acknowledgment and the woman smiled before quickly leaving the backstage area. As he waited for Miss Springfield to grace him with her presence, he looked around and took in his surroundings. The space looked like any other backstage area of a stage: dark, filled with props and tech supplies, and people dressed in black wearing headsets and running around frantically. He could see the bright spotlight coming through the openings of the black velvet curtains which led to the stage. The crowd was getting restless. He could tell by listening to the loud constant hum from the combined low voices of the audience. A combination of very important voices to be exact. He smiled as he thought of the copious amount of important people from all over the world currently sitting in the theatre. They had all come to hear him speak about his latest research on emotion. Emotion was a very interesting topic in the science community, as it was widely believed that pure science was without any emotional influence. Purely logical. After all, the best scientists were logical ones.

While Joshua was observing two tech staff argue about which colour to use for the stage background, an attractive brunette woman emerged from the stage. She looked in his direction and smiled, and then enthusiastically walked straight towards him.

"Hello, Dr. Lacombe! My name is Danielle Springfield, and I will be your M.C. for tonight. It is such a pleasure to meet you!" The energetic Miss Springfield held out her hand towards Joshua. He obliged, and shook her delicate hand while also returning her charming smile with one of his own.

"The pleasure is all mine, Miss Springfield," he said in a low voice. Danielle's charming smile instantly turned into a flirtatious one, as she held his hand for one second too long before retracting her hand.

"Well Dr. Lacombe, let me give you a quick rundown on the order of things. Please, sit down." She gestured towards a small table with two chairs next to a collection of very large old speakers. Joshua sat down as directed. The young woman looked directly into his eyes as she began to speak:

"Alright. So first of all, I will start out by welcoming everyone. You know, acknowledge all the VIPs, the sponsors, pretty standard stuff. Then I will give a brief introduction about you and your work. After that, a five-minute video will play, giving more details and background on your project. It's the one that your staff sent to us, so I assume you know it and I don't have to go over it?" She had spoken in such an eloquent manner without pausing thus far, that it took Joshua a second to realize that she had meant to ask a question.

"Yes, I have seen the video. There is no need to explain it to me Miss Springfield." He replied in an equally eloquent manner.

"Perfect! And please, Dr. Lacombe, call me Danielle!" Her flirtatious smile returned once more. "Okay, so right after the video I will introduce you to the audience, and from there you have the stage! After your presentation I will return to the stage to give the closing statement, and then, that's a wrap!"

She held her hands up in a dramatic fashion to end her very brief information session.

"Is everything clear to you, Dr. Lacombe, or is there something that you would like to go over again?"

"I don't think that will be necessary. You have made everything perfectly clear, Danielle." Joshua smiled, showing off his pearly white, straight teeth.

"Well I am glad you think so, Dr. Lacombe! Is there anything I can get you before we start? A water, coffee…." She quickly glanced down at her watch before finishing her sentence.

"Oh dear! You're going to have to make that coffee an espresso, because we are on in two minutes!" she looked up at Joshua with excitement in her eyes.

"Don't worry, I just had a coffee before I came here. We can start whenever you are ready. I don't need anything."

"Fantastic! Oh and before I forget, here is the remote to change the slides of your presentation. Just press this button here to go back and forth between each slide," she pointed to the middle button of the remote as she handed it to him.

"Thank you," Joshua said politely, taking the remote.

"Danielle! You are on in one minute!" one of the tech staff yelled from across the room.

"I guess that's my cue!" she said enthusiastically with a big grin. "Wish me luck!" she said to Joshua.

"I would happily wish you luck, but it appears that you don't need it." Joshua smiled slyly as he said this.

"Hmmm, that's very true, Dr. Lacombe. It appears that you are smarter than you look!" she winked and quickly turned to rush towards the stage curtain before Joshua could reply. Leaving him sitting alone at the table, open-mouthed and with raised eyebrows, watching the sassy, beautiful woman walk onto the stage. He was now very curious to see what this woman was like on stage, in front of an audience.

Danielle's performance was impressive, this he had to admit. She had such eloquence when speaking, and was able to hold the audience's full attention even when speaking about less than exciting things like the donors and sponsors of the night. She made the opening ceremony pleasant and enjoyable, throwing in a few jokes here and there to lighten the mood. When she finished, the lights went dim and the video began to play. Danielle moved off stage and went to stand next to Joshua. She leaned into him and whispered,

"Are you ready to tell the world about your breakthrough, world-changing research?" she said the last four words with obvious sarcasm.

"I am always ready, Miss Springfield." His intense look towards her was definitely felt by Danielle, but not fully seen through the darkness.

"In that case, I would wish you luck but it appears that you don't need any," she replied sassily. Proud of herself for using his own words against him.

Joshua had to laugh at this, "Good one. I see that you possess both beauty and wit," he said with a wink as the video came to an end. Danielle rolled her eyes and flipped her hair in response as she went running back to the stage, feeling a bit perturbed that she did not get the chance to use one of her many comebacks on the doctor.

"Now, without further ado, please give a warm welcome to the man we have all been waiting for… Dr. Joshua Lacombe!"

The audience applauded as requested. Joshua walked onto the stage with such a confident demeanour, winking at Danielle as he passed by her, and stopped when he was directly in the middle of the stage. He stood centre stage and waited for the crowd to quiet down. Once the applause stopped, he stood omnisciently for a few more seconds (for dramatic affect) before he spoke.

He stood with his hands in his perfectly tailored suit pants, and wore an amused look on his face. Joshua looked way too calm and collective to be standing in front of the most influential and powerful scientists, doctors and investors in the world. He appeared at ease in the silence in front of such a significant crowd. Finally, he opened his mouth to speak:

"You have all come here tonight to hear about my latest research on emotion in the human brain." He paused, looking around at the anticipating audience. His voice was strong with a hint of playfulness. "But what you don't know, is that tonight you will hear more than just mundane research results. For today I have much more than ground-breaking research to tell you. Today, ladies and gentlemen, you will be the first to hear about a discovery that will eventually save the entire human race. This discovery will in fact, rid the world of prejudice, racism, sexism, and even war. Ladies and gentlemen, I have found the answer. I have found a way to fix the one major flaw of human beings. The one flaw that prevents us from universal peace, equality, and intelligence. I have found the cure."

It was here that Joshua paused and turned around to face the gigantic screen behind him. The title slide of his presentation appeared, brightly projected onto the white background. During this second of silence as he turned around, the theatre filled with whispers from the audience. Some of excitement, some of anger, and the majority of disbelief. A picture of the human brain appeared on the massive screen, with specific parts highlighted.

"This, ladies and gentlemen, as you know, is the most complex organ of the human body. It is the part of the body that we know so much, yet so little about. It has taken countless years of research just to get a general picture of what the brain really does. I myself, have spent the past five years specifically working on emotion in the human and animal brain. Five years of performing endless experiments, failing, and trying again. Nevertheless, I was determined to complete my research goal. And it is with this unwavering determination, that I am proud to say I have finally cracked the code. I have solved the problem. I have pinpointed the exact location in the brain responsible for dispersing emotion to the prefrontal cortex of the brain. And with this discovery, I have stumbled across what will be the future of the human race!"

Joshua dramatically raised his voice at the end of his monologue, and paused to hear the audience's reaction. The loud hum of voices that resulted from the pause were, ironically, a fury of emotions. The tension in the room grew to such a level that one particularly frustrated gentlemen felt the need to yell out from the crowd:

"Will you quit with the dramatics and just show us some of your research?! I did not travel nineteen hours to hear you make ridiculous claims about saving the human race! Show us this "world-changing" research already!" the angry man said the last few words with utter disgust. Other audience members agreed with the boisterous man and clapped for his little outburst. Joshua waited for the crowd to become generally quiet again before he continued. He smiled, completely unaffected by the insults,

"Well my friend, I never make a claim unless I have sufficient research to back it up. You should already know this about me if you have read any of the eleven scientific articles that I have published. In fact, today you will get to witness the internal cause of your little emotionally charged outburst. And after my presentation, you will know which exact part of your brain is making you feel embarrassed and ashamed as you walk out of this theatre in the next 45 minutes." He stopped to look around at the audience, "Is there anyone else who has doubts about my research?" The crowd fell completely silent. "I didn't think so. Let me continue."

Joshua changed the slide on the giant projector screen. Pictures of dissected parts of the brain revealed themselves one by one on the screen.

"As I am sure you all know; our current knowledge of the brain and its relation to emotion is severely lacking. We have only just identified general areas that are associated with emotion. For example, the amygdala, the hippocampus, the thalamus, the prefrontal area, etc. We have previously thought that emotion was distributed throughout different parts of the brain that interact together. And while this may be true, that not just one area is responsible for emotion, there is in fact one part that can completely stop the process of emotion. What I mean to say is, the brain is full of connections and I have found the connection that distributes emotion to the prefrontal cortex. The area of the brain that is associated with your very thoughts, personality, and your logical, decision-making skills. Simply put, if you cut this connection, emotion ceases in the brain. I have experimented on mice, rats, birds, monkeys and an elephant, and I have seen the exact same results in every case. Let me now show you the most profound results from two specific case studies." He switched the slide.

"Here we have 'Daisy the Elephant', a 23-year-old African elephant from a travelling circus. A year ago, Daisy gave birth to a daughter. Unfortunately, due to a heart defect, her daughter died at four months old. Daisy was utterly devastated by the loss of her daughter. She refused to eat or drink anything and was in a permanent state of mourning. On a side note, we know that elephants have a great capacity for emotion. Even in the wild they will mourn the death of a herd member and have a burial ritual. They are amazing creatures.

Anyways, I heard about Daisy and contacted the circus. They agreed to do the surgery as Daisy was close to death, and they had exhausted all other options. I performed the surgery in the precise manner as I had done with all previous surgeries, almost exactly a year ago on January 11th, 2017. The very next day when Daisy awoke from surgery, she immediately ate and drank like the starving elephant she was. Daisy no longer rejected the attention from the circus staff, and was able to perform in a show later that night. It's been a year now, and my staff still does regular checkups on the elephant.

Since the surgery, the staff has reported Daisy in perfect health. But what's even more amazing, is that she no longer has her famous temper tantrums, she is able to move from place to place without any shock whatsoever, and she has learned a total of thirteen more tricks with ease and precision. I don't know about you, but I would call that a success. What is even more interesting, is that Daisy still walks over and looks at the corner of the pen where she gave birth to her daughter. Acknowledging the fact that she had a baby, but no longer mourning. Due to the severed connection in her brain, she no longer has an emotional connection to her daughter, but she still retains the memories of the event. The facts still remain". At this moment, Joshua stopped to take a drink of water from the glass situated on the side podium.

"If this is not enough to convince you of the significance of my discovery, let me draw your attention to the next slide." He pointed the remote at the screen and changed the slide. A picture of a chimpanzee appeared on the brilliant screen.

"This is Keekay, the chimpanzee. Now Keekay is a beloved family member to a lovely elderly couple, who are retired zoologists. They found the abandoned baby chimpanzee on their last research trip and decided to raise him as their child, as they had no living children of their own. The couple were fully aware of the dangers of having a wild animal, so they moved out of the city onto a spacious acreage. For the most part, Keekay was a gentle soul, and had no problems with the adults and children that came to visit his family. However, once in a while he would have violent episodes in which he would destroy anything in his path, and would be completely inconsolable for about five to ten minutes. Thankfully, his owners were accustomed to these violent outbursts and could usually spot out specific behavioural patterns before an episode. Once they recognized these signs, they would place Keekay in his own room where he could have the outburst without hurting himself or anyone around him.

This being said, one particular week when the couple had guests at the house for an extended period of time, Keekay got a bit jealous, possibly from the lack of attention he was receiving, and he had one of his infamous violent episodes. Unfortunately, his owners did not recognize his change in behavioural pattern, as they were occupied with entertaining their guests, and he became violent in the same room as the guests. Keekay attacked a 64-year-old man, tearing up the left side of his face which resulted in putting the man in hospital for two weeks, and months of recovery from facial reconstructive surgery. The attacked man knew how much Keekay meant to his friends, but was also traumatized from the event and did not wish it upon anyone else. So he gave the owners a choice: either euthanize Keekay or keep him locked up in a secured cage at all times. For the owners, putting down their precious chimp was out of the question, but they also could not stand the thought of having him locked up 24/7. They fervently researched other options about anger management therapy, and this is how they stumbled across my research on emotion. They contacted me, asking if I could rehabilitate their chimpanzee. But what I gave them instead, was much more successful than any form of therapy. After the surgery, Keekay has had zero violent episodes and I can guarantee that he never will again." Dr.

Lacombe paused to let the audience take in the permanency of his last statement.

"I have many more success stories similar to these two, but no failures to show you. All seventeen surgeries have been successful. Now you might be asking yourselves, 'this is a very interesting and breakthrough discovery, but how is this the cure for the human race?' Well, ladies and gentlemen, I want you to imagine a world without emotion for one second. Just imagine a place with no fear, no hate, and no anger. There would no longer be prejudice, nor racism, nor sexism, as these concepts stem from both fear and hate. The cycle of poverty would be broken, as logically speaking, anyone born on this earth has the potential to become successful. There would be no more war or terrorism, as these acts are results of hate. There would be no more quarrels or wars over religion. Because logically, the fact that someone believes in a different God than you should not physically affect your life and therefore, should not be an issue. People could believe what they wanted and get along peacefully. But hypothetically speaking, if everyone thought completely logical, would the world believe in only one God or no God at all?" The question garnered some heated whispers from the audience. Joshua ignored them and continued his speech:

"Furthermore, people would be able to live in peace as they would no longer see each other as enemies, but as the key to survival. Because it takes the work of many to provide food, shelter, clothing and all the necessities of life. The world would change their focus to the needs of the people, animals and plants of the earth, and less on useless material goods. Pollution of the earth would dramatically decrease, as it does not make logical sense to kill your own planet. So this, ladies and gentlemen, is your cure! I am offering you a world without hate and without war. This is an opportunity to create a peaceful world, where instead of concentrating all our resources on making guns and bombs, we can put our energy into things that really matter. Like universal access to clean water and education, and improving the equality of life for everyone. I have no doubt in my mind that in a world with purely logical minds, the future would be limitless. Think of the amazing medical and scientific discoveries that could happen! Cancer would be a thing of the past, and previously incurable diseases would now have a cure.

A logical world is the New World. With logic, we would move past the Information Age and discover the next chapter of our history: The Age of Intelligence. And unlike many, I am not afraid to start this new worldwide Movement of logic. This is why, I have begun testing the surgery on human subjects."

The crowd roared with fury. A vicious wave of anger, disbelief and fear covered the grand theatre. Yet despite all this commotion, Dr. Lacombe stood unfazed and confident. As he already knew that the crowd would react this way. Because even the most intelligent and logical humans in the world are scared of a successful world. As this meant the rest of the world would see that they really aren't as smart and important as they make themselves out to be. Joshua knew that it would be impossible to get consent for human testing for this very reason. People are too scared of change. Even if that change would create success on a world wide scale. So he took the liberty of starting it himself. As he stood centre stage staring into the violent crowd, he knew that he had sparked a Movement that would change the world.

A Movement that would result in universal peace, equality, and intelligence.

This was the birth of the New World.

A new race of human beings was about to be born.

And so began the Cold Cognition Movement.

PRESENT DAY

Chapter Three

I woke up the next morning to a soft whimpering sound and a gentle tug on my bed covers. I felt so groggy and hungover from the night before that it took me a few moments to realize that the whimpers belonged to Nikita, and that the tugging was her gently pawing at my bed.

"Ugh. What do you want?" I said as I painfully rolled over to face my whining husky. But instead of changing her mood to insanely energetic (which she usually did when I gave her attention), she continued to whine whilst holding her ears back and her bushy tail between her legs. Now this was extremely rare behaviour for Nikita, I couldn't remember the last time she had acted this way. But in my current state of pain I was too tired to analyse the situation further. I slowly turned back over to face my bedroom wall again, pulling the covers over my head and hoping that this hint would shut her up.

Unfortunately, this action only caused her to whimper even louder. The whining quickly escalated into full out barking, and then to jumping right up onto my bed and pouncing on me. I tried to play dead for as long as I could (hoping that like a bear, she would get bored of my dead-like state and leave me alone. Honestly I would never try this with an actual bear, because apparently it only works with certain types of bears. And if I was ever in the situation where I was face-to-face with a bear, I doubt that I would have the composure to calmly detect what type of bear it was and whether or not I should run, play dead, start screaming… I really don't know exactly), but once Nikita pounced directly on my already pounding head, all of my motivation to play dead ceased immediately.

"Oh my god! Okay, I am up you crazy animal!" I yelled as I flailed around trying to untangle myself from the blanket trap and the feral beast on top of me. This process resulted in the both of us falling off my delightfully warm bed, and onto the cold hard floor.

"There. Are you happy now?" I yelled in defeated frustration, still tangled up in my blankets with my disheveled hair pointing in every direction. Even in this moment of defeat I could still appreciate the humour of how ridiculous this whole scene must have looked from an outsider's perspective. Nikita on the other hand, felt no such humour and slunk off to the opposite wall of my bedroom. There she backed herself up against the corner and returned to her whining. I gave her a strange look,

"I just can't please you today, can I?" I sighed heavily. 'I guess I should probably get up and do something since I'm up already', I thought to myself.

I pathetically crawled across the dark hardwood floor to where my purse lay by the half open bedroom door. I must have drunkenly dropped it as I stumbled into my room in the wee hours of the morning. A wave of dread washed over me. I just realized that I had no clue how I got home. Hopefully this meant that it was a good night. I tried hard to remember the events from yesterday as I half-heartedly searched for the cellphone in my bag. Blurry memories of the party slowly crept into my mind. I remembered dancing like crazy, having an amazing game of beer pong (which in sober reality most likely meant that I lost very badly), being amused at Dawson's flirting methods with multiple girls, making out with some guy from Saskatchewan, and trying to convince Devon not to go streaking outside in the minus thirty weather. I remembered her saying something along the lines of: "Teslin, I need to do this. It's my destiny." However, I could not recall whether or not she went through with her streaking destiny.

I finally found my phone and got a sudden shot of adrenaline to see all the drunk messages and photos that were no doubt on my cell phone. Of course with my luck, the cell was dead. I said a few choice words under my breath as I stumbled over to my bedside table where the charger lay and plugged in my phone. But nothing happened.

"What the heck?!" I said loudly. Nikita began howling even louder in response to my outburst. I had to use all my strength to stand up and walk to the other outlet in my room. Still nothing. 'Well maybe the power just went out', I thought to myself. I vaguely remembered there being a blizzard last night as I somehow tipsily made it into the taxi-cab. The storm probably caused a power outage, it had happened before. So I decided to go downstairs to flip the breaker, even though all I really wanted to do was slink back into my luxurious bed.

After what seemed like hours, I finally got out of my party clothes and into something warm and comfortable. I then made my way downstairs with Nikita following closely behind me. As I staggered down the steep flight of stairs I couldn't help thinking that the house felt eerily quiet.

"Mom?... Dad?" My shouts were met with utter silence. They probably just went out for breakfast or lunch, I had no idea what time it actually was. I finally made it to the breaker just as I felt my body wanting to give up. I switched the breaker off and on. Nothing. I tried again, still nothing. Again and again I flipped the breaker and to no avail.

"Oh come on! That's not fair!" I cried out, exasperated. I angrily stomped my way into the living room and dramatically planted myself onto the big leather sofa. I sat there pouting with my arms crossed and Nikita laying by my feet. Although she had stopped whimpering, she was still unusually quiet and docile. I ignored her weird behaviour, and turned to face the large window behind me, pulling back the covers to peak outside.

The bright sun reflecting off the fresh white snow almost blinded me. Once my eyes adjusted to the light I was able to see the winter wonderland more clearly. Outside everything was covered with a fresh coat of glistening white powder. So pristine and calm was the scene before me that I felt my anger quietly slipping away. I was hypnotized by the enchanting frosted wonderland, when something caught my eye and broke nature's spell.

There across the street, two doors to the left, were Mr. & Mrs. Killam and their two children walking down the sidewalk in their pajamas. What an odd sight to see, especially since it had to be at least minus thirty outside. They must be freezing! But what was even stranger about this sight, more so than Mr. Killam's exotic taste in pajamas, was the manner in which they were walking. It was as if they were in a daze or a dream of some sorts. Maybe they were sleep walking? 'No, Teslin, that's ridiculous. An entire family sleep walking together doesn't seem plausible'. I pressed my face up to the window and squinted my eyes to get a better look. I almost wished that I hadn't. For what I could now see that I hadn't before, was six people dressed up in white from head-to-toe pushing the family towards a large white bus.

My heart began pounding frantically in my chest. 'What the hell was going on? Was I seeing things or was this actually happening!?' My mind chaotically tried to make sense of what I had just seen, but none of the thoughts swirling around in my head were able to explain it. I focused all my attention to the scene outside, hoping for more clues that would give me some logical answer. I anxiously observed as the six soldier-like figures put the Killam family into the bus, and closed the door. The bus moved a few feet forward to the next house, while the white soldiers moved on foot. The soldiers marched up to the front door in an orderly fashion, effortlessly broke through the door and entered into the Robson's family home.

I was so stunned that my body was unable to move, frozen in shock. About thirty seconds later the White Soldiers returned with the Robson family, who also walked in a trance-like state. 'They aren't dreaming. They are being drugged!' my mind screamed at me. 'And the strange people dressed in white have to be soldiers. Look at the way they move, so unified, skillful and fast!' But there was one question that I could not wrap my head around: What were they doing with my neighbours? What did these White Soldiers want with my humdrum neighbours? Maybe I don't want to know, I thought as I noticed another white bus on my very own street. It was only two houses away. White Soldiers also accompanied this bus, and they seemed to be continuing the same pattern as those soldiers across the street. That meant they were most likely coming for me as well. Either way I wasn't going to hang around and find out.

My mind instantly went numb as my body went into survival mode. I felt like I was having an out-of-body experience as I watched myself run up the stairs, grab my bag, car keys and jacket. I half put on my winter coat as I ran down the stairs towards the front door.

"C'mon Nikita!" She didn't need to be told twice, she was practically stepping on my feet as I ran out the door to my car. I didn't even bother locking the front door, they would break it down anyways. I made a direct bee line to my car, patiently waiting in the front driveway. Parked on the street right behind my car was a white bus. My body started to quiver with fear. My fingers almost stopped working completely as I fumbled with the car keys, trying to open the frozen door.

"Calm down and open the frickin' door, Teslin." I said aloud to myself. By some miracle I managed to open the door. I rammed the keys into the ignition and turned them. But instead of being greeted by the familiar roar of the engine, there was only silence. Crap! Of all the days for my car not to work, it had to be in a life-threatening situation! My whole entire body was now shaking uncontrollably as I stumbled out of the car and ran to the front of it. There laying in front of the car in a pile of snow, was the unplugged extension cord. I picked up the cord feeling confused, because I distinctly remember plugging in the block heater yesterday night before I left for Devon's. But it didn't matter now, the engine was frozen. It would take too long to thaw it out. Using my car as an escape was out of the question. I was still holding onto the extension cord when I heard the familiar crunching sound of footsteps on the frozen ground. I looked up to see the White Soldiers to my left, leading my neighbours to the white bus parked at the end of my driveway. They saw me too. I froze, looking directly at one of the soldiers. I could feel his piercing stare even through the blacked-out face shield of the white helmet that he wore.

"Teslin, stay calm. We are here to help you," the White Soldier spoke in such a powerful and assertive voice that I almost wanted to obey him. And maybe I would have if I hadn't of looked down at the small victim he was holding in his arms. Little five-year-old Lilybelle, the sweet child that I had been babysitting since she was born. Her white blonde curls framed her delicate little face in a way that made her look like a porcelain doll. Even through the haziness of whatever drug they gave her, her big dark grey eyes were fixed on mine. And in her musical and innocent voice, she whispered the words:

"Run, Teslin."

I instantly began to slowly back away, moving down the driveway towards the direction of the street.

"Teslin, you don't need to run. We are your friends." The same soldier spoke again, this time with a soothing and kind voice. 'How do they know my name?' I wondered as I continued backing away.

"Teslin. Stop." His voice was firm and commanding again, and before I could process what he had said, my physiological flight response took over my body and I ran.

"Teslin!" I heard a voice yell behind me, but I didn't turn around.

"Don't worry about her. She has no place to run. We will collect her by the end of the night with the others."

This was the last thing I heard before I raced away from my home. I didn't know where I was running to, however, my legs seemed to know where they were going. I ran with my mind blank as the white snow under my feet.

I kept running until I came to the town centre, about five minutes from my house. It was completely dead. This never happened on a Saturday. My feet came to an abrupt stop as they didn't know where to go next. Nikita, who had been running behind me the entire time, lay down beside me and panted heavily. Not a single person could be seen and every store was closed. It was utterly and entirely empty, like a ghost town. And I just stood in the middle of the town, without even a sliver of an idea of what to do next.

I fell to my knees and sat there like that for a while, stroking my exhausted husky half-heatedly and wondering what the hell was going on. I hoped that this was all just a very bad dream, and that I would wake up and it would all be over. But I knew that this was reality, my heart pounding against my chest kept reminding me of how very real it all was. Suddenly Nikita lifted her head from my knee where she was resting it, cocked her head back and forth, and then bolted towards my favourite café about ten metres from where we were sitting. She started barking and clawing at the café front door.

"Nikita, be quiet!" I ran over to her as fast I could to put a halt to her incessant barking. When I reached the café and tried to grab her, I almost screamed with joy, because in the glass window of the café stood Mrs. Rundle, the café owner (who was also a dear friend to my family). She motioned for me to come inside quickly. I didn't hesitate, and neither did Nikita. Mrs. Rundle opened the door and closed it so hastily that I was surprised we even made it inside. Before I could say anything she embraced me with the biggest hug I had ever received from her in my life. I was a bit taken aback as Mrs. Rundle was not known for being affectionate, but I wasn't going to say no and so I hugged her back just as tightly.

"Oh Teslin, words cannot describe how happy I am to see you," Mrs. Rundle practically sang, her strong voice was mixed with fear and relief.

I took a step back and looked at her intently, "Are you okay, Mrs. Rundle?" I asked. I looked the sturdy older woman up and down to check for any visible signs of duress, but she appeared to be fine. Her momentary affection for me instantly passed, however:

"Don't look at me like I am some decrepit old woman, child! I am perfectly fine. It should be me asking if you are alright! You look like a hot mess with that hair all over the place, your makeup is a disaster, and…" she paused for a second. "Oh god, what is that I smell on your breath, alcohol? Goodness gracious child, it's a wonder how you've even survived this long!" she threw her hands up in a dramatic fashion to emphasize her point. I couldn't help but break out into a big grin. Mrs. Rundle really was okay, and feisty as ever.

"Stop smiling like an idiot and help me board up this door," she said as she began to move a heavy oak table towards the front entrance. My millions of questions and thoughts that I had been suppressing in my head since morning, poured out all at once as I helped her with the table.

"Mrs. Rundle, I'm sorry if I offended you. I didn't mean to. I am just so happy that you are okay. But do you know what the hell is going on? Where is everyone?! And why are there strange people dressed in white taking all of my neighbours into white buses?! Have you seen my parents? I don't know where they are! I just want to know what's going on, Mrs. Rundle. I'm scared that it's something bad. Something really bad. I can't explain it, but I just feel like I am in some sort of horrible nightmare with no way of waking up." I paused to catch my breath. I was about to go on but I noticed that

Mrs. Rundle had stopped boarding up the door, and stood motionless, staring outside through the glass door. Something about a silent Mrs. Rundle sent an eerie chill up my spine. I fell silent as well, not knowing what to do or say. Finally, after what seemed like ages of stillness, Mrs. Rundle spoke in a quiet voice while continuing to gaze outside.

"They came for us late in the night, about two in the morning. I had gotten up to use the washroom when I heard the front door open and footsteps coming up the stairs. I panicked and hid in the hallway closet. I could see from the crack in the door that there were men dressed in white walking into my bedroom. They pulled my husband out of bed and threw him into the hallway. They asked him where his wife was, but he said that I wasn't there, that I was visiting my sister up north. They hit him a few more times until they were satisfied that he was telling the truth. Then they released some kind of fumes from a canister and I can't remember exactly what happened next. I just know that I somehow made my way over here to find help, but I couldn't find anyone. So I boarded myself up in my shop and then that's when you came along."

She turned to look at me, pushing her long white hair behind her ears, giving herself a second to compose herself.

"I don't know what's going on, Teslin. But I do know that we aren't going to get any help from around here. We have to get out of this town and we have to do it fast."

My heart sank, she spoke that truth that I didn't want to hear. We were on our own. There was no one to help us. I stared into Mrs. Rundle's honest hazel eyes. She was my only life line until we figured out what was going on. We had to stick together.

"Okay," I said. "So how do we do that exactly? Get out of here, I mean. My cell phone isn't working, my car is out of commission, and I assume you are in the same situation?" I raised my eyebrows questioningly.

"Correct," she replied matter-of-factly. "Whoever is responsible for whatever is going on must be serious about rounding up everyone in this town, as they cut off the electricity, gas, water, and all forms of communication. And I imagine that someone as smart as this would also have all the major roads blocked off as well. This means that we can't escape using any road." Mrs. Rundle began to pace back and forth around the front of the café, tapping her chin as she thought. I just sat down on a chair and watched her with my mind completely blank.

"C'mon Teslin, don't leave all the thinking to the old lady now. How are we going to get out of this predicament of ours?" she put her hands on her hips and scowled at me.

"I'm sorry, but what can we do!? We don't have a vehicle and we can't use any roads. What are we going to do? Put on our snow boots and hike up the mountain?" I said sarcastically. Mrs. Rundle's scowl changed into an evil grin.

"Teslin! That's exactly what we are going to do! We will escape through the mountains! No one knows the mountains better than you do! You practically live up there!" she began running around the café saying that we needed to pack supplies for our long journey ahead, and asking me what kind of tea I preferred. How this woman was so positive and energetic was beyond me.

"Mrs. Rundle, I was joking! There is no way we would survive for more than a day in the mountains! They are dangerous and we do not have any of the right supplies. We would freeze to death before we were even close to finding…" I was cut off by the loud ringing of my cell phone. Both Mrs. Rundle and I stared at each other with a confused expression on our faces. 'How was my cell phone ringing when it was utterly dead this morning, and when communications were supposed to be shut off?' A surge of hope went through my mind. Maybe this was all some big misunderstanding and everything was okay now. I held onto this idea as I rummaged through my bag and pulled out the ringing device. The call display said it was my father. I jumped to my feet with both excitement and relief, and answered the phone.

"Dad! Where are you? Are you okay?!" I shouted into the speaker.

"Teslin, I am so glad that you are fine. Don't worry, I am good. And what about you? Where are you?" my dad's voice sounded a bit forced, but I was too relieved to be talking to him to care.

"I'm safe too! I am here with Mrs. - "

My phone was yanked out of my hands before I could finish my sentence. Mrs. Rundle had just grabbed the cell phone out of my hands and was now covering the speaker, looking at me with wild eyes.

"What the hell are you doing?!" I asked angrily.

"I have a bad feeling about this, Teslin. Do not tell your father where you are." She said in a very stern tone of voice.

"What are you talking about? It's my father! He is going to help us!" I practically yelled at her.

"I'm not joking around young lady. Promise me you will not tell him where you are or I'll break your phone right now!" she said this in such a forceful tone that I knew there was no changing her mind.

"Okay, fine. I promise," I said through gritted teeth. I just wanted my damn phone back from the crazy old lady. She handed me back my phone as she promised.

"Dad, are you still there?"

"Yes, I am. Honey, where are you?"

"I am… I am safe," I said, scowling at Mrs. Rundle.

"Why won't you tell me where you are, Teslin?" my father asked.

"It's a long story, dad. But where are you? I can meet you somewhere." There was a moment of silence before he spoke again.

"Of course. Meet me at the house in an hour. Can you do that?"

"Yes, I can!" Memories of the terrifying morning flooded my mind. "Listen, dad, this is going to sound crazy, but there are White Soldiers going around abducting everyone in town. It's not safe! I don't know what's going on." I said with a shaky voice.

"Darling, don't worry. I know you must be scared, but you have to trust me. Everything will be okay. Meet me and your mother at the house in an hour. We will make sure you and whoever else you are with are safe. Okay?" my Dad said all this with a calm and steady voice, like he knew exactly what was going on. But how could he know everything and be so calm about it? Something didn't make sense.

"Okay, sounds good. See you in an hour," was all I said before the phone went dead. Now I felt even more confused than I did a few moments ago. Mrs. Rundle walked up to me and took my hands into hers.

"Sweetheart, please don't get mad at me but I have a really nasty feeling about this." She had obviously overheard the entire conversation and felt just as uneasy as I did. "I know that he is your father, but I don't think you should trust him. We have to find help from someone outside this town. We have to go through the mountains, Teslin!"

I let go of her hands and took a step back.

"I understand why you feel that way, but he is my father and I trust him." Even I could hear the doubt in my voice as I said this. "I at least need to hear what he has to say." I quickly added.

Mrs. Rundle gave me a weak smile, "Alright, Teslin. But I am still going to get all the supplies we need for the mountains. I am going either way, with or without you. But I do want you to come with me. I will wait for you by the lake we always start our hikes at in the summer, close to the Nordic Centre, remember? I will wait there until mid-day before I start trekking north to Banff, okay? There's got to be someone that can help us there. We just need to inform the RCMP about all the mass abductions and it will blow up into a big news story. There will be nowhere for those horrid people to hide, and I will get my sweet husband back."

Mrs. Rundle said all this in an overly confident manner. I couldn't help but laugh at this. Of all people to be stuck with in this town, I was glad it was with Mrs. Rundle. She was such a tough and matter-of-fact person who always got the job done. She had never been afraid of hard work. I could learn a lot from this woman.

"Alright, Mrs. Rundle, I'll tell you what. I will for sure meet you at the meeting point. I will either be coming to you with good news or bad news. Let's hope it is good news for our sake. There has to be a reasonable explanation to all of this madness, and I'm sure my father will have the answer. Everything is going to be just fine." I tried to say all of this in an equally confident voice, however, judging by the skeptical look on Mrs. Rundle's face I was not successful.

"Whatever you say child. Now, help me with the packing, would you?"

****

For the next half hour, I let Mrs. Rundle boss me around: telling me what to pack, how to pack it, and how horrible I was at packing. Under normal circumstances I would have probably only lasted about five minutes before I started an uprising against the authoritarian woman. Fortunately for her it was not a normal day, and I welcomed the constant commands as an alternative to thinking about other things.

I was still most definitely in denial about what I had seen this morning. There had to be some reasoning for this, as well as a justification as to why my father seemed to be unaffected by the mass abductions. I refused to believe that he had anything to do with the White Soldiers, but the alternative seemed to fit together much easier than my wishful thinking. I pushed these thoughts to the back of my mind and focused on the current task of packing the last of the baked goods into an already overflowing backpack.

"You better get going, missy. You're gonna be late."

I was so concentrated in my own little world that Mrs. Rundle's loud voice made me jump in fright. Mrs. Rundle gave me a sympathetic look. I probably looked exactly how I felt: like a complete nervous wreck. She walked over to me and helped me put on my jacket. Then she gave me a warm scarf, a wool toque and some heavy-duty mitts.

"It's gotten even colder out my dear. You are going to freeze with just your winter coat," she said as she finished wrapping the scarf around my neck.

"Thank you." I wished my voice didn't sound so pathetic, but I couldn't help it. I was scared. Mrs. Rundle walked me over to the café front door, but just before she opened it she embraced me tightly and whispered in my ear:

"When you get to your house, run straight upstairs before you talk to your parents. Grab your backpack and pack as many warm clothes as you can." She then pulled out of our embrace so that we were face to face. She put her hand gently on my cheek, "Now this part is important, Teslin. Please don't fight me on it. Make sure you have some kind of weapon with you when you go down to talk with your parents." The growing horror in my eyes was surely visible as she spoke those last words.

"Why would I need a weapon to talk to my parents?" I asked, dreading the answer.

"I hope to God that you do not need to use it, but just have it with you in case. Okay? Promise me you'll do this, Teslin. Promise me, please."

She looked at me with so much care and concern, a look that she had never given me before. I had no idea that Mrs. Rundle cared about me this much, and I did not want to let her down, so I nodded my head. This made her smile and tear up, consequently making me tear up as well. She opened the door and gently pushed me outside.

"Be safe. I'll see you soon" was the last thing she said before she closed the door and I was completely alone.

The piercing cold instantly brought me back to the present, and a gust of icy wind took my breath away completely. The harsh cold always brought me back to reality, it had no room for emotional thinking. When it was this cold you just focussed on the task at hand and nothing more. As a result, I became highly aware of my snowy surroundings. There was no creature or human to be seen, except for me and my faithful husky. I looked down at Nikita, who stood protectively by my side. She looked back up at me with her icy blue eyes. I didn't have to tell her anything, she already knew how I felt. They say that dogs, and animals in general, have a sixth sense and are able to tell how people feel and can even predict natural disasters. I personally believed that people could also do this, but we are just too self-centered and so wrapped up with the craziness of life to ever notice that we have this ability.

Another gust of unbearably frigid wind hit my face, almost as if it was slapping me and telling me to get a move on. Not wanting to stay out in the minus thirty something Celsius degree weather for more than I had to, I started trudging through the fresh pile of snow that was supposed to be the road. Pushing myself forward through the biting snow and the frosty air made me feel stronger. If I could survive living in one of the coldest places on the planet, I could handle whatever the future held for me. And this is the thought that I held on to as I made my way towards my waiting parents.

I reached my house about ten minutes later. At this point the frozen cold didn't even bother me anymore. The idea of what I might find inside my house was far more daunting than the harsh weather. I reached the front door of my house and turned the knob. It was unlocked. My hands began shaking uncontrollably as I pushed open the heavy door. I took one last deep breath of the sobering cold air and forced myself to walk inside. Then I closed the door so quickly that I almost caught poor Nikita's tail in it. I had forgotten that she was even behind me, she had been so quiet. As I stood facing the door, I heard two familiar voices speak in unison:

"Hello, Teslin."

I turned around slowly, and there past the living room and in the kitchen, stood my parents, directly in front of me. They stood with impeccable posture and they looked at me with big smiles on their faces, waiting for me to reply. 'Well this is already weird,' I thought to myself. 'My parents are never this happy to see me, something is definitely not right here'. I didn't know how to respond to this so I simply replied:

"Hello, mother. Father." My words sounded so strange to even my own ears. It was like I was talking to a pair of strangers. Yet my parents didn't seem to be phased by my overly strange polite response.

"Come join us in the kitchen to talk, dear." my mother said, still smiling. I was just about to listen when I remembered the promise that I had made to Mrs. Rundle.

"Umm… yeah, for sure. Just give me one sec, okay? I need to grab something from my room." I ran upstairs before they even had a chance to reply.

As I entered my room, I felt oddly comfortable and peculiar at the same time. Obviously the feeling of calm was from being in the house that I had lived in for all of my twenty-two years of life, however, the strangeness that I sensed was from something that I couldn't exactly put my finger on. I think because, in all honesty, I had never experienced such a day as I had today. And it still wasn't over. All of my answers as to what was going on in our quaint little town could possibly be answered by the two people standing in the kitchen downstairs. But for whatever reason, I didn't feel happy or relieved about this prospect. In fact, I was sort of dreading it.

'You have to stop over-thinking things and just do it! Like a Band-Aid, rip it off fast and then it's all over.' I advised myself most sternly. Although this metaphor stood the test of time for most, for me, it just reminded me of the last encounter I had with a Band-Aid (a horrible incident in which took me 26 minutes to slowly pull off a Band-Aid from my right arm that was covering a minor cut. Needless to say, Band-Aids were not my friends).

"Keep it together, Teslin!" I said aloud. This wasn't the time nor the place to let my mind wander as it pleased. I finally got myself back on track and went about grabbing my biggest backpack and stuffing all of my warmest clothing inside. I was just about to go back downstairs with my barely closed backpack, when I remembered Mrs. Rundle's warning. I needed to have a weapon. 'What kind of weapon did I need to protect me from my parents? What were they gonna do, lecture me to death?' I thought sarcastically. Still, I promised Mrs. Rundle and I was a woman of my word, so I searched around my room looking for something that resembled a protective item of sorts.

It was while I was rummaging under my bed that I pulled out my box of keepsakes. An embarrassed smile crept onto face, 'Holy crap, I do have a weapon in my room! My lipstick Taser!' I tried not to giggle as my fingers grasped the bright pink Taser in the form of a common cosmetic. Memories of the story behind this small little bad boy came rushing back as if it was only yesterday when Dawson, Devon and I, snuck Tasers across the border as a dare. Tasers are of course illegal in Canada, however, that doesn't mean we can't get our hands on them if we wanted…

It was about two years ago when the three of us decided to take a road trip. We all really wanted to go somewhere out of the country for spring break, but we were so poor from school that we couldn't afford to go to places like Cancun or Miami. Nonetheless, we were determined to get out of the country, so after we put our resources together we were able to afford an exotic vacation down to Great Falls, Montana. Whilst enjoying our wonderful vacation in Montana, I became particularly fascinated by all the guns, knives and Tasers that were so easily accessible. I especially fell in love with the sparkly pink beauty that I currently held in my hands now. But at the time I told myself that it was a silly idea. Tasers were illegal in my country after all, I couldn't take it home with me. No matter how much I wanted it. Dawson had noticed my looks of admiration, however, and dared me to try to sneak it over the border. Not one to back down from a dare, I immediately purchased the small Taser. Not wanting to miss out on the fun, both Dawson and Devon also bought themselves Tasers. I remember it so clearly, the moment when we drove up to the border crossing and the border officer asked me, "Are you in possession of any firearms or weapons?" My heart was practically beating out of my chest as I innocently answered: "Nope." After a few more standard questions we triumphantly crossed the border back into Canada! Unscathed, and with our precious cargo intact. I felt so free and alive! Truth be told, that was probably the most badass thing I had ever done in my life! Consequently, the moment I arrived home, I ran up to my room and hid it in my keepsake box. This is where it had stayed for the past two and a half years, safe under my bed.

"Okay, Mrs. Rundle, I have that weapon you wanted," I whispered to myself as I stood up from the floor. I threw my backpack on my shoulders, hid the Taser in my jacket pocket, and walked downstairs. Walking down the stairs I felt a bit more confident, and also a bit insane as to why I was carrying such an item to go talk to my parents. I also noticed how cold it was in the house. That meant nothing had changed from this morning, the power was still out. 'Maybe the White Soldiers had just evacuated everyone and took them somewhere with heat so they didn't freeze?' I thought doubtfully to myself. I couldn't avoid my parents any longer without being suspicious, so I got up from the bottom step (where I had sat down to procrastinate a bit longer) and walked towards the kitchen.

As I turned the corner I observed a strange scene indeed. My mother and father stood behind the kitchen table (again with unusually good posture) looking emotionless, while Nikita stood on the edge of where the living room turned into the kitchen. She stood on the carpet but would not cross over onto tile. She stood in a defensive position with her ears back and her body low to the ground, her eyes never leaving my parents. This was NOT a good sign. Ironically it was my dad who taught me to always trust the instincts of a dog, and now it was my dog warning me not to trust my own father. My pulse once again went sky rocket so I could hardly hear my own thoughts.

"Teslin, darling, please come sit down." My mother gestured to the chair next to her. 'It's facing the wall, there is no quick escape from that position. Do not sit there,' I was shocked at the warning voice in my own head, but I listened submissively.

"No thanks, I think I will just stand here," I replied talking a stand next to Nikita - not crossing over into the kitchen. My parents both looked at me and then to Nikita. Their faces were expressionless and therefore I could not decipher what they were thinking.

"As you wish," my father said. He began slowly walking towards me as he spoke, "I can imagine how confused and scared you must be, to see the things that you did. But those White Soldiers you spoke of were not actually abducting our neighbours. They were saving them." He stopped about a foot in front of me, and I swear that I could hear a faint growl in Nikita's throat.

"What do you mean by 'saving them'," I asked warily. "Is it because there's no heat or water? Did the snow storm do something to the town's power? Is that why?"

My father locked his eyes on mine. He only did this when he was judging whether or not he should tell me something. 'Then it must not be a simple explanation such as a power outage,' I quickly realized. My mother's voice interrupted our intense staring contest, and I turned my gaze towards her. She also began walking towards me as she spoke.

"Your father and I have been chosen to be part of a world-changing Movement, Teslin. A Movement that will finally bring peace and equality to this world." She stopped beside my father and held his hand. They looked at each other and smiled. 'Oh my god, my parents have gone insane', I couldn't help thinking. 'What were they taking about? A 'world-changing movement' that would bring peace and equality? What did that even mean?' My confusion was turning into frustration at this point.

"What are you guys talking about?" I said a little too loudly.

"It would be easier just to show you, rather than try to explain it to you," my dad replied. "You won't understand right now. You're angry and confused. You're not thinking straight. Please come with us and we will show you everything. Once you receive the Cold Surgery it will all be very clear to you." He outstretched his hand to me, waiting for me to take it. Nikita's growls were undeniably audible now, and I took a step back instead of taking his hand.

"You guys are making no sense, whatsoever! Have you been drugged or something? And what do you mean give me a 'Cold Surgery'? What the hell is that!?" I was shouting at them.

"Teslin, you're allowing your emotions to affect your thought process. Stay calm, and we will explain everything as I said before."

"How can I stay calm, when you and mom are acting like crazy people?! And telling me the whole town has been saved by some world-changing Movement? Do you realize how insane that sounds?"

I had passed the point of frustration, and now I was completely furious. I still had no idea what was going on, my parents were insane, and I somehow got in the middle of all this. I just wanted to wake up from this dreadful nightmare already.

My mother and father gave each other a look, and then my father had my left arm in a tight arm lock before I even had a chance to react.

"You must come with us now. Everything will be okay." he said as he held me tightly. Then I saw my mother pull out a black canister from her purse. 'It must be that drug Mrs. Rundle was talking about. The one the White Soldiers have been using on everyone. My parents are going to drug me and take me away like the rest of the town.' I could feel the adrenaline rising in my body. It was only a matter of seconds before my fight-or-flight response took control of my body. And it did; but this time instead of running, I fought.

Without thinking, I kicked the back of my father's knee. As he fell, I took this opportunity to use my free hand and grab the Taser hidden in my pocket. I pulled the cap off and tasered my father in the back. His body slumped to the ground, writhing in pain. I turned to my mother who held the canister in her hand and a thick scarf over her nose. She was only able to disperse a small amount of gas before I kicked the can out of her hand. This didn't even phase her, as she ran straight at me, knocking me to the ground and constricting her hands tightly around my neck. I lay helpless on the ground. She sat on top of me using her weight and legs to strategically disable me from moving, while she gripped my throat tighter and tighter. I couldn't move or breathe. The world started spinning and turning black.

'This is how it's going to end' I thought as I went in and out of consciousness. 'I'll never know what actually happened', this was my last thought before I felt all the weight of my mother being lifted off of me, and the violent pressure on my neck vanishing. I wondered if this is what death felt like, silence and darkness. It felt so peaceful. But then the most heinous of agony came up through my lungs and assailed my tortured throat. It took me a moment to recover from the ghastly pain and to realize that I was breathing again. I was not dead.

Consciousness quickly returned to me and I could hear the most gruesome and grisly sounds. This was enough to get my heart pumping and my body to jump to its feet. Through the haziness I could see what was making those horrible noises. My mother was screaming as Nikita stood on top of her, making the most ungodly noises and gnawing at my mother's throat. Red was everywhere. I covered my mouth, almost vomiting from seeing the bloody scene. But since I had nothing in my stomach to throw up, it was only a false alarm. I steadied myself from falling over and hoarsely yelled out:

"Nikita!"

She lifted her head up from my mother's raw neck and turned to look at me. Her patches of white fur were dipped in crimson red, and her eyes mirrored the fierce yellow eyes of the wolves she descended from.

"Come here!" I demanded, my voice still not my own. She obeyed. Then I saw my father crawling over to my bleeding mother. My mind went absolutely numb, and I turned and ran out the door onto the glistening, white-covered streets.

I raced faster and faster away from home. Thinking that the faster I ran, the faster the memories of what I had just seen and done would become distant, far-away memories. I kept running, up into the mountains, until I saw Mrs. Rundle in the distance. She was in the exact place where she said she would be. As I came closer, I could see that there were more figures standing with her. But the closer and closer I got, the blurrier and blurrier they became. I finally reached Mrs. Rundle and collapsed into her arms. I could hear a loud hum, like she was talking to me, but I couldn't hear anything more. I no longer could see anything either. The world began to change into a swirling pool of black darkness. Then there was nothing.

Chapter Four

I dreamt of a peaceful winter morning. Light snow fell through the rays of warm sun. The Rocky Mountains smiled as the falling feathery snow tickled their sides. The mountain goats played a game of chase along the mountain tops, expertly jumping across the dangerous peaks. The birds danced through the air, sweetly singing in harmony, thankful for another beautiful sunny day. I was hypnotized by the spectacular scene before me.

And then suddenly a little bird dropped from the sky. It fell to the ground so delicately that I thought it had done this on purpose. That is, until the white snow around its tiny body turned bright red. For in reality, the innocent little bird did not fall down, it had been shot down. Then another, and another. One by one the tiny birds were shot down from the clear blue sky.

I tried to yell and warn them to fly away, but I had no voice. It felt as if someone was behind me, holding my throat tightly so that I could not scream. I turned my head to see if someone was behind me, and that's when I saw the White Soldiers. They were crouching amongst the thick trees and holding strange crystal guns that reflected in the sun. I wanted to scream and run at them, but I still had no voice and my body refused to move. I stood there helplessly on the side of the mountain, listening to sweet, innocent songs turn into horrid screams. The screaming got louder and louder, until it didn't sound at all like screaming anymore. Instead, it reminded me of voices in a heated argument. The voices became louder and more comprehensible until I realized that I wasn't dreaming anymore. My heavy eyes continued to stay shut as I listened in on the surrounding voices:

"Not yet! The poor thing is exhausted and no doubt traumatized. Give her at least twenty more minutes of peace." The voice was from a woman. It must be Mrs. Rundle.

"We have to wake her soon. We are losing daylight and we are like sitting ducks out here. We have to go much further and deeper into the mountains if we are going to have any chance at all." This voice was from a man. But not a familiar one. It was a very deep and strong voice that had some sort of accent attached to it.

"I agree with Calmar; we are only putting ourselves at risk by staying out in the open. We are wasting precious time by waiting here." Another unfamiliar voice spoke. It was a soft spoken female voice. Yet even though the voice was small, there was something powerful about this speaker that I could not put my finger on.

"Let me wake her up then. I'll do it gently, and she won't be afraid because she knows me." I instantly recognized this voice. It was Dawson. He was okay! A little bit of hope instantly started to grow inside of me. 'Maybe Devon was okay too!' Before I could continue to think about who else may have avoided the White Soldiers, I felt a warm hand touch the left side of my face.

"Hey there, sleeping beauty. It's time to get up now." Dawson was speaking in his sweetest voice. He used this same voice when he was attempting to get me to lend him money. I slowly opened my eyes, but shut them quickly due to the burning sun reflecting off the snow.

"Hey asshole," I said half-heartedly through squinty eyes. He laughed at this.

"She's going to be just fine everyone!" he announced. This news caused quite a kerfuffle throughout the group. I slowly stood to my feet with the help of Dawson. Then I almost fell back down as Mrs.

Rundle charged at me with a big bear hug. Before I could even react she was stuffing my mouth with a muffin.

"Eat, young lady!" she commanded. I did not put up a fight. I didn't realize how hungry I was until I devoured the muffin Mrs. Rundle forced upon me. "That's a good girl," she said, stroking my hair as if I was a dog.

'A dog.' My mind went instantly to thoughts of my own dog.

"Nikita!" I cried out. "Where is she?"

My question was quickly answered by a bounding bundle of fur knocking me over and licking my face to death. I hugged her tightly and buried my face in her thick black and white fur. This hyperactive creature had just saved my life, and may have killed my mother in the process. I didn't know how to comprehend that possibility. I just knew that right now, I wanted to hold on tightly to this dog that I loved so much. I felt a pair of arms embrace me from behind. It was Dawson.

"You're okay now, Teslin," he said gently. "What happened with your parents?" he asked in an uneasy tone. His question sent a shiver down my spine. I did not want to retell the gory events to everyone, especially since some of those people were strangers. So instead I simply lifted my head up from Nikita, found the eyes of Mrs. Rundle and said:

"You were right."

Mrs. Rundle pursed her lips and frowned.

"She doesn't need to tell us right now, you idiot!" she directed towards Dawson, along with a fierce glare. He glared back at her. The two of them didn't have the best history of getting along.

"Now Teslin, there are some people that I want you to meet," Mrs. Rundle held her hand out and I took it. She walked me over five steps toward a young Native American woman sitting on a wooden bench.

"Teslin, this is Sylvan and her beautiful baby boy, Nisku."

Sylvan expertly balanced her baby in one hand and held out her free hand for me to shake. She smiled as we shook hands, and I couldn't help but be taken aback by her beauty. She was probably one of the most beautiful woman I had ever seen in my life. She had flawless tanned skin, high sculpted cheekbones, long silky black hair that rolled down to her waist, and a pair of loving dark eyes.

"Nice to meet you, Teslin." she said in a musical and quiet voice. She was the voice that I had heard talking before.

"Nice to meet you too, Sylvan." I politely replied and then smiled down at her young child. As the plump little child returned my smile, I realized that Sylvan was still holding onto my hand. I thought this was a bit strange, so I looked up to find her eyes looking deeply into mine, as if she was peering into my soul. I was lost for words, but thankfully she spoke up:

"You are very strong, Teslin. Stronger than you think. Don't let fear and doubt tell you otherwise." Then she let go of my hand. I didn't know what to think of what she just said, or what to do, so I simply said: "Thank you". She gave me a gorgeous smile in return.

"Now, over here -", Mrs. Rundle began speaking as she moved me towards a tall man who must have been in his late twenties, "- is Calmar. He's from Australia." She said rather bluntly.

"Nice to meet you, Australia." I said, poking fun at Mrs. Rundle. Calmar laughed, along with Dawson and Sylvan. However, Mrs. Rundle didn't seem to find the humour in this, and proceeded to give me dirty looks.

"Nice to meet you too," he said shaking my hand. "So do you prefer being called Teslin or Canada?" he asked mock seriously, continuing the joke much to the dismay of Mrs. Rundle.

"I'll proudly respond to both," I replied, trying not to laugh and further provoke poor Mrs. Rundle.

"Well now that we've all been properly introduced we better get a move on. It's going to get dark in a few hours and we have to get as far away from here as possible." Calmar was no longer joking as he said this. He was completely serious.

"Up the mountain and then north to Banff, right?" I asked, feeling hopeful that with a group on our side we could easily put a stop to whatever Movement my parents were talking about. Calmar and Mrs. Rundle exchanged worried looks as I said this.

"Actually we can't go to Banff," Calmar said hesitantly. I gave him a confused look which encouraged him to explain further. "We can't go to Banff, because it's currently being raided by the White Soldiers. I just barely escaped, and ran here thinking I could get help. But apparently that's not an option." He looked at me, waiting for my reaction. I couldn't give him one, because frankly I couldn't speak.

'What exactly are we dealing with? How did these soldiers, this Movement, or whatever it was, move so fast? And where do we go for help that won't already be too late?' All of these thoughts stampeded through my mind at once. I was getting so tired with my growing list of questions, and frustrated by the utterly unknown situation we were currently in the middle of.

Calmar's voice interrupted my internal dialogue, "Teslin, I know it's hard, but if you tell us what happened with your parents, maybe that'll give us an idea as to what's going on." He gave me an encouraging smile, while Mrs. Rundle looked at me like I was about to have a mental breakdown any second.

"Okay," was all I said. I felt everyone take a step closer, no doubt dying to know what had made me run towards them like a maniac and why Nikita was covered in blood. I took a deep breath and retold the events that occurred in my living room. I told them every word that was spoken between my parents and I. I didn't even spare them from the grisly details of the attack. I swear Dawson was about to get sick when I described what Nikita did to my mother.

After I finished, I stood in silence and looked around at the four and a half people standing in front of me. Even baby Nisku seemed to be affected by the bloody tale; the six-month-old stared at me with big brown eyes. Of course, Mrs. Rundle was the first one to break the silence, "How in the hell did you get your hands on an illegal weapon missy?" she asked in horror.

"Are you kidding me?" I retorted. "My mom might be dead and you're going to lecture me on that?! You're the one who told me to have a weapon in the first place!" I pointed out loudly.

"I mean really, Mrs. Rundle, have some sympathy for goodness' sake," Dawson mimicked the voice of Mrs. Rundle as he spoke. She turned towards Dawson and was just about to let him have it, when a loud Australian accent filled the air.

"Okay everyone, we need to stay focused." We all turned to face Calmar, who apparently took it upon himself to be the group's moderator. "So your parents said they were a part of some "world-changing Movement" that's supposed to create peace and equality before they attacked you?"

I nodded, "Yeah, and they also mentioned something about a surgery. A "cold surgery" I believe is what they called it. They also kept saying how I shouldn't let my emotions affect my thought process. I don't know if that's relevant but it's something that they've never said to me before."

"Okay. Thanks, Teslin," Calmar smiled at me. "What would you guys think if we start walking up the mountain for a good two or three hours? Then we can find somewhere to set up camp. After that we should discuss any ideas or theories as to what this Movement has to do with everything we have just been through, and what we should do next. I am sure that we can piece it all together and come up with a decent plan of action." He looked around the group for agreement. No one opposed. Mrs. Rundle clapped her hands together loudly, startling Nikita who barked at the high pitched sound.

"Alrighty then, everyone, take a backpack and a sleeping bag. We will take turns carrying the baby." She already had her backpack on and was starting to walk up the mountain trail before she finished giving orders. Sylvan and Nisku walked behind her, followed by Dawson, then me, and Calmar taking the rear. We kept that order for the entire first hour. The only thing we said was the occasional, "Mind your step" or "Watch out for the tree branch". The snow was so deep, and it took twice the energy to take each step; therefore, small talk was not really an option as we were all huffing and puffing and trying to conserve as much energy as possible. Up and up the six of us went. In utter silence, we pushed our way up the unforgiving mountain.

****

At about the halfway point of our journey, the silence was starting to drive me absolutely insane. Not only that, but the thoughts in my head proved to be very unhelpful: Replaying the living room scene over and over again, and trying to find a clue of something that could explain my parents' behaviour and why my mother tried to kill me. Attempting to make sense of a senseless day was slowly making me senseless in the process. I had to talk to someone. I needed something to distract myself from the twisting dark thoughts inside my brain.

I looked to the front of the line where Mrs. Rundle was marching at a speed the military would be proud of. I'd rather not find out the consequence of interrupting her rhythmic marching. Next in line was Sylvan. I had no idea of how to even start a conversation with such a beautiful woman. 'This must be how guys felt when they wanted to talk to a pretty girl,' I thought to myself. I didn't feel particularly confident today, so I looked at Dawson, who was walking directly in front of me carrying baby Nisku. I wanted to ask him about Devon and the rest of our friends, but I couldn't handle any more disappointing news. So I looked behind me at the Australian; my last resort. I knew nothing about him whatsoever, so it should be easy to make small talk. Maybe he even had an interesting life story to tell me (I was very desperate for any kind of temporary distraction). Making up my mind, I slowed down my pace so that Calmar caught up to me and we were walking side-by-side.

"Ski or snowboard?" I asked him casually. This was a perfectly normal question to ask, as it was extremely common for Australians and other foreigners to live and work in Banff so they could enjoy our beautiful mountains.

"Snowboard," he replied. "You too?" he asked.

"No way, I'm a skier. I like to face the mountain head-on," I replied.

He just smiled and shook his head, not saying anything else. I waited a moment more before I spoke up again.

"So you're quiet when it comes to conversation, but apparently not so much when it comes to giving orders," I concluded with much more sass then necessary. Nonetheless, my plan worked. It got his attention. At first he looked a bit taken aback from my comment, then he quickly replied:

"Sorry, just a reflex I guess. I was in the military for seven years. Giving orders is a bad habit of mine." He managed to say all this without making eye contact with me.

"So I presume you're not in the army anymore, what made you stop? Didn't like it anymore?" I asked nosily.

"I loved it. However, I had seen enough to last me a few lifetimes. I needed a change," he said flippantly like it was no big deal.

"Did you ever kill anyone?" the words were out of my mouth before I could stop them. I looked at him with wide eyes full of shock and uneasiness, not sure how he would react to my inappropriate question. To my surprise, he didn't seem the least bit phased. Instead, he finally turned to face me. It was the first time that I had gotten the chance to really look at him. He was actually quite handsome. Not in the obvious way that Dawson was, but in a subtle, more rugged way. He had strong features, lightly tanned skin, and dark brown eyes that held many secrets. I also couldn't help but feel the desire to run my fingers through his thick, loosely-curled black hair. I almost blushed at this thought, but managed to hold myself together as he was staring right at me and would have noticed.

"Yes, I have," his eyes appeared to get even darker when he said this. My stomach turned. I had no idea how to respond to this answer of a question I should have never asked. 'Should I say "I'm sorry?" or maybe try to bond with him and say: "Oh I know how you feel. I may have gotten my mom killed this morning. It's a bummer." ???' I thought in panic, unsure of how to proceed. God must have taken pity on me, as a sudden loud voice redirected our attention.

"Damn, Mrs. Rundle! I can see that you've been doing your squats lately. Good work on that booty!"

'Thank you for Dawson and his stupid comments,' I silently prayed as the tension between Calmar and I was completely shattered. Our full attention was now centered on the no-doubt-dramatic-show unfolding before us. Mrs. Rundle whipped around to face Dawson, consequently smacking Sylvan with her backpack (as she was standing right next to Mrs. Rundle) and causing her to fall over into the deep snow. Mrs. Rundle was too angry to even notice that Sylvan had fallen, as she began screeching at Dawson:

"You nasty little boy! When did you become such a disrespectful brat? You used to be such a nice boy until you hit puberty. After that, you decided to stop using your brain and let your little pecker do all the thinking!"

I had to cover my mouth to stop from laughing hysterically! I couldn't believe Mrs. Rundle had just said that to Dawson! What was even more hilarious was how true it was! Dawson used to be such a sweet boy, until he realized that he could get away with murder by using his charm and good-looks. I was still struggling with not laughing when I looked over to Dawson. He had obviously expected her to say something like this, and pretended to be unaffected by her comments.

"I was giving you a compliment! You don't have to get so defensive!" he weakly retorted back.

"Oh for goodness' sake, give me that child!" she said as she grabbed baby Nisku from his arms (it had been his turn to carry the peaceful child). "You are going to corrupt the little angel. Here, Teslin, you hold Nisku. At least you'll set a good example for him," she exclaimed as she placed the smiling child in my arms.

"Oh yeah, a really good role model there. She tasered her father and let her dog attack her mother, but she's great with kids!" Dawson said loudly and sarcastically.

Everyone instantly went silent and stared at him with disbelief and shock. He then realized the severity of what he just carelessly said, and looked at me with regret. I could tell that he truly did regret his hurtful words, but it was too late. He already said them. My blood began to boil and sharp cutting words began gathering their way into my mouth. I was just about to release them, when Mrs. Rundle beat me to the punch, literally. She simply walked up to Dawson, gave him the scariest death stare I had ever seen, and slapped him hard across the face. Then she turned on her heel and continued walking up the mountain. Without a word being said, we all followed suit. No one spoke a word. A strong gust of wind blew by us, and with it, it took my last flicker of hope. How would we ever survive this impossible situation, if we couldn't even get along for a couple of hours?

After about another hour of complete silence we reached a somewhat flat opening in the mountainous forest. In my eyes it looked like a glorious sanctuary in contrast to the steep, thickly wooded terrain we had been struggling with for the past few hours. I still had Nisku in my arms. He had been fussy for the past half an hour, and now he began to cry. I gave Calmar a look that I hope said, 'We should probably stop now.' He received the message clearly.

"I think this will be a good place to set up for the night," he announced loudly so he could be heard over Nisku's cries. Nisku suddenly stopped crying and strained his neck to look at Calmar. Then he gave him the biggest toothless smile as if he understood that we were finally stopping. Calmar appeared to be a bit unsure of how to react to the smiling child, but then he smiled back instinctively.

"He likes you," a soft voice said. Sylvan walked over and took Nisku from me. "I bet you are a hungry little wolf, aren't you?" she said to the now giggling baby. Calmar cleared his throat, he was in his commanding officer mode again.

"Alright. How about Mrs. Rundle, Sylvan and I stay here and set up the tents, while Teslin and Dawson go collect firewood?" he made a point to look at me for approval.

Actually our whole dysfunctional group looked at me, waiting for me to speak. This day was getting stranger and stranger.

"Sounds good," I said to Calmar. "Let's get to work everyone. C'mon, Dawson." I turned from the serene haven and trucked into the heavily wooded forest, never checking to see if Dawson was actually following me. To be quite honest, I was still a bit perturbed by his earlier comment, and as a result, I really didn't care if he was following me or not. I almost wished he wasn't. And then I heard "Hey, Teslin!" not too far behind me from where I was crouching down picking up broken branches. I sighed loudly. It was just not my day.

"What do you want?" I said sharply.

"I just want to say I'm sorry for what I said earlier. You know I didn't mean it. I was just upset with everything that's going on. I mean, we don't even know what's going on, how messed up is that?"

"Very," is all I replied, not giving him any eye contact whatsoever. He pulled my arm and spun me around to face him. I had no choice but to look into his dark blue eyes, which were looking at me very anxiously.

"You scared me, Teslin." His tone was eerily serious, almost too serious for my liking, and I frowned in confusion. It took him a second to realize that I would need a more detailed explanation, and he took a deep breath before he spoke.

"When you were telling us about what happened with your parents, you just seemed, I don't know, so cold about it. Like you were retelling something you saw on TV. And I could have never in a million years thought that you would Taser your dad, or let Nikita attack your mom. You would never do something like that. Your mom and dad are like family to me too; I care about them and you very much. I just don't know what to think, Teslin."

During his explanation, his eyes never left mine. They were so sincere, probably the sincerest that they had ever been. I couldn't possibly be mad at him. Taking his hands in mine, I calmly explained myself, or what I thought was myself:

"Look Dawson, you weren't there. You didn't see them. They looked like my parents, and sounded like them, but they didn't act like them. It was like I was talking to strangers. Then when my dad grabbed me so quickly, it caught me off guard and I just reacted without thinking. Also, I didn't LET Nikita attack my mom. The only reason she attacked my mom was because she was choking me to death! As soon as I regained consciousness and figured out what was going on, I told Nikita to stop. Now, tell me what I should have done differently in that situation?! I had no choice, Dawson! I would probably be dead or God-knows-where if I hadn't of fought back." I let go of his hands and took a step back, the snow crunched loudly under my feet. He looked at the ground and avoided my eye contact.

"I'm so sorry, Teslin. I guess that after everything that has happened, I had just hoped we would get some answers when Mrs. Rundle told me you were talking to your parents. But that wasn't the case, and I took my frustration out on you. I'm sorry." His voice was genuinely apologetic. I smiled at him and hugged him tightly.

"I forgive you."

He hugged me back even tighter. The warm feeling in my body was suddenly overtaken by my horrid curiosity, and out came the question that I had been dreading:

"What happened last night? I know that you and a bunch of others crashed at Devon's place, and -" I couldn't finish the sentence. Dawson lowered his head. He looked ashamed for some reason. I didn't want to push him further.

"You don't have to tell me."

"You need to know, she is your best friend too," he was referring to Devon. He started fidgeting with a tree branch before he began to talk, "I don't exactly remember what time it was, very early in the morning I'm sure. Most of us were already passed out, and the ones still awake were pretty wasted. Anyways, I really needed to take a piss, but of course all the washrooms were full. So I put on a jacket and boots and went outside. While I was taking my time outside, I heard some strange noises out front, so I went to see what was going on. I walked around to the front of the house, where I saw a bunch of soldier-like-guys dressed in white taking everyone out of the house and piling them into a white bus. I should've done something, but I couldn't move. I was frozen. I hid in a spruce tree and watched the soldiers pack everyone into the bus, and then do the same at the next house. I didn't know what to do. So I grabbed my stuff from the house and ran. I was wandering around in the trails when I found Mrs. Rundle, and she told me you were okay," he finally looked up at me and gave me a crooked smile. "I was so relieved to know that you were alright, Teslin! Hell is a lot easier to handle with your best friend," he ended in a solemn voice.

I rolled my eyes at him, "You are so dramatic!" I exclaimed. "This is not hell. First of all, we're not dead. Second of all, hell would not be this freaking cold!" I gestured to the frozen landscape all around us. Dawson let out a soft chuckle.

"Okay, you got me there. This is not hell. But then tell me, what is it?" he asked with raised eyebrows. I tried to come up with a quick sassy comment, but alas, I had no clue as to what our situation would even be defined as. Mostly because I don't think it had ever happened before, as far as I knew anyways. As an alternative to a clever comeback, I decided to tell him the unavoidable truth (something I normally only did when I was too lazy to think of a snappy retort).

"I honestly don't have the slightest idea. Although, whatever it is, I am positive that we will figure it out and get through it together, ok?" I hoped that I had sounded more confident than I felt. It seemed to have worked, as Dawson was now wearing his infamous Cheshire Cat grin.

"Whatever you say boss. Now stop slacking and get back to work. We don't have all day you know!"

I looked down at the small pile of broken branches and twigs in my arms, and then at the non-existent pile in his empty hands. I raised my eyebrows and then threw a deadly look in his direction. He simply smiled sweetly and went off skipping into the woods. I shook my head after him, 'How is it possible that I feel like hugging him and strangling him at the same time?' I thought as I continued on with my task. I guess that would just have to forever remain as one of the world's many mysteries.

****

The reflection of the orange flames danced in Sylvan's eyes. She was sitting between me and Mrs. Rundle, telling us a story about her grandfather who had spent a week living off only what the Rocky Mountains provided. I'm sure that her tale was meant to be encouraging to our group, unfortunately, I think that it only made us feel even less confident and more helpless than we already did. I looked around at our interesting group. All of us were so very different, yet we all had a common goal: we wanted to find answers. Dawson and Calmar were sitting across the fire from me, both mesmerized by the colourful flickering of the bonfire. It was hard to tell if they were even listening to Sylvan's story. They both looked as if they were in a trance. I directed my attention back to the girls: Mrs. Rundle was currently telling Sylvan the best way to put a crying baby to sleep is by putting a little whiskey in the baby's bottle. I could tell that Sylvan was not completely convinced by the confused look she wore on her face. I looked around our eccentric group once again and felt compelled to do something that would bring us closer together. If we were going to spend so much time together, we might as well try to get along. I went with my gut and blurted out the first thing that came to my mind.

"Hey, do you guys want to play a game or something?" I said loudly. Mrs. Rundle and Sylvan stopped debating over the ethics of giving a child alcohol, and the boys both tore their gaze from the fire to look my way.

"What kind of game do you want to play, Teslin?" Dawson asked slyly, raising his eyebrows up and down.

"Definitely not whatever game you're thinking of," I snapped back. After Dawson's remark, everyone looked quite doubtful that we would be playing any sort of game. 'This was a stupid idea, it isn't going to work,' I panicked to myself. But I wasn't going to go down without a fight. "I'm talking about a kind of group bonding game. I know it sounds stupid, but we aren't exactly getting along all that well, and I thought maybe this could help." My statement sounded more like a question.

"That sounds like a lovely idea, Teslin!" Sylvan said, smiling encouragingly. I smiled back, happy to actually have one recruit on board with my idea.

"I'm in," the voice came from Calmar. My smile grew even bigger.

"I'm only playing if Dawson promises to behave," Mrs. Rundle announced. Now everyone looked at Dawson, who appeared quite amused at this request. He paused for dramatic effect before he bowed his head to me and said:

"You have my word, Your Majesty." I stifled a laugh.

"So what kind of game is it?" asked Sylvan, who was clearly the only one really excited to play the game.

"Well -," I began, as I really had no idea of what kind of game we would play. I was honestly just making it all up as I went along. "- it's a game where... we go around the circle, and everyone has to tell the group something about themselves." I stopped to make sure that I still had everyone's attention. Feeling like they still had some kind of interest I went on, "It can be anything really. A funny story, a sad story, something very personal, anything." I paused for a second to point at Sylvan, who had her hand raised in the air as if she had a question. She did.

"Does the game have any rules?" she asked. I thought about it for a second.

"Yes, of course it has rules," I said, creating the rules in my head as I said this. "The rules are that the story has to be one hundred percent true. Also, when someone is telling their story everyone else is not allowed to talk or to judge the speaker in any way or form. Got it?" I asked, scanning around the fire.

"Well, that sounds like a lovely game!" Mrs. Rundle exclaimed. "Who gets to go first?" she asked excitedly.

"Teslin goes first. It's her game after all," Dawson said, smiling at me with evil eyes. He obviously knew that I was completely making this up on the spot, and he wanted to continue putting me on the spot to entertain himself.

"Fine. I will go first," I said with my head held high to spite him.

"I can't wait to hear your story," he said in a charming tone.

Though I hardly heard what he said, as my mind was so busy running through all the different kinds of stories that I could tell.

There were so many of them that I did not know which one to choose, and whatever story I chose would set the tone for the rest of the stories. I had to choose a story that was balanced. Nothing too dark, but nothing too funny either. Something personal, but not too personal. My eyes scanned the campsite around me, looking for some inspiration. I looked at the three small tents set up to the left of me. They did not arouse a good story out of my brain. Next I looked to my right where Nikita was laying on the ground, chewing on a bone she had found. She was busy gnawing away, unaware of my gaze, when I suddenly knew what story I would tell. I cleared my throat to notify the group that I was ready to begin, and they politely waited in silence. After a few seconds of making myself comfortable on the log that we were currently using as a bench, I began my story:

"Six years ago, something very important happened in my life. You see, it was my sixteenth birthday and there was only one thing that I wanted for my birthday… a dog. I begged my mom and dad for so many years, but they refused to let me have one. They decided this, not because I wasn't responsible enough, but because of my extremely short attention span. They were right, of course. In the past I had started many new projects and activities, but I rarely finished them as I would get bored so quickly and had to start something new. Although I assured them that with a dog it would be different, they didn't believe me, or so I thought.

Anyways, the morning of my sixteenth birthday came and my father woke me up, telling me that there was a family emergency and we had to leave at once. So my mother, father, brother and I all got in the car and drove. I was still half asleep so it didn't even occur to me where we were going or what was the family emergency. We drove for about twenty minutes before my dad turned off the highway and drove up to an old farm house. He turned the engine off and we all got out of the car and walked up to the home. My dad knocked on the door, and an older lady whom I did not know opened the door. She greeted my parents and then looked to me and said, "Oh you must be the birthday girl. Come with me!"

I was obviously very confused at this greeting, however, my dad gave me a nod of approval and so I followed the strange lady into the house. I followed her into the living room of the old house, where a large pen was set up in the middle of the room. The pen was full of Siberian husky puppies. I almost screamed for joy, but of course, I didn't want to scare the puppies. Instead, I sat down next to the pen, and the woman took out all seven of the puppies, placing them all beside me. I was in heaven with all of these furry little angels licking, biting, and nuzzling me. All of the puppies were jumping up on me, so overjoyed to meet me. All but one that is. For there was one puppy who stood about three feet away from me. She was smaller than the other pups, but for what she lacked in size she made up for in spirit. She was staring me down, not sure what to think of me. I was so enchanted by this little husky and tried to coax her to come to me. With her head down, she slowly crept towards me. She was still unsure about me, but her curiosity got the better of her. When she was close enough, I picked her up and held her right in front of my face. I looked into those piercing blue eyes and I just knew she was my dog.

Apparently she knew as well, because she started wagging her little tail and licking my nose. When I put her back down she had also fully decided that I was hers, and began barking and biting at the other puppies until she scared them all away. Everyone laughed at this feisty little dog defending me from her evil siblings. I remember saying to my dad:

"See, Dad, you don't have to worry about me looking after her. She's gonna look after me!" And ever since then she's done just that. I know that I have lots of wonderful friends, but the truth is people aren't perfect. They make mistakes. They let you down. But Nikita… Nikita has never let me down. Not once. I am her world. And just knowing that one creature on this planet would do anything to save me, makes me want to be a person worth saving."

I was staring at Nikita as I said this last part, and by pure chance (or maybe because she heard her name), she stopped chewing her bone to look up at me. I pretended that she knew what I had said, or at least felt it at some emotional level. As I was so grateful for this dog for so many reasons, saving my life included. Mrs. Rundle took my silence as the end of my story.

"Oh what a lovely story! I had always known that you and Nikita had a special bond, but I didn't know it started. How precious! Can I tell my story now?"

I smiled, glad to see how enthusiastic she was about the game.

"Of course you can. The floor is yours," I replied. And with that little introduction, Mrs. Rundle cleared her throat and commenced her story:

"Now, those of you who know me may not believe me, but I speak the truth when I say I was a bit of a wild child back in my day. Quite the rebellious bad girl, dare I say! All of the boys in my town wanted me to be their girl. But I was a free spirit. And I had all the boys wrapped around my finger. Why would I pass that up for just one?! I didn't think there was a man on earth that could ever sweep me off my feet. I lived life on the edge as a free woman and I never wanted that to ever change for anyone, especially no man.

Then one day while I was working – Oh and by the way I worked as a bartender at this cool new club. I was twenty. – Anyways, while I was working late on a Saturday night, all the girls were going crazy over this new guy who just moved into town. My friends were beside themselves talking about how gorgeous this new guy was, and what a talented dancer he was. I was just about to tell those girls to smarten up and stop talking like a chicken with its head cut off, when out of nowhere someone cranked up "Twist and Shout" on the stereo, and yelled for everyone to come outside. Suddenly everyone ran out of the bar. And as soon as they made it out the door, I heard the girls start screaming and the boys start hollering! So I left the bar and ran to see what all the commotion was about. And boy, did they ever have a reason to be cheering. Because there, a few yards in front of me, was a spitting image of James Dean, dancing on top of a brand new '64 Mustang. I fell in love almost instantly. I knew he was the man I had tried so hard to avoid all my life. He would be the man to sweep me off my stubborn feet. I just knew it.

Anyways, after all the craziness died down and everyone left, I was stuck cleaning up the bar. While I was cleaning, none other than the man of my dreams struts in and tells me to pour him a drink. I told him the bar was closed, and I wasn't pouring him no drink. I also told him that he should beat it out of my bar before I beat him. And you know what he said to that? Well, he slowly looked me up and down and said: "Where have you been all my life?" Then we made passionate love right there on that bar. We got married seven months later. Do you know that it's our fifty first anniversary this January? Oh how I miss him. My darling husband. I really hope he's okay, wherever he is."

Mrs. Rundle began tearing up and Sylvan instinctively put her arms around her.

"You have been blessed with such a wonderful man, Mrs. Rundle. Some of us have not been so lucky." This was a natural transition leading into Sylvan's story. She continued to hold Mrs. Rundle as she spoke:

"Just as Mrs. Rundle said, I too fell in love with my husband from the first moment we met. He was such a lovely man, and always took the time to make sure I felt beautiful and loved. I couldn't believe how well everything worked out for us. Right after we got married we both found great jobs, we bought a brand new home together, and we were still so in love. It almost felt too good to be true… and it was.

As the months went on, he kept saying how we deserved better things: a nicer house, a fancier car, a bigger television, things like that. I kept telling him that I was perfectly content with what we had, and that I didn't want anything more, but he became obsessed. He spent thousands of dollars on things we didn't need and we were coming close to declaring bankruptcy.

Around this time, he started drinking to cope with everything. The drinking brought on a lot verbal abuse, and the verbal abuse quickly turned into physical abuse. I was running out of lies to tell my co-workers of why I had so many bruises on my body. Finally, when I found out I was pregnant with Nisku, I had enough. I could not bear the thought of bringing up a child in this kind of toxic environment. Leaving my husband was the hardest thing I ever had to do, because I knew deep down he was still that same caring and loving man. But I had to do what was best for my baby and my life, so I divorced him and got a restraining order so he could no longer hurt me.

At twenty-five years old, I was divorced, jobless, pregnant, and alone. My husband had taken a lot from me, but he had not taken my determination or my baby. I moved far away from him, found a job that could let me work from home, and started a new life. This was an extremely hard thing to do. But when I got to hold Nisku in my arms for the very first time, I knew that all the struggle was worth it. He is my world, my guardian angel. He saved me from an unhappy and harmful life. I owe him everything."

Sylvan kissed her sleeping baby on the forehead as she finished her story. Everyone was sitting in silence, her story had quite an effect on the group. I had a sneaking suspicion that Sylvan was more than meets the eye, but I didn't realize just how strong she was. I looked at the woman with such admiration, wishing that I could be as brave as her. A mumble of voices interrupted my wishful thinking, it was Dawson and Calmar discussing who should go next. It was decided that Calmar would go next. He loudly cleared his throat, folded his hands together, and gazed into the fire as he told his story:

"I guess it's my turn then. Well, there was this one time, a few years back, when I was on a mission in Afghanistan, and… it didn't go exactly as planned. My eleven men and I were on a Special Forces team, and we received information from a reliable source that the Taliban would be meeting in the area, so we went to check it out. Everything was going according to plan, until we got to the site. An old abandoned warehouse with no one to be found. I had a strange feeling about it and I ordered my men to fall back, but it was too late.

Bullets started flying at us from all directions. We tried to take cover behind the debilitated shelving but it did no good. My men were getting hit and going down fast. We radioed for backup as we dragged the injured men out of the building, trying to avoid bullets at the same time. I just about reached the door with the two men I was extracting, when a sharp and powerful force went through my shoulder and knocked me down. It didn't take me long to figure out that I had been shot. The large amount of blood spilling from my shoulder was a dead giveaway. Anyways, I managed to get back up and continue pulling my men to safety, but the blood loss was getting to me and I started to fade quickly. Another bullet hit me, on the left side of my back. I fell to the ground again, but this time I didn't get back up. I just lay there on the hard dusty floor, losing consciousness. I thought I was going to die, that this was the end of the road for me. The last thing I heard before I blacked out was the sound of bullets flying through the air.

By some miracle I didn't die. And when I woke up, I was lying in a hospital bed. They told me that I was going to be deployed back to Australia to recover from my injuries. They also told me that seven of my men had been seriously injured and two had died. It took months to recover physically from my wounds, though I don't think I've ever recovered mentally. Almost dying made me realize how precious life is and how quickly it can end. I think that if everyone had this kind of experience they would appreciate what they have a whole lot more, and be more kind to their fellow man. Every day after that I secretly wished that one day I would go to work and they'd tell me I was out of a job. Not because I was fired, but because there wasn't a need for soldiers anymore, because people had stopped fighting. I hate to say it, but that's the only thing we can always be certain of. People will always fight. There will never be peace in this messed up world we live in."

Calmar looked up from the fire, and because I was sitting directly across from him, he ended up staring directly into my eyes. I had never seen such intensity behind anyone's eyes ever before. They were full of so many emotions: hurt, anger, bitterness and confusion. I could not tear away from his gaze; he held me captive and I was almost afraid to look away. While I was spellbound by the fire that reflected off his dark eyes, I could have sworn that amongst all the hostility in his eyes, I saw a flash of hope: a small wish that things could get better. He finally switched his gaze off me and towards Dawson. Apparently I had been holding my breath the whole time as I was now gasping for air.

"Your turn, mate. What kind of story do you have for us?" he asked Dawson.

Dawson, who was clearly affected by the darkness of the last two memoirs, didn't look at all enthusiastic about the game. Nonetheless, I knew that he would go through with it, as he never was one to give up at anything. Even a silly game. He looked at me, for support I think. I smiled at him, hoping that this would be enough to give him confidence. Opening up and sharing his inner thoughts wasn't really his strong point, despite all my years of trying to help him. He weakly smiled back at me as he commenced his story:

"I don't really have any interesting stories to tell. I mean, I've travelled a lot with my parents and went on many awesome adventures, but nothing life changing. I guess the most life changing thing that ever happened to me was when my parents divorced a couple years ago. It's kind of weird to admit, but all my life I had admired the love my parents shared. You could just tell by the way they looked at each other, the way they laughed together, and the way they would sneak in a kiss when they thought I wasn't looking. They were so in love. It was the one thing that I could count on to always be the same. Their jobs changed, their house changed, their friends changed, but their love never changed.

And then for some reason, which I still have no idea why, one day it just stopped. They stopped laughing and kissing, and they started yelling and fighting. I couldn't do anything to make them go back to the way things were before. For a while I thought it was somehow my fault that it happened, because I was never really home. I was too busy partying and caring about unimportant things. I don't know, maybe it was partly my fault. I mean, I still can't comprehend how something that I thought was so set in stone and forever, can just stop, and it's like it never happened. If you saw my parents together now, in the rare occasion that they are in the same room, you would never in a million years guess that they had been so utterly in love for twenty-one years. You would probably only see how they absolutely hate each other with a passion. And you would be right. It's just a depressing thought to realize that nothing lasts forever. Not even the most precious things. But I guess that's life, right?"

Dawson looked around the campfire for agreement.

"You got that right, mate," Calmar piped in. Then everyone was silent for a few moments, soaking in all of the accounts we had just heard from the group. I was especially touched by Dawson's story. I had no idea that his parents' divorce had been so hard on him. He had always shrugged it off like it was no big deal. I felt a pang inside my heart. I wished that I had seen through his front and could have helped him through the divorce. I guess he was a better actor than I thought.

Our group was now in quite the solemn and reflective mood as we all stared into the dancing flames. I knew that I should say something, it was my game after all.

"Well, I think that was a successful game!" I spoke up, smiling as I said this. I paused for a second. I felt like I needed to say more than a superficial comment, so I went on:

"Look guys, I don't know what's going on or why our whole lives are suddenly turned upside down. I also don't know what my parents have to do with this whole "Movement" or whatever this thing is. I don't even know what we are going to do tomorrow. But I do know that I am with a group of very strong and courageous individuals. And I am really glad that we have each other."

To my surprise, my little speech actually worked. Everyone looked at me and had, what I believe to be, hope in their faces. I couldn't help but smile at them; my unconventional makeshift family.

"I am glad that we have you too, Teslin." Sylvan's smile was contagious, and the whole group was smiling now.

"I couldn't agree more!" the voice came from Mrs. Rundle. "Now that was a wonderful game, but I believe it's time for bed now. Everyone off to their tents! Sylvan and Nisku in one tent. Teslin, Nikita and I in another, and the boys in the other. Good night everyone!"

We all quietly chuckled at Mrs. Rundle's sudden concern for our bedtime curfew, even Mrs. Rundle herself. So we said our good-nights and went into our designated tents. Mrs. Rundle, Nikita, and I, snuggled together in our small tent to create as much body heat as possible in order to fight off the freezing cold. As we slowly drifted off to sleep, I heard Mrs. Rundle mumble to herself, "I'm sure we will be just fine. It will all be better in the morning." Man, did I ever wish she was right. I imagined warm tropical beaches as I let the exhaustion of the day devour my body and pull me into a deep sleep.

Chapter Five

Soft voices intertwined with the crackle of burning wood gently nudged me awake. Not surprisingly, it was another frosty morning. I turned to my right where Nikita was sitting patiently; waiting for me. She gave me the usual morning kiss before she proceeded to get rambunctious. As she bounced around the exceptionally small tent, I realized how cold it must have been last night. This was from the white frosted tips on Nikita's black fur. Only half of her body wasn't icily frosted (the half that had obviously been pressed up against my sleeping bag during the night). I shifted to the left where Mrs. Rundle should have been, but that side of the tent was empty. 'She must be already up and busy building us a luxurious cabin,' I thought sarcastically. Nikita's energy was now too large for the tiny two-person tent; I zipped open the tent and released the hound. She thundered out of the tent and plowed her way into the nearest snow bank, rolling around and growling like a cat that just inhaled a ton of catnip.

A sudden shrill scream made my heart drop to the pit of my stomach. I was just about to go into full panic-mode, when my mind finally registered that the sound came from a joyful little Nisku; He was laughing and giggling uncontrollably at the sight of Nikita tumbling about in the snow. I put my hands on my head and gave it a shake.

"Get a hold of yourself, Teslin. At this rate you're going to become completely crazy by next Tuesday!" I said, a bit too loudly than I had intended. I hoped that no one had heard this or they might question me on why I chose Tuesday as the day I would lose my sanity.

Needing a moment to compose myself, I took a deep breath and garnered up all of my strength (in case it was another day similar to yesterday) before I crawled out of the tent. As I stood up, shaking the fresh powder off of my snow pants, I noticed Nikita had finished her little hyperactive episode. She was now sitting proudly on top of the conquered snow bank, panting heavily. I then pivoted to face the gloriously warm campfire, which apparently everyone but me had been invited to. I couldn't believe my eyes! The four adults were sitting peacefully next to each other: smiling, chatting, and even laughing as they passed around warm food. My mouth almost dropped. 'Could these really be the same people that were so painfully hard to get along with yesterday?' I thought to myself as I continued to observe the group in disbelief.

"Well look who finally decided to grace us with her presence. Good morning, Your Majesty!" Dawson looked fairly pleased with his run on joke from yesterday. Since I didn't want to offend the cheeky peasant boy I replied in my most Royal Queen voice:

"Good morning to you too my humble servant. I presume that you have my breakfast and morning tea ready?" I sashayed over to the fire, and elegantly planted my royal buttocks on the free space of log next to Calmar.

"Of course, my Queen. Here you are, two duck eggs, fresh caviar, imported wild Salmon from British Colombia, a freshly fluffed scone from London, and your breakfast tea." Dawson got up from his seat and handed me two strips of bacon and a muffin.

"Thank you, peasant."

"You're most welcome my beautiful ruler."

"Now tell me, Harold, what is on the agenda for today?"

"Well, I do believe that we must pay a visit to Princess Josephina today."

"Oh god, not that horrid woman! You know I can't stand her, Harold!"

"I know that! But Your Majesty must be courteous nonetheless, it is your sovereign duty."

By this point the both of us had adopted horrible British accents, and the rest of the crew were looking at us like we were escaped patients from the psych ward.

"Well I don't want to go! Why can't you go instead?" I pouted dramatically.

"Your Majesty, I would love to go in your place, however, I am not of royal blood."

"Well, that's where you're wrong, Harold."

"What does Your Majesty mean?"

I gave Harold a very grave look. I could only hope that he would be able to handle the shocking truth that I was about to drop on him. I took a deep breath before I dramatically spoke the secret that I had been hiding from him for the past twenty-two years of his life:

"You're a princess, Harold."

"I'm a what!?"

We couldn't hold it together any longer and we both burst out laughing. The others joined in, and laughter warmed the icy air. Even Nisku laughed, and Nikita started howling so as not to be left out. This made us laugh even harder. I laughed until tears rolled down my face and almost instantly turned into icicles.

"You guys are hilarious! I can see why you two are best friends!" Sylvan said, shaking her head at us.

"Yeah, I wasn't really sure what was going on there at first… but you two really make quite the improvisational comedic pair. Well done." Calmar said, also shaking his head at us. His thick curly locks delicately danced about from side to side.

'Oh my god, what is it with you and your obsession with Calmar's hair? Stop it!' I reprimanded myself and turned my attention to Mrs. Rundle, waiting for her to comment and shake her head at us as well. Instead, she made an unimpressed face and said:

"Well come on, finish the story. I want to know what happens to Princess Harold."

"That was just a free preview, Mrs. Rundle. If you want the show to continue we're talking at least a fifty-dollar bill here." Dawson smiled innocently. Mrs. Rundle responded by throwing a snowball at his head.

"How's that instead?" she asked, smirking wickedly.

I rolled my eyes, "Alright children, no horseplay at the dinner table!"

"But, mom!" Mrs. Rundle whined like a bratty little child.

I couldn't help but laugh out loud. It was the first time Mrs. Rundle and Dawson were sort of getting along, and it was in such an odd way too! I was about to further reprimand my horribly behaved children when Calmar's voice stopped me:

"So, I don't want to put a damper on things, but, what exactly is our plan today?" Calmar's legitimate concern instantly murdered all laughter and smiles. We all fell silent and looked around at each other. Eventually everyone fixed their eyes on me.

'How the hell did I get myself volunteered into being ringleader of this weird, dysfunctional group?' I thought to myself in honest confusion. I couldn't come up with any logical answer. So I blankly stared back at them. Unfortunately, pretending that I did not notice my apparent election win wasn't going to work. I sighed and decided that I might as well embrace my unwanted leadership role. Someone had to do it, and apparently that someone was me.

"Guys, the only option I see is to head east towards Calgary. There has to be a town or some place on the way that the White

Soldiers haven't touched. I mean even if they have, there is no way that they could take over an entire city as big as Calgary. That's impossible. We just have to make it there without getting caught, or freezing to death. Mrs. Rundle, how are we on supplies?" I surprised myself with how naturally this being-in-charge thing came to me.

Mrs. Rundle did some mental calculations in her head before she replied, "We have enough food to last us about two days, two and a half days at the most. Thankfully we don't have to worry about water though, as we can easily boil snow over the fire."

"Okay, so that gives us a time limit of two days to find help. All we really have to do is find some place with cell coverage and we can contact the authorities. It shouldn't be that hard to do." I calculated in my head that it would most definitely take us more than two days to reach Calgary at the rate we went. I prayed to God that we would find help before we ran out of food. However, I didn't dare share my doubts with the group. Doubt was the last thing we needed. In an attempt to override any current doubtful thoughts of my comrades, I tried to sound as positive and encouraging as I could.

"So now that we have a plan we should probably start packing up and get moving as quickly as possible. You guys cool with that? Any other ideas?"

"Nope. Sounds good to me. I'll start taking down the tents." Calmar said.

"I'll give you a hand with that," Dawson piped in.

"I'll clean up around here and put the fire out." Mrs. Rundle announced.

"Here, let me give you a hand with that," came from Sylvan, who put down her baby in a makeshift cradle she had carved out of snow.

The whole group went to work, and I was left sitting dumbfounded on a log. Nikita trotted over to me and put her head in my lap. I gave her a pat on the head, "This is so weird. People are actually listening to me!" I whispered into her big velvety ear. She shook her head in response to my warm breath tickling the insides of her ear. I smiled and gave her a good rub down before I went over to help the boys with the tents.

It sounds silly, but I felt a lot better now that we actually had somewhat of a plan. We still had no answers or no clue about anything, yet somehow having a purpose made the unknown a little less scary. I think this thought comforted the others as well, because there was a happy, light air around us as we packed up our small campsite. Everyone worked so quickly and efficiently; we were done in no time.

As we began our long journey, I took one last look at our safe haven. Looking over my shoulder, I watched a powerful gust of wind blow in with such a force, that it left a fresh blanket of snow overtop our campsite. Now all evidence of our footsteps were completely covered, making the area appear as if it had never been touched. I smiled to myself, at least Mother Nature seemed to be on our side.

****

Walking through the blinding white snow didn't seem to be as much as a chore as it was yesterday. Probably because it was a bright sunny morning; if you stared up at the big blue sky, you could have sworn it was a pleasant summer day. So I continued looking up at the warm blue sky, and this helped distract me from the reality of knee-high snow and bitter-cold air. Another noticeable change from yesterday, was the amiable atmosphere surrounding our group. We were all getting along quite well, and this apparently made all the difference. I did a quick scan around the area to check up on my group members which I was growing fonder of by the hour. Sylvan and Nisku were in the lead along with Nikita, who took it upon herself to provide entertainment for baby Nisku. She walked alongside the pair protectively, and every once in a while she would jump up to lick Nisku or frolic in a snow bank. Nisku would always respond the same: with a big belly laugh. The kind of laugh that made you want to laugh along as well. He didn't know it, but every time I looked at him, it stirred up a mix of emotions. On one hand, I was jealous of him. He had no clue what was going on. He didn't have to worry about anything. How I longed for a day where I didn't have any responsibilities. A day where I could simply be myself, and everyone would adore me and accept me for exactly who I was. But on the other hand, I felt saddened that bad and unexplainable things happened to even the most innocent people. It wasn't fair that such a young child had to be uprooted from his home, and forced to survive in the harsh Northern climate like the rest of us. He had never done anything wrong. I doubt he even knew the concept of right and wrong. He was completely helpless without the protection from others. Thank God his mother was Sylvan. She would fight for him.

A stab of betrayal pierced my heart as I thought about my own parents. They had always fought for me. All my life they supported me and encouraged me in whatever I did. For this very reason it made no sense as to why my parents would ever want to put me in danger. They would never want to hurt me. The only way I could see them wanting to harm me is if they were brainwashed, or hypnotized, or something like that. I closed my eyes tightly, trying to forget the living room scene that still haunted my thoughts so frequently.

I took a deep breath and observed the pair walking in front of me. Mrs. Rundle and Dawson were having what appeared to be a heart-to-heart conversation. Taking a break from their usual boisterous arguments, they were conversing in low voices and looked very serious. This made me desire to know what they were saying even more, so I strained my ears to listen in on their conversation:

"It's not something you can just force, my boy. It's something that happens naturally, and sometimes when you least expect it." Mrs. Rundle said in a motherly tone.

"But that's just it. How do you know when it's real? I'm sure people have faked it before." Dawson's reply held a hint of frustration.

"Well of course you can fake it. I faked it all the time with many boyfriends before I met my husband. But when it's real, you know. You can feel it and there's no denying it."

"Well then, tell me. What did it feel like? How did you feel the moment you knew you were in love?"

Mrs. Rundle paused for a long moment before she replied.

"It was like we were the only two people in the world. The world went on spinning around us, yet time stood still for the two of us. Then I felt a warm sensation rush over by body, originating from my core. I was so attracted to him that it felt as if a powerful magnet inside of me, was pulling me towards him. But it's not that kind of attraction that you feel when you pass a good-looking guy on the street, or the type you feel when you get to meet your gorgeous celebrity crush. No, it's something much more than that. It's like your whole entire being wants to protect, and love, and care for that person. Your whole world now includes this person. And deep down, you know that no matter what happens in this life, as long as you have each other everything will be ok." Mrs. Rundle turned to smile at Dawson. "I'm sure it's different for everyone, but for me that's how it felt. And that's how it has felt for all of these years. You would think I'd have gotten bored of my husband after all this time! But in fact, I love him even more than I did that first moment we met."

Dawson took a few seconds to take all this in before he spoke, "That's really beautiful, Mrs. Rundle. I really am happy for you. But if love really is that amazing, then how can it so easily dwindle away to nothing? How can so many people fall out of love? Seriously, it seems like everyone is getting divorced these days. Does being in love even exist or mean anything nowadays?"

Poor Dawson, he was really struggling with this. I wished I could give him an answer, but unfortunately, I didn't know too much about love either. Although apparently Mrs. Rundle did, and she put her arm around Dawson as she wore a nostalgic look on her face.

"Let me tell you a little story, Dawson. My great-grandparents came from Ireland, and one of the only things I can remember about them, was the wonderful fairy tales they used to tell me and my siblings. They told us magical tales about fairies, giants, leprechauns, banshees, and basically every other mystical creature out there. We of course believed every word! But as we grew older, my siblings eventually stopped believing in the stories and said they were nothing but a bunch of silly folklore. I told them I agreed with them, but I secretly kept believing that they were true.

Anyways, about eleven years ago we all decided to take a trip to Ireland for a family reunion. One of the tours we did took us to a field with a great big fairy ring - something that my great-grandparents had told us many stories about. The tour guide retold one of these stories, and warned us not to cross over the fairy ring or the fairies would curse us. My siblings and their spouses all laughed at this, even their children said it was stupid. Yet in spite of their mockery, they still didn't dare go into the fairy ring. I had a sneaking suspicion that they didn't want to take their chances of getting cursed. Just in case.

Well, after they had a good laugh and took some pictures for the family album, it was time to get back on the tour bus. But I stayed behind just for a second longer. And in that second, I saw a flash of wings flutter under a mushroom. It was only for a split second. If I had blinked my eyes I would have missed it. But I know what I saw was real, because I believed it. You see, Dawson, my family would have never seen it, because they would never entertain the idea of its existence. Once you cease to have faith in something, it will cease to exist in your mind. Love is exactly like magic. You can't see it or feel it unless you believe in it. And just like magic, if you stop believing in it, it starts to die.

You know, I've lived for quite a few years on this planet and what I've seen really saddens me. It seems to me that no one cares to use their imagination anymore. Children aren't outside playing in the woods pretending that they are brave warriors or great adventurers, but rather they are inside watching television and playing video games. They don't have to use their imagination at all. And adults are only making things worse by encouraging their children not to use their imagination. In fact, it's a sign of maturity when children stop believing in Santa Claus or the Tooth Fairy. Parents want their children to be little bright logical thinkers, just like mom and dad. This is why I think so many people are divorcing and falling out of love, Dawson, because love is not logical. Love doesn't work that way and it never will. True love doesn't exist unless you work for it and you believe in it."

Mrs. Rundle took her arm off of Dawson and they walked in silence for a couple of minutes. They began speaking again, however, I didn't get the chance to hear what they were discussing because Calmar walked up beside me.

"How's it going, Commander?" he smiled cheekily.

"Oh not too bad. You know, the usual. Giving out orders, coming up with tactical plans, saving the world, nothing too exciting." I replied nonchalantly.

"Sounds like a normal day to me."

"Exactly. I'm actually thinking of changing careers. I need some more excitement in my life."

"Oh really? What were you thinking of?"

"Hmmm, something really dangerous and life-threatening. Like becoming an accountant or owning a llama farm."

"Ah, Yes. I've heard those llamas can get quite violent."

"It's true. Especially during shearing season. I hear they can bite your whole hand right off!"

We both laughed. I liked it when he laughed. It seemed that all the darkness in his eyes vanished when he was laughing. 'Maybe that's how his eyes always looked before he became a soldier', I wondered.

"But seriously, Teslin. How are you?" he gave me a meaningful look.

"I think I'm ok. I don't really know how I'm supposed to feel. I've never been in this kind of situation before." I replied honestly.

Calmar smiled sympathetically, "Neither have I. But we seem to be doing just fine."

"I guess so. I mean it's hard to say how we are doing, when we don't even know what we are up against."

"True. But in this kind of situation you just have to trust your gut, and trust those around you."

"Trusting people isn't exactly my strong point. There's only a few people in this world that I truly trust. And apparently I'm down two as of right now." I hung my head slightly as I thought of my estranged parents.

"You don't know that for sure, Teslin." He placed his hand on my shoulder as he said this.

"Yeah, I do. There's no other explanation. Anyways, I think that it's better that I embrace the truth sooner than later. It's better for all of us."

Calmar was quiet for a second before he replied.

"You know, you're probably the strongest person that I've ever met, Teslin."

I had to laugh at this, "I don't know about that! I also don't know who thought it was a good idea to volunteer me as team captain either."

He had to chuckle too, "C'mon, it's obvious why we did it."

I looked at him, bewildered. I honestly had no idea if his last statement was actually serious or not. It couldn't be.

"Honestly, Calmar, I have no flipping clue."

He was now looking at me like I was joking! I frowned, and he slowly realized that I was serious.

"You're a fighter, Teslin. You do what you have to do to survive. No matter how hard it is. We all realized this when you told us what happened with your parents. You had to act quickly, and you did. I don't think I could have done what you did. It takes a strong leader to be able to put their personal affairs aside for the good of others. But you do it, and you do it well."

I couldn't believe that the person he was describing was me. I guess I've been told I was a good leader before, in school and at work, but I always thought that anyone could do it. I just happened to be the one that always got stuck with being group leader, because no one else wanted to do it! So it was very strange to hear someone telling me that I was chosen not because I was the last resort, but because they thought I was an actual leader.

"Oh. Well. Thank you," was all I could think of to say.

He smiled, "You're welcome." Then he completely changed the subject, "So what were you doing before all this happened? Are you a student? Are you working? You have any big life goals?"

I couldn't believe it. Who was this talkative man all of a sudden!? And why was he asking me so many hard questions, giving me compliments, and consequently making me feel very uncomfortable? I know he was only trying to be friendly. He couldn't have possibly known that my biggest pet peeve was when people asked me what I was doing with my life. Because in fact, I did not know what I was doing with my life. Of course I had dreams. I wanted to become a psychologist. But it was going to take a few more years before that happened. Sometimes it was hard to keep being positive about my dream when it felt so far away. Especially because my current situation was not the ideal place where I wanted be at twenty-two years old. Yes, I did complete my undergraduate degree in psychology, but I was also still living with my parents and working as a sled dog tour guide. I guess I shouldn't be complaining, my life wasn't a complete disaster, but I still felt a bit lost. I had always thought that I was meant for greater things in life, that I could make a difference in this world. Maybe I was just disillusioned though. I am sure that everyone thinks they are special and meant to change the world in some way. This thought had crossed my mind once or twice, but even so, there was a small part of me that hoped it was true. That one day I was going to make a difference in this huge yet small world we lived in.

"Teslin?"

Calmar's voice startled me. I was so wrapped up in my own head that I had completely forgotten about the questions he had asked me.

"Oh, sorry. Umm…" I stumbled over my words, trying to think of what to tell him. "Well, I finished my undergrad degree last year, so I am just working this year to save up money. My best friend and I are planning on touring Europe for a few months in the summer. Then after that I will be going back to school for quite a few more years."

"What are you going to school for."

"Psychology."

"Very cool. So I'm guessing you really like it then, if you're going to be going back to school for a few more years?"

"I do." Unfortunately, instead of simply leaving it at that, my mouth felt the need to spill how I really felt. "It's scary though. I'm investing so much money and so many years of my life into this. What happens if after only a couple of years I end up hating being a psychologist? What then?! I will have wasted so much of my life, and probably have a terrible mid-life crisis that will secure my dark lonely future involving a whole lot of cats."

Calmar stopped me in my tracks and put his hands on my shoulders. His dark eyes pierced straight through me.

"Teslin, that's not going to happen. And even if it did, you would find a way to get back on your feet, be successful, and learn to love all of those cats."

I couldn't help but feel a warm wave come over my body. Whether it was from his kind words or from being so close to him that I could kiss him, I didn't know.

"Thanks, Calmar." I spoke quietly so that my emotions didn't give me away. I think he interpreted my quietness as insecurity, because he responded by giving me a big hug. Either way, I wasn't complaining, and I hugged him right back. Even through the many layers of clothing and the thick winter coat, I could tell how muscular he was. 'Probably from all the years of physical training he had to do,' I thought to myself. And then it hit me. I think he knew exactly how I felt. He was probably feeling the same way, maybe even more so. He spent so many years in the military and now he was doing something completely different.

I had to ask, "Do you ever feel lost? I mean, you're doing something new and so different from what you are used to. Do you ever feel like you are just wandering around, without a purpose?"

He extracted himself from our hug and looked at me thoughtfully.

"I'm not gonna lie, sometimes I do feel a little bit lost. But then I think of it as an adventure to find the next chapter in my life, and it becomes a lot more fun and exciting. Life is all about perspective, Teslin. Everyone has the ability to create their own happy and fulfilling life. It's not easy, but if you really want it to happen, it will. Unfortunately, too many people let the bumps and obstacles in life determine their path instead of bulldozing right through them."

I smiled to myself. His words reminded me of what my father used to tell me when I was feeling discouraged: "Never let people tell you what you can and can't do. They don't know you like you know yourself. If you are motivated and work hard you can do anything you want. Simple as that."

I think my father and Calmar would get along if they ever happen to meet. Calmar began walking again and I followed slightly behind him. We quickly caught up to the others and once again I could overhear the conversation between Dawson and Mrs. Rundle:

"It is true, my husband and I fight over the roles of men and women all the time. We came from an era where traditional roles of men and women were still favoured, you know. So we always fight over who wears the pants in our relationship." Mrs. Rundle said matter-of-factly.

"That problem can easily be solved if you both don't wear any pants at all." Dawson said with a devilish grin. Mrs. Rundle raised her eyebrow and gave him an amused look. Dawson was apparently more curious about this topic, and proceeded to question Mrs. Rundle further.

"What do you do then? Do you cook and clean and let him do all the manly stuff?" he asked.

"If by "manly stuff" you are referring to sitting on his butt and watching hockey, then yes, he does a lot of manly stuff. But I also make sure he helps me with the household chores or he doesn't get fed. We both have full time jobs, you know. I own my own successful café and he works as a civil engineer. It's not fair that we both come home, tired after a long day of work, and I have to continue working at home, but that's life. A woman has to take care of her family."

Dawson rolled his eyes at this, "Hey, it's not like guys do nothing. We have to work hard to buy our women the nice house, expensive clothes and fancy silverware to keep them happy. And even then, they still aren't happy! We are always doing something wrong, and because we aren't mind readers we can never figure out why!

And I seriously have to take out a loan just to afford a girlfriend. Women say they want equality but then they expect men to pay for everything. Dinner, drinks, jewellery, flowers, you name it. Do you know how many times girls chatted me up at the bar just so I buy them a drink, and then they run off after? Or how many times girls have gotten me to pay for not only their drink, but drinks for their friends too? Girls can get away with anything. They just have to smile and bat their eye lashes to get out of a speeding ticket. Girls have it so easy."

Dawson's last statement was just too much. I couldn't keep quiet any longer listening to the way he spoke about women. He really had no clue what women had to go through on a daily basis. I spoke loudly, consequently getting the attention of everyone.

"Yeah, you know what, Dawson? You're right. Being a girl is so easy. It's so great how women get paid less than men for the same amount of work, or that after a day of work they have to come home and cook, clean, take care of the kids and their husbands. It's also awesome that when a woman is in a position of power, she has to work twice as hard as a man just to prove herself worthy. Even then, if she is as successful and ruthless as her male counterparts, instead of being respected for doing her job she's called a bitch.

And it's so easy to deal with cramps and bleeding, not once a year, but once every month for a good chunk of my life. Did you know that some women get cramps so bad that they have to get pain medication to cope? It's great, isn't it?! Oh, and on top of that, I have to worry about getting pregnant too! How exciting! And if I did get pregnant, I have to decide whether or not to keep the baby, because I know the father won't be helping me out with raising the kid. Men are so brave and strong, but for some reason they run for the hills at the thought of a helpless little baby. And even if I wanted to have the baby and give it up for adoption, I would have to go on maternity leave and take a major pay cut. So the other option is abortion, and then I would have to deal with the psychological trauma of ending the little life form growing inside of me.

Oh and I almost forgot, not only do I have to work, cook and clean, deal with periods, and worry about an unwanted pregnancy, but I also have to make sure I look beautiful and sexually appealing to men while I do all of this. I mean, because everyone knows a woman's worth is based on how physically attractive she is. So I spend hours of my time and thousands of dollars so I can look like what society tells me is beautiful, and get depressed when I never achieve that perfect photoshopped look. However, when I do achieve an acceptable attractive appearance, now I have to be careful not to walk alone at night, because I could not only get mugged but raped as well. But if I did get raped it would probably be my fault because I was wearing lots of makeup and a low cut dress, right?

I'm sure I'm forgetting some other things, but either way you're right, Dawson. Women have it so easy because guys buy us drinks and dinner and we can get away with the occasional discrepancy."

I was practically seething when I finished my rant. I probably looked like I wanted to kill Dawson, because I definitely felt that way. I couldn't take my eyes off his stupid, entitled face. He better not say some idiotic comment, or I wouldn't be able to control myself as to what injuries I inflicted on him. But of course, Dawson being Dawson, couldn't help himself:

"So you agree with me then. Girls have it easy."

I lost it. I tried to run at him but a pair of strong arms held me back. Calmar, who obviously anticipated the attack, had his arms locked around my torso. I tried to shake him off but it was no use. He was too strong. So I yelled out instead, "Let go of me!"

The voice that came from my throat hardly sounded like my own. It was fierce and wild and terrifying. Calmar was stunned as well, so I took advantage of his state of shock and broke free from his grip. Dawson looked legitimately scared. I stood there, glaring him down and imagining all the ways I could kill him, when the image of tasering my father flashed across my mind. It completely threw me off. 'When did I become so violent?' I didn't know, but I did know that I didn't like it.

I became fully aware of my surroundings; everyone was staring at me with either fear or uncertainty in their eyes. I didn't want to scare them, but I did want to get away from them as fast as I could. I took a deep breath and began speed walking away from all the stares.

Nikita tried to follow, but I didn't even want her around me, "Stay." I spoke in a harsh and emotionless voice that didn't sound like me either. She lowered her head and softly whined, but she listened. I walked past Sylvan and Nisku, who were the furthest ahead, making no eye contact. I pushed my sore legs as fast as they would go through the untouched deep snow. I went ahead without once looking back. I wanted to leave everything behind me. I needed to be alone. I needed to clear my head. I needed to figure out who I was.

****

My legs were burning. I had been power walking through the abysmal snow without stopping for the past twenty minutes. When I looked behind me, there was no sign of any life forms. Only snow, trees and silence. Ahead of me there was a clearing on the mountain. A nice break from all the trees. Simply white snow with no distractions. It almost helped me think clearer as I walked through the open mountain area.

I replayed all the events in my head starting from when I woke up yesterday, up until the present moment. I don't think it had even been twenty-four hours since my life turned upside down, but it felt like weeks had gone by. So much can change in so little time.

Apparently that applied to people as well. They say that a person's true colours show when they are in a life threatening situation, so did that mean I was an innately violent person? A fighter, as Calmar had said? I liked the idea that I was strong in the face of adversity, but not too crazy about how fast I resorted to violence. No wonder Dawson was scared of me when he heard about what I did to my parents; I was becoming scared of myself too. I had to get a hold of myself before I did something horrible. This whole ordeal was getting to my head. I had to figure out the truth about my parents, the White Soldiers, and the Movement before it was too late. I just had to keep moving forward, keep pushing, and stay positive. We would find help and we would find answers. It was only a matter of time.

'Yes, that's the spirit, Teslin! Stay positive and keep moving!' I encouraged myself. I did feel a bit better after I decided to be positive about things. It was no use worrying about something that I couldn't control. However, I could control what I did, and what I was going to do was to find answers. My mind finally felt clear and decisive about something in what seemed like ages. Unfortunately, my body did not feel the same way. The frozen temperature, exhaustion, and hunger had finally caught up to me, and my body began to quiver.

Nonetheless, I was resolved to keep pushing forward. I continued to move my shaking legs, one in front of the other. I did not take more than ten steps before my exhausted legs finally gave out, collapsing into the soft white powder. There was no way my worn body was going to move an inch further. So I sat there on my knees, looking at the ground, and giving my body the rest that it demanded. It had to be about ten minutes that I sat there, motionless in the snow. I figured that the group would have caught up to me by now. Maybe they had stopped to eat something. I silently cursed myself for not thinking of packing some food before I stormed off. All I had in my backpack was clothes, blankets, and a sleeping bag.

Nothing even remotely edible. I finally felt like I had mustered up enough energy to walk back to the group, when I heard a noise. I looked up from the blinding white ground and directly into a pair of deadly yellow eyes.

I couldn't breathe. My body couldn't move either. Not from exhaustion but from fear. For there, just inches away from my face, stood an enormous black wolf. The wolf stared me down, its yellow eyes were both mesmerizing and terrifying at the same time. It was completely still, and I hoped that if I stayed perfectly still it would get bored and leave me alone. But I knew this was only wishful thinking. I knew this would most likely be my end. There was no way I could fight off a massive wolf in my weak condition. I was going to die.

Strangely enough, I felt rather peaceful about dying. Probably because I was under the spell of the lethal creature in front of me. Even though my body was brimming with terror and panic, it couldn't mask the deep awe and admiration that I had for the wolf. She was magnificent. So powerful and beautiful. Her fur coat was thick and black as night. Her body was muscular and lean. But more striking than anything, were her glowing eyes. They pierced deep into my soul, causing my heart to stop beating. I couldn't stop my hand from reaching towards her. I thought I might as well get the chance to touch the beautiful creature before it killed me. I slowly moved my hand towards the thick black mane just under her bone crushing jaw. She didn't move. She continued to stay perfectly still and stare into my eyes. Just as my fingers brushed the tips of her fur, she jerked her head to look over her left shoulder, as if she was looking for something or someone, or maybe for the rest of the wolf pack that was going to devour me. Then she turned back around to give me one last piercing stare before she lifted her head back so her nose pointed to the sky.

The blood curdling howl she released from deep inside her throat made the hair on the back of my neck stand up, and now my heart had not only stopped, but it dropped to my stomach as well. I felt like I was also going to pass out from the lack of oxygen as I was still not breathing. Suddenly without any warning, she stopped howling and ran past me, knocking me over onto my back as she barreled full force towards the forest behind me. The blow had me gasping for air as I lay on my back. I forced myself to turn to my side and see if she was coming back for me. As I lay on my side, completely defenseless, I saw five other wolves about fifteen yards away run past me towards the trees. They didn't even look my way; they were so focussed on running into the forest. A second later my attention was drawn back to the clearing, where a large flock of birds were coming towards me, flying towards the thick forestry. As the screeching birds flew over me, I lay in the snow completely baffled as to what the hell was going on. Now not only people had me dazed and perplexed but the animals as well! And then it hit me. These animals were running from something.

I felt like I was about to get sick. My imagination ran wild with ideas of the kinds of things a pack of wolves would run from, and this gave me the adrenaline boost I needed to push myself up onto my feet. As I struggled to not tumble back down to the ground, I heard the familiar sound of a helicopter getting closer and closer by the second. I wanted to believe that it was a rescue crew that was sent for us, that all our struggles were over. I wished that this was true and that we were going to be safe, even though deep down I knew that it wouldn't be the case. I should have run towards the forest like the rest of the animals, but the flicker of hope made me stay. I stood determinedly in the snow, prepared to meet the truth. Not ten seconds went by before the sound of the helicopter became deafening. A second later and I could see the chopper rising above the ridge of the mountain. It was about 100 yards from me and yet I could still clearly see the pilots, dressed in white from head to toe.

'Why did you think it would be any different?' I asked myself, completely defeated. The angry flying machine began whirling towards me. The logical voice in my head was now furious with me: 'Why are you still standing here like an idiot?! They found us! They are not here to help us, Teslin. Run!' My body instantly obeyed, and before I knew it I was running with all the strength I had left towards the tree line. The forest wasn't too far ahead of me. It would be my only chance of evading the White Soldiers.

As I got closer I could see the others. They had made it out into the clearing. I yelled out as loud as I could as I ran towards them, "Run! Back into the forest! Run!" It took them a second to register what was going on, but when they saw the helicopter coming behind me they understood perfectly, and began to run as well. I looked back over my shoulder to see how close the chopper was. It was too close for comfort. However, what was even more uncomfortable was the fact that four White Soldiers were hanging from a rope ladder, shooting guns at us. I screamed at the others to run faster, but my voice could no longer be heard over the sound of the helicopter. I had almost caught up to the group and we were so close to the tree line. Then Mrs. Rundle, who was no more than twenty feet in front of me, started staggering and finally fell to the ground. I was completely stunned, I almost stopped running from shock. She was shot.

Suddenly running became so hard, and I wobbled over to her side. Calmar was there as well, sitting at her side and yelling something to me. But I couldn't hear him very well. Come to think of it, I could hardly even hear the chopper anymore. Everything was starting to spin. Calmar had his hand on my shoulder, still trying to tell me something, but he kept swaying back and forth and didn't make any sense. He started saying the word 'tranquilizer' over and over again, and I finally got it. They weren't shooting bullets at us, they shot tranquilizers. I watched Calmar as he slowly drifted off into a deep sleep. Then I somehow pushed myself up, and started walking like a zombie towards the forest. We were so close. I felt something sharp hit my back. I kept going. It felt like everything was in slow motion. To my left I saw Dawson fall down into the snow, and to my right Sylvan slowly tumbled to the ground. Poor little Nisku was crying as he lay helplessly on the frozen ground. I kept going. I was about six feet from the forest when I felt another sharp pain in my back.

Instead of walking, I was now crawling. Slower and slower. I couldn't hear anymore. I started to lose my vision and my motor skills finally quit on me. I lay sprawled out on my stomach, reaching for the forest which was now just inches from my grasping fingertips. Not wanting to give up, I kept fighting the impending unconsciousness that was gradually taking away my chance of escaping the White Soldiers. My eyelids were now too heavy to keep open. But right before the tranquilizers rendered me senseless, I caught a glimpse of a pair of yellow glowing eyes hidden within the trees.

Chapter Six

A bright light shone directly into my eyes. It moved from one eye to the other. Back and forth it went until it became rather annoying. I instinctively went to shield my eyes from the light with my right hand, but it wouldn't move. 'That's odd,' I thought to myself. I tried my left hand with the same results. I even tried moving my legs. Nothing. My brain, who was clearly on a hiatus, sluggishly began to theorize possible reasons of why my body wasn't responding as per usual. The thoughts formed about as fast as molasses. Nonetheless, slowly but surely my neural processing started to speed up as the light in my eyes grew brighter.

Foggy memories of trees, wolves and helicopters danced in my mind. Faster and faster the memories spun around together, as if they were trying to weave themselves into a picture. The image was finally formed and my pulse rose exponentially. I could feel the trillions of neural connections in my brain all coming to life at once. Everything became crystal clear. I now knew exactly why I couldn't move my extremities, as I could feel the cold metal restraints against my wrists and ankles. I could feel a flimsy mattress under my body and a sharp foreign object buried deep in a vein of my left arm. I could hear the beeping of machines and the sounds of people bustling around in a hurry. I could smell the overbearing antiseptic stench that always brought back unpleasant flashbacks. It was obvious to me that I was in some kind of hospital or clinic, attached to an IV, and restrained on top of a cheap hospital bed.

The piercing light in my eyes was now so irritating that I could no longer ignore it. I opened my eyes to find a strange man holding an apparatus with a bright light on the end. He switched off the light a second after I opened my eyes.

"She's awake, Dr. Grove."

I intuitively tried to jump off the hospital bed as a response to hearing my father's name. Unfortunately, the metal restraints would not comply with my wishes. The man with the light continued to speak, his sentences were abrupt and to the point:

"She seems to have completely recovered. All of her vitals are normal. It took five hours for the tranquilizers to wear off. Much longer than the others, however, she was injected by four highly dosed darts. The others went down with only one or two. According to our sources she didn't even react to the first tranquilizer, and hardly at all to the second. A third and fourth dart were necessary to render this one unconscious."

He walked around to the other side of my bed, where he then proceeded to remove the needle from my arm. As he did this, he revealed the figure of my father - who was standing directly behind him, by the opening of the curtains that surrounded my bed. I didn't know what to do or say. I felt completely helpless and at the mercy of whatever he decided to do. It was the first time in twenty-two years that I was truly afraid of my father. So I simply stared back, waiting for him to make the first move. He stood in silence as well. His eyes looked fixedly into mine, as if he was trying to read my thoughts. I attempted to do the same to him, but his emotionless face gave me nothing to go on. I had no way of knowing what he thought of me. Was he angry, sad, or indifferent? I had no idea. He began walking towards me, and a flashback of watching him writhe on the ground after I tasered him made my pulse quicken. What was he going to do to me? I wanted to shout out at him. To ask him what the hell he was doing, or maybe even tell him I am sorry for what I did. I don't know. I wanted to say so many things, yet instead I continued to remain completely mute as my father now stood inches away from me and placed his cold hands on my shoulders. Then what he did next completely astounded me. He hugged me. Since I was still a prisoner of the metal bed, I had no other choice but to accept the hug, whether I wanted it or not. My father then pulled out of the embrace and smiled.

"I am so glad to see that you are okay, Teslin."

"I am glad to see that you are okay too." I replied in an anxious voice, not daring to ask if mother was also alright.

"We've been watching you and your friends. You assumed the role of the leader just as I predicted. I am proud of you." He continued to smile.

"Wait. What do you mean, you were watching us? For how long? Dad, tell me what's going on right now. I am so tired of not knowing anything." I was no longer afraid, but angry and determined to find answers.

"I will tell you everything you want to know and more. Come with me. Oh, and there's no need for any more violent surprises, honey. You are safe with us." He undid my restraints as he spoke. It was obvious he was referring to the living room scene, and maybe to my outburst at Dawson too if he really was watching us.

"I have to say, we never could have predicted that you would have done that, Teslin. I had always known you were a leader, but I never knew that you were such a fighter. But you can imagine what a nice surprise it was for us." He finished unlocking the metal cuffs and turned to smile at me yet again.

"Tell me what's going on," was all I said in response. I was done with the strange niceties. I needed to know answers, and I needed to know now.

"You just want to get right down to business, don't you? That's what I like to hear. Your transition here will be seamless." He offered me a hand, but I pushed myself off the bed by myself. I didn't want his help until I knew exactly what he was involved in.

As I steadied my legs on the hard ground, I looked down at my clothes. Naturally, the attire was all white. I was wearing a long sleeved shirt, fitted pants, and steel-toed boots. For some reason, the material of the clothing was foreign to my skin; it felt soft to my body, yet to the touch of my fingertips it felt impossibly strong and hard. I wanted to ask my father what the outfit was made of, but I didn't want to further delay the truth. I did however, notice that my father was wearing the exact same thing. The same attire was worn on everyone else that we passed as we walked down a long white hallway. I was baffled at just how many people there were as we walked through the exhaustingly long hall.

People of all ages and ethnicities were going in and out of the copious amount of doors that lined the ivory coloured walls. Every door had a number painted on it, which I noticed as I passed by door number 127. I wondered how many doors were in this place, and also where and what exactly this place was? I had a feeling it was underground since I hadn't seen any windows or doors leading to the outside. Wherever it was, it was no doubt highly secured and unknown to the authorities. It had to be. Unless this was some kind of secret government facility. But then what did the government want with my father? He was a surgeon, not some kind of secret agent. The possibilities began to pile up in my mind, and I almost accidently ran into a passerby.

"Sorry," I said instinctively without even looking up at the person.

"Teslin, do watch where you are going." My father's voice echoed loudly off the empty walls.

"Sorry," I repeated.

This hallway really was never ending. It twisted and turned like a sinister snake. I would have never been able to find myself back to where we began if my life depended on it. Finally, after what seemed like hours later, we came to a set of large doors. My father paused before opening them.

"Teslin, I want to introduce you to our Enlightenment Program. I would ask that you keep quiet, as outside noise is sometimes still a distraction to the young ones."

He looked at me for compliance. I nodded my head, although I had no clue what I was agreeing to. He pushed open the doors, and what was revealed behind those doors… I hardly had the words to describe it.

The room behind the doors was humungous to say the least, the floors and the walls all possessed a sapphire blue tone that gave the room a calming vibe. The main floor stretched out at least fifty yards and equally as wide. It was surrounded by seven open levels, that circled the outside of the main area and went up so high that I had to crane my neck to get a glimpse of the seventh storey. Each level possessed light blue glass panes facing the front of the room where we stood. They were only about four feet high, so people could still see over the panes and down to the bottom level of the room easily. I could only imagine how big each floor was, as all I could see was what the see-through glass allowed me.

Nevertheless, it had to be the biggest and most impressive room I had ever seen. The word 'room' really wasn't even appropriate, more like 'magnificent theatre hall' for the exceedingly rich and famous. Although I would need binoculars to watch a theatre show from the highest floor, it was that tall. Yet something even more amazing was not the room itself, but what filled every square inch of the main floor and the seven raised levels.

Children of all ages occupied every seat on the main floor, and from what I could see, every free space in the above floors as well. They all sat in front of their own state-of-the-art computer. All of them were fixed on the screens in front of them. Some of them were typing away madly, others clicking frantically, and some were whispering softly into the microphones of their headsets in languages that I did not know. There were also adults, whom I assumed to be the teachers, pacing back and forth through the rows of students, stopping occasionally to address any questions that a student had. There must have been at least a few thousand students in this room; yet it was so peaceful. Which immediately struck me as a very odd thing indeed, as children were never this quiet. Something did not seem real about this whole scene, it felt almost surreal to be exact. I turned to look at my father, who had obviously been entertained at my reaction to the "Enlightenment Program" as he so casually called it.

"What do you think?" he asked with a hint of pride in his eyes.

"I think… I think it's impossible. How are these children able to concentrate and behave so well? I've never seen anything like it." I answered honestly.

My father gestured for me to sit down at the long empty table situated directly in front of the grand room. 'It's probably used for the most important people when addressing the entire student body,' I thought to myself as I sat down two chairs from the end, leaving room for my father to sit down beside me. He had his hands folded together, and placed in front of him on the beautiful black walnut table. He always did this with his hands when he wanted to talk to me about something serious. I braced myself for the worst.

"Teslin, do you remember when I mentioned something about a Cold Surgery to you, when we were in the house?"

"Yes. What is that?"

"It's an amazing neurological surgery developed by a famous Neurosurgeon named Dr. Joshua Lacombe. It's a surgery that takes less than five minutes to perform with the most incredible results: Removing emotions from the process of decision-making.

Dr. Lacombe managed to pinpoint the area of the brain that is responsible for sending emotional information to the frontal lobe – where, as you know, much of our mental processing occurs. Once this connection is destroyed, emotion can no longer affect your decision-making abilities. This is a phenomenon also known as Cold Cognition. Emotion still exists in the brain and can sometimes still be felt by the body, however, it cannot reach your frontal lobe. The surgery is quick and essentially painless.

A thin, needle-like drill is inserted at the top of the scalp, then drilled through the skin, the skull and finally into the brain. Once inside the brain, we are able to use advanced medical technology to manipulate the flexible drill, and disconnect the targeted neural connections that transfer our emotions. Because of Dr. Lacombe's very precise coordinates, we are able to find this specific bundle of connections rather flawlessly, and the surgery occurs without little to no mistakes.

Teslin, do you know what this means?"

It took me a second to realize that he had stopped his explanation, and was now asking me a question. I was still trying to process the horrifying implications of what he just told me.

"So… you're basically kidnapping people and giving them glorified lobotomies to rid their minds of emotion?" I asked in utter disbelief, hoping that I was way off the mark.

"It's much more than that, my dear. Look around you. These children learn for twelve hours a day, only stopping to eat and sleep. They would never be able to learn and process the large amounts of information that they do, if they had emotions interfering with their mental processing. Children have a huge capacity to learn - significantly larger and faster than that of adults. After the surgery, this capacity increases to an amount that we have not yet determined. Mainly because the children are continuously surprising us with their knowledge:

We have six year olds that can speak fluently in five different languages, ten year olds that can perform mathematical and scientific problems designed for advanced doctorate programs with ease, fifteen year olds that can design impenetrable communication technology, and the list goes on. Although each student is required to learn a certain amount of material in Mathematics, Physics, Biology, Chemistry, Psychology, History and Languages, once it becomes obvious where their strength lies, we focus their education strongly in that direction. For example, one girl showed extreme mastery in languages at the age of five; she is now ten and she can speak twelve different languages. She is one of our head interpreters."

"Wait a minute!" I had to get this straight. "So if she began learning five years ago, how many years have you been working on this program?! How long have you been lying to me about your job, and about giving surgeries to children in some underground secret liar?!" I whispered angrily.

"We've been working on the Cold Cognition Project for six years now. And I never lied to you. I always told you that I was studying the brain, which is one hundred percent true. Our facility was the first of its kind. Dr. Lacombe wanted a safe and unsuspecting place in the world where we could test out the surgery and technology. However, today our Movement is international. There are 64 other facilities just like ours around the globe.

Yesterday, was a monumental and world changing day. After six years of intense preparations, we finally began the Cold Cognition Movement. We were so successful that Dr. Lacombe authorized the other 64 locations to begin the Movement as well. We are making history, Teslin. We are creating a world of intelligence, peace and equality. We are saving humankind, and consequently, we are saving the planet." My father believed every word he spoke, and for some reason I was starting to believe them as well. But I still had questions that needed to be answered:

"Okay, I can see how creating intelligent beings is important, but how exactly does it save the world?"

"Teslin, the world we live in now is full of selfish and hateful people. There is so much disparity between the rich and the poor. Prejudice, racism, and sexism run rampart throughout the planet. Constant wars plague the Earth, all because of power, pride, religious and cultural beliefs. People are not getting any smarter, in fact, they are starting to regress.

Therefore, there will never be peace in this world if we do not change the people. Words can only change people so much, Teslin, at some point action has to be taken to be successful. Think of a world without war and prejudice, a world where only completely logical and intelligent beings exist. Imagine all the things we could accomplish. We would all focus on ways to keep our people strong, increase our longevity and the lifespan of our planet. We would direct all of our energy to advancing the medical and scientific fields. We would find the best ways to produce food and minerals from the earth. We would all work together, as we would no longer be citizens of individual nations, but citizens of the world. The only thing that is stopping us, is emotions. They are what hinder people from world-change, simply because people are scared: Scared of change, scared of success, scared of themselves and those around them.

Hardly anyone volunteered to have the Cold Surgery, even though its potential benefits were more important than their very existence. People illogically tend to think that their lives are special, and worth an invaluable amount. When in reality, we are extremely replaceable. If I died today, there would be a replacement of equal merit and skill to take my place by the end of the day. That's the truth that no one wants to hear. But we have to accept this if we are ever going to change the world for the better. Lives must be sacrificed for a noble cause. Our cause is to create intelligence, peace, and equality on world-wide scale. We hope that you will join us, Teslin. We could greatly use your talents of leadership and logical decision-making. People naturally follow you, and that is a very rare gift."

My father finished his speech and waited for my reply. I had a feeling that I didn't really have a choice in the matter. I turned my eyes to the strangely quiet children that stared fixedly at their computer screens. They didn't seem scared or under duress in any way, but they weren't laughing, smiling, or playing either. They weren't real children. Apparently without emotions, children were like little robots who sucked up as much information as they could. It was amazing and sad at the same time. And the whole Cold Cognition Movement thing was a bit confusing as well. To my understanding, we were bringing peace and intelligence to the world by forcing people to undergo a surgery that removed emotions in such a way, that it only affected a person's reasoning capabilities, making them purely logical beings. I really didn't know how I felt about all this. I didn't like how people were not given a choice in the matter, but I did see my father's point. There was a small chance that people would voluntary allow emotion to be removed from their prefrontal cortex, even if they did see the benefits. Maybe we would be better without emotions messing with our brains.

I looked over at the children again. I saw a little boy of about fourteen lean over to the much younger girl sitting next to him, and asked her about a math equation. She answered quickly without any extra small talk, he thanked her, and they went back to their appropriate screens. The whole interaction struck me. I don't think I had ever seen a boy ask a young little girl for advice, let alone in mathematics. Even at a young age, I remember hearing people say that girls weren't as good at math as boys, because our brains were not as logical as boys. Apparently, women and girls were too emotional. I never truly believed this, as I usually received a better math grade than most of the boys all throughout elementary and high school, but this sort of thinking still affected me to some extent.

Like the winter my brother's older friends told me I couldn't play hockey with them because I was a girl. I had played with them for the past four winters before, but apparently now that they were older (about thirteen years and I was ten at the time) they were stronger and smarter than me. What made me even more furious, was that they let a boy who was exactly my age play with them. So I knew the only reason I couldn't play was because I was a girl. It was the first time I really experienced injustice in my life.

I again looked at the boy who asked the young girl for mathematical advice; he asked her because he knew she would have the answer. He didn't hesitate, he had no prejudice or sexism towards the little girl. It was so refreshing to see, and it made me smile. I began to really like the idea of a logical brain. Perhaps the sacrifice of emotion is what it took to have equality. I never really thought of how emotion fueled prejudice, sexism and racism, but I guess it was true: that it was illogical emotions of fear, anger and pride, that conceived such horrible concepts. For all anyone knows, this Cold Surgery could be the next chapter of the human race.

"I'm interested. Tell me more." I smiled at my father. I guess he really did know what he was doing. He wasn't the brainwashed monster that I pictured in my mind for the past day and a half. All he wanted was equality and peace. That couldn't be so bad, could it? I truly hoped not. My father smiled back at me.

"Come with me. There are other things I want to show you."

We walked out of the massive blue masterpiece-of-a-room, and back into the white labyrinth-like hallway, passing by many more people and many more doors as I followed closely behind my father. Again the hallways turned and twisted, until we came to a room which had multiple large windows (allowing you to view the activity of the room from the hallway). My father stopped by one of the large windows.

"We don't need to go inside for me to explain what happens in here," he said, gesturing at the see-through windows. "This is our Textile Factory. It's where we make our uniforms, with the most advanced technology in the world."

I peered through the spacious window to see an enormous room full of large machinery, assembly lines, and sewing machines. The textile workers in the room worked in such a fast and skilled manner, that it was mesmerizing to watch them glide from one machine to the next, completing the uniform a bit more at each step. Everyone moved in such a choreographed way, that it almost resembled a dance. I noticed at the end of the assembly lines, where the newly made uniforms were quickly piling up, the workers could hardly keep up with transferring the clothing from the assembly line into large shoots in the wall. It was amazing how many uniforms they could make in what seemed like seconds.

'They must need them for quite a lot of people,' I thought. I still couldn't imagine for how many people. My father said this was a world-wide Movement, but was that really possible? To change the whole world? I wasn't so sure, but everyone in this facility seemed to believe it, and worked the hardest I had ever seen in my life to achieve it. I wanted to change this dangerous subject in my mind, so I asked my father a question:

"So what kind of material is this?" I asked, pointing to my own uniform.

"I am glad that you noticed, because it's not like any other material you have felt before."

He smiled at me, but there was no emotion behind the smile. I began to realize that all of his smiles had been like this, fake. I began wondering if it was just a side effect from having emotions for so long, or if he smiled because he knew it would make me feel more comfortable, when his answer interrupted my thoughts:

"It's a material that was developed in our very own Medical and Technology lab. An area that I will show you next. Our experts created a material that on the inside, holds body temperature and is extremely soft to the skin, however, on the outside, it is a flexible and durable material that is completely fireproof, waterproof, and bullet proof. We want our people to be protected in every way possible. If you wear one of our uniforms, you have our promise that you are protected."

I looked down at my own uniform.

"And the shoes?" I asked.

"The shoes have a more durable material in them. Since your feet endure the worst, they are built for the worst."

"Very interesting." I said coolly, like it was no big deal. However, on the inside I felt invincible! Neither fire, nor water, nor bullets, could stop me! What an interesting concept, to be invincible. I had never really thought of it until now, and I have to say, it felt great! I felt like I could do anything. I felt like I could conquer the world! My stomach churned, at the thought of taking over the world. Wasn't that what we were attempting to do, in a way, to take over the world? Suddenly I didn't feel so powerful. I felt… uneasy… strange. I felt like the whole world was spinning at high speed, and I was simply a bystander, watching the world go on without me. And it only took two days for my world to be completely derailed and leave me behind. I was only one person, there was no way I had a say in any of this. This was too big for me. I might as well just go along with everything, get the surgery done, and then my uneasy feelings would be a thing of the past.

'I suppose it's my best option,' I thought as I listened to my father further explain how the machinery worked. I usually blanked out when people started explaining to me how complex machinery worked. I was much more interested in how people worked. In fact, I always found myself focusing on a person's eyes and body language a bit too much that it sometimes freaked people out. Apparently I came off as "too intense" according to Devon. 'Devon!' I had to ask my father about her! I cut my father off mid-sentence, as he was describing the details of their testing process, and blurted out my question:

"Do you know where Devon is!?"

My voice sounded desperate and surprisingly loud, that my father instantly stopped talking. He turned from the window and looked at me.

"Yes, I do," he said rather bluntly. Then he promptly returned to his explanation as if the interruption never occurred. I didn't want to cut him off again, but this answer gave me absolutely no information whatsoever. I had to at least know if Devon was okay.

"Can I see her?" I asked, again speaking loudly to be heard over his powerful voice.

Once again, he instantly stopped talking and stared at me. But this time with an entirely emotionless face. I had never seen my father look at me this way before. Deafening silence surrounded us for a few painfully long seconds, before he finally decided to answer me.

"If that's what you want. I can have it arranged for you to meet with Devon. But only for a short while, as we all have very important jobs to do here, Teslin."

"Of course, I understand. I only need a few minutes with her. Thank you!"

He simply nodded his head in agreement, "We will now proceed to the Medical and Technology Laboratory. This way, please."

And with that, he began walking away from the windows of the Textile Factory, without even a second glance to see if I was following behind him. I, of course, did follow him. Mainly because I didn't know where else to go in this confusing maze. He probably already realized that, which is why he never bothered to look back.

The third room we visited, the Medical and Technology Laboratory, was almost identical to the blue mystical palace of the Enlightenment Program. However, it was all white instead of blue, and a tad bit smaller (boasting only five floors instead of seven). This being said, it was still a luxurious laboratory to say the least. Brimming with microscopes, test tubes, flasks, funnels and beakers, all filled with colourful liquid that I could only begin to imagine its purpose. Curious looking equipment and machinery also lined the sparkling white countertops of the laboratory. Scientists of all sizes and ages were rushing to and fro, carrying glass vials and folders stuffed with papers. To an unknowing eye, the whole scene resembled something of a mad house. Yet if you continued to stare for more than a second, you would come to see that there was a logical order to the frenzied chaos. With all the running around you would think someone would have bumped into someone or something, or tripped over the many wires running along the floors connected to alien machines, but this was not the case. Instead, the uniformed scientists all walked in a logical, thought-out sequence which was executed flawlessly. If you watched long enough, it almost looked like the motions were all repeated exactly, but with different people. What an odd thing to see. They looked like very well-rehearsed robots. One of these robots happened to look right at me, and then at my father. He stopped in his tracks and began walking towards us. As he walked closer, I got a better look at him. He was very young, about sixteen or seventeen.

'Maybe he was an intern?' I thought questioningly. That could explain why someone so young would be allowed to work in such a grand laboratory.

"Good evening, Dr. Grove. I am glad that you are here. I wanted you to be the first to know that we altered the treatment in the way you suggested, and we now have the world's fastest and fully-effective cancer treatment." The adolescent boy spoke in a very confident tone, seemingly unaware of his young stature. Although I was not as curious about the boy himself, but about the statement he just declared.

"A fully-effective cancer treatment?! What wonderful news! This treatment will be life-changing for so many people!" I beamed at the young man, "That's amazing news! Congratulations!"

He simply nodded in acknowledgement to my praise, and then directed his attention to my father, who stood to the right of me looking very serious (a look which I still hadn't gotten used to. I missed his crooked smile and how his whole body shook when he laughed. I suppose that was all in the past now).

"Very good, William. Run the test one more time on ten new test subjects. If the results are all successful, you and your team may begin mass distribution of the treatment to our other locations."

"Yes, sir."

Then the boy turned around and walked away, ending the conversation. I knew they couldn't be excited about this great news, so I was excited for them:

"Dad, this is amazing! You can help so many people now that you have the cure for cancer!"

My father looked down at me, showing not even a hint of pride or happiness on his face, "Teslin, the cure for cancer was already discovered about eight years ago by a scientist in Belgium."

I frowned in confusion, "Wait. What do you mean? That doesn't make any sense. If there was a cure, we would know about it. News like that would be celebrated all over the world!"

He simply shook his head and said, "You overestimate the goodness of people, Teslin. The cure was rather inexpensive and would be very accessible to everyone. That being said, the very powerful and excessively greedy pharmaceutical companies did not want to lose billions of dollars on the cure. They currently collect countless dollars for their somewhat effective treatments, painkillers, and the myriad of other drugs that counter unwanted side effects. These companies would have taken a huge financial hit if the cure was ever released.

So they paid the inventor a very generous amount of hush money and pretended like it never happened. It is unfortunate that greed and selfishness - some of man's biggest flaws - are the reason that the cure is not known.

In our New World, this will never happen, Teslin. You heard us, we improved the cure so it works in under a day, and after our final testing is successful we will share this miracle with the rest of our people. We want to make our people strong and healthy so they can give back with their talent and skill, not with their money. Actually, money will be a thing of the past. It is something that only lesser beings desire."

Apparently he was done with our conversation, because he abruptly finished and walked out of the laboratory. He left me alone in the busy hum of low voices and machines. I didn't know how to begin to process the information my father had just dropped on me.

'There was already a cure? How many people had died because of this secret? And if it was indeed true, what else had the people in power hid from us?' These thoughts created a horrid shiver that ran down my spine. Maybe I didn't want to know the answer. Either way, I knew I had to continue following my father through this endless maze. There wasn't much else I could do. I suddenly felt so hopeless and infinitesimal, like I never had a choice in my life. I always did what was expected of me by my peers and society. I guess this was the same thing. I would do what was expected of me by this Movement. What other choice did I have?

They seemed to have noble goals, even if the means to their goals were a bit questionable. They wanted peace, intelligence, and equality. How was that a bad thing? There was still something that didn't feel quite right about the whole thing, but what could I do about it? I watched the scene in front of me, there were no smiles or laughter, just limited talking when it was deemed necessary. This isn't how people are supposed to interact, so coldly. Once I got the surgery I would be the same, and then I suppose it wouldn't matter anymore. I wouldn't feel the need to smile or laugh either. I tried to clear my head of these distressing thoughts, and ran out of the lab to find the man who controlled my future.

****

I caught up to my father in the white hallway. He had never once looked behind him to see if I had followed him. Even though his indifference was not surprising to me anymore, it still felt strange. I silently walked a few feet behind him, falling in step with his fast and determined pace. As we walked, I noticed that the walls abruptly changed from blazing white to a silver colour. My fingertips were met with cold metal as I ran my hand along the wall. I didn't know much about metals, but I could tell that this specific metal was extremely durable and strong. 'What could possibly be hidden behind these walls that needed such protection?' I thought curiously. I had to know.

"What is behind these metal walls?"

He answered without a pause in his step, "Our military wing."

My pulse instantly rose at the thought of the White Soldiers. The metal wall went on forever, and I could only imagine how large the room behind it was, and what was residing within it. The large metal door leading into the military wing possessed a number of locks and deadbolts. Seeing the number of locks on the door only made me want to get inside of that room even more. A surge of meddlesomeness came over me when I observed the small window at the top of the door. I know that curiosity killed the cat, but I couldn't help myself. I stopped and tried to peer through the tiny window. Unfortunately, even on tiptoes I could only see the bottom rim around the small opening. I would have to jump to be able to see anything at all. So I bent my knees getting ready to make the jump, when a strong force yanked me off my balance and away from the door. It was my father's strong arm that had torn me away so swiftly. He continued to hold my arm painfully tight as he pulled me down the hallway, marching away from the silver door.

"You are not authorized to go in there, Teslin." He quickened the pace even more so.

"I only wanted to see! What's so wrong with that?!" I yelled, whilst simultaneously ripping my arm free of his grip. "What are hiding in there that you don't want me to see?!"

This seemed to have struck a chord with him, and he stopped marching and whipped around to glare at me. He came towards me, and stopped just inches away from my face:

"There are somethings that I cannot tell you until after you have the Cold Surgery. Only then will you be able to think logically and understand what we must do in order for our Movement to be successful."

I was tired of being intimidated and scared, so I stared harshly back at him.

"You mean kill people. Right?" I tried to keep my anger at bay, but it was becoming impossibly harder to do so. There was going to be nothing peaceful about this Movement. I now knew that for sure.

"Teslin, we can't expect the rest of the world to simply stand down and agree to the surgery. People are afraid of change. Even if it is for the better. It would be very naïve to believe that everyone will agree with our noble cause, mainly because humans are not logical creatures. We will be met by opposing forces. And we will have the military support to defend ourselves. We have to be able to protect ourselves if this Movement is going to be successful." He returned my stare with such a fierceness that I felt my anger subsiding, making room for the fear which was slowly taking its place.

"Now stay close and no more distractions. There is one more place I want to show you before you can see Devon." My heart did a little skip at the mention of Devon's name. I wanted to see her so badly, so I followed my father obediently. As I did this, I became consciously aware of how good my father was at manipulation. He knew that if he mentioned Devon I would forget all about what was behind those metal walls, and act submissively so I could see my friend. It was a clever ploy indeed. He knew right away what to say to deter me from questioning him anymore on the military wing. And it worked. I didn't know whether to feel impressed by this or worried at how easily my mind could be changed. Though I didn't get the time to decide which one it was, as my mind was once again distracted by yet another grandiose room.

"Here we have our Communications Headquarters. This is where you will be working, Teslin. Providing information and orders to our teams of White Soldiers on the ground." He made a sweeping gesture with his arm to further emphasize the magnificence of the scene in front of me. This was quite unnecessary, as anyone would be impressed by the Communications Headquarters. So much so, that I hardly registered the fact that my father said I would be working here, aiding the White Soldiers of all people. These words fluttered to the back of my mind as I took in the splendour of the room before me.

It reminded me of a massive lecture theatre, with rows upon rows of black wooden desks crammed with strange holographic computers and very serious looking people in white uniforms. The people were skillfully and rapidly turning, pushing, and pulling the holographic information from their computers, while also relaying intelligence through the microphones on their dark blue headsets. The impossible amount of holograms spinning and moving around was overwhelming; so many different colours and sizes constantly changing and shifting. It looked more like a show of dancing lights than a room full of computers. Each individual computer had its own eloquent dancing light, while also joining all the other fellow lights to create a spectacular performance. I was so utterly enthralled in the dance, that for a moment, I forgot all about the world. I forgot about my confusion, my doubts, and my fears. The fact that I was about to be a part of a Movement that I did not completely understand or agree with, temporarily escaped from my memory. For the first time in what seemed like weeks, I felt light and free. I was not weighed down by the unknown, but lifted up by the mesmerizing lights around me. It was like I was in a fantastical dream; the problems of the world were far behind me. Enchanted by the forever altering aurora, I followed the colours across the vast space until my eyes rested upon the huge screen that encompassed the entire front wall of the lecture hall. Although it was only one large screen, there were multiple screens projected onto it, projections composed of maps, detailed mathematical equations, satellite information, live feed from the White Soldiers, and other important looking material which I couldn't even begin to comprehend. A smorgasbord of data. I didn't know how anyone could focus on just one screen at a time. While my eyes adjusted to the overload of visual information, my brain began to register the hum of the computers, the sound of low voices all speaking at once, and a very loud and confident voice that could be heard clearly above them all.

My ears followed the commanding voice until I came across its owner: a very tall, dark-skinned woman. She was pacing back and forth behind her desk (which was much larger than the others), while also yelling out commands and occasionally manipulating data on her computer. For some reason I hadn't noticed her before, which was odd because she was unmissable as she was so loud and the only one standing up in the room (other than my father and I, of course). Even from far away she was very intimidating. She held herself in such a powerful and aggressive manner, as if she was daring you to challenge her. She was the kind of person that you always wanted on your side, not as your enemy. And she was also the very person that my father was headed straight for. I slunk quietly behind him, wary of what was to come of our interaction with this woman.

My father spoke first, "Good evening, Armena. This is my daughter Teslin."

The woman did not bother to reply. Instead, she looked me up and down with a stone cold face. I tried my hardest to bravely look right into her humourless eyes. To this she replied in a harsh and rude tone:

"She hasn't gotten the surgery yet. Why not?"

Father replied without hesitation, "She is still recovering from the effects of four highly-dosed tranquilizers. We need to be sure her body is in perfect condition before the surgery, hence why she will receive treatment first thing tomorrow morning after a full night to recover."

Armena simply nodded her head, "Very good. I will see you tomorrow then, Teslin. Get some rest. We have lots of work to do tomorrow."

For some reason, Armena scared me to the point that I was utterly tongue-tied and all I could do was nod in agreement. Thank goodness she seemed to take my nonverbal response as acceptable, since she immediately went back to yelling out orders. There was no hiding my apparent fear of Armena. Working with her was the last thing I wanted to do. I instinctively looked up at my father for reassurance. He gave me none.

"Come along, Teslin," was all he said. Holding back tears of frustration, I clung on to the belief that everything would be better after I got to see Devon. And I repeated this to myself as I quietly followed the man whom I used to trust with my life.

****

We continued down a new hallway, which I was certain was new, because the walls were now blue instead of white. A dark majestic blue that had the effect of calming my frazzled nerves and spinning head. There was also a lot more people down the blue hallway. People were steadily going in and out of the many doors lining the walls. They were blue as well, with gold door handles. It was strange to see that out of so many people, not one person made eye contact with me, not even accidentally. Instead, they all wore impassive expressions on their faces and walked in a very determined manner.

'It's like they're not even real people anymore,' I thought to myself. 'They seem more like robots than humans.' This notion engrossed my thoughts in such a significant way, that I almost did not notice my father had abruptly stopped in front of me. Thankfully, I managed to stop myself before I crashed into him. He had halted in front of one of the blue doors, knocked three times, and then let himself in without any kind of verbal announcement. I followed after him, into the small blue room. It was alike an upgraded hostel room, lined with several bunkbeds, with a large closet, a washroom, and a tiny round table. And everything was in a calming shade of blue. But what I was most interested about, was not the odd blue room, but the person who was sitting at the tiny blue table… Devon.

A huge smile burst across my face at the sight of seeing my best friend. I ran towards her and embraced her tightly.

"Oh Devon, I am so happy to see you! I was so worried about you!"

I had known her all my life, but suddenly the body that I was embracing seemed foreign and strange. She only lightly hugged me back, not at all like herself. I pulled out of our embrace and looked at her closely. She looked worn, and wore not a trace of make-up. Her long blonde hair was tied back in a high ponytail. This was all very unusual for Devon. She loved wearing make-up, and always had her wild platinum-coloured hair flowing free.

"Devon, are you okay?" I looked deep into her hollow brown eyes, and sat down beside her.

"Of course I am okay, Teslin," she replied in an emotionless voice. A voice very different from the familiar one I knew, full of excitement and dramatics. She continued speaking in this strange tone.

"I am working in the textile factory. I've caught on quite quickly as apparently I have a natural knack for this kind of thing. The people here get along so nicely, Teslin. No one fights or argues at all. Because we all agree on the most logical solution to every problem. You are going to love it here, Teslin. You always said you wished you could live to see the day that world peace was realized. Now you can."

She made the effort to smile after she finished speaking. I was not sure how to continue this conversation, something I had never thought was possible with Devon. We could talk for hours about absolutely nothing. And yet, right now I couldn't come up with a single thing to say to her. For she was no longer my Devon. She belonged to the Movement now.

'Maybe I could get the old Devon back if I could just talk to her longer. Remind her of all the crazy adventures we had together.' The thought ignited a small flame of hope just big enough to try.

"I'm happy to hear that, Devon. So what else have you been doing while you've been here? Have you seen any of our friends? Like Dawson? What are they up to? Oh, what happened with that guy you liked at your birthday party!? Have you talked to him? Are there any good parties here in this facility? Surely you already started planning something, haven't you!?" I asked in a very energetic voice, which would have worked the old Devon into a complete frenzy. She would have squealed in delight to give me all the details, as she always knew everything about everyone. But instead of answering my many questions, she calmly replied with a statement I could not believe was coming out of her mouth:

"Teslin, what we are doing here is much more important than you, or I, or any of our friends. We have a chance to change the world for the better. To have peace, equality and intelligence on a world-wide scale. There is nothing more important than that."

My heart sank when she said this. She really was gone. The surgery really had worked. I slumped back into my chair and looked down at my shoes.

'Was world peace really so important if we lost ourselves in the process? Or maybe it was, maybe I was just being selfish not wanting to give up my emotions. I didn't want to be an emotionless robot. But I suppose that was the only way humans could have peace. Sacrificing our emotions for the good of the world was just a small price we had to pay. It was possible that I was making too big of a deal about the surgery. If it really did bring peace amongst the people as my father, and now as Devon had said, then it couldn't be all that bad. I mean, isn't this what I always wanted, world peace? Devon was right, now I had the chance to be a part of a Movement that would create world peace. Why was I fighting it?'

I looked back up at Devon, she smiled at me.

"You looked tired, Teslin. You should get some rest." She reached over, still smiling, took my hands in hers, and spoke softly, "Good night, my friend. May all your dreams come true tomorrow." Then she let go of my hands and I stood up to leave.

I walked out of the small blue room with a strange calmness that I hadn't experienced for a while. I took a deep breath as I waited for my father to close the door to Devon's room.

"Now I shall take you to your room. I have a surprise there waiting for you." He said this with a hint of excitement. I cocked my head in curiosity. I did love surprises, so I forced my tired legs to move on, my inquisitive nature giving me the energy boost I needed.

About twenty doors down from Devon's room, is where my father opened another blue door. The blue door of my new room. It was a lot smaller than Devon's room, but that was because it housed only one bed. I had my own private room. My father held it open and gestured for me to enter. I did. I wanted to question him as to why I got my own room, but upon taking one step into my blue accommodation, I was violently bulldozed over by a large black-and-white creature! Pinned down to the ground, I found myself staring into the icy blue eyes of my beloved Nikita. I laughed out loud from pure relief and joy at seeing my husky! The one thing in my life that hadn't changed. My parents and my friends may have all been altered, but Nikita remained the exact same furry butt she had always been. I didn't even care that she was licking my face like a maniac, I was too happy to be upset by a little saliva.

Then I heard a soft Slavic voice from in the room speak, "Nikita, leave her alone. You are going to smother her completely."

My body instantly froze, for that voice was one I could recognize before I came out of the womb. It was my mother! She wasn't dead! I immediately pushed Nikita off of me and sprung up to my feet. There, across the room, stood my mother, wearing the same white uniform that we all did.

She looked beautiful like always, and wore her usual sweet, loving smile. Standing in front of me now, she didn't appear different at all. In fact, she looked quite normal to me. This was very odd, as everyone seemed to be so drastically affected by the surgery, so why wasn't she?

My feet began to walk towards her against my own will, they seemed to think she was still my mother too. I was about two feet in front of her when I saw something that made me gasp, and caused my feet to stop dead in their tracks. Dark red and purple scars covered her entire neck and collarbone. Some of them were long and thin, while others were short and wide. I stared at her neck, remembering how the scars were made, by deadly teeth and claws. I looked down at my Nikita, who was currently standing next to me licking my hand. How could such a sweet creature like her be responsible for butchering my mom's neck? My mother must have known what I was thinking, for she attempted to make me feel better.

"Teslin, it is okay. It's not Nikita's fault." She gestured to her wounded neck, "This was all a misunderstanding. She was merely trying to protect you because she thought you were in danger. But it's all in the past now, okay? We have much more important things to focus on right now. So don't be worried about me, darling."

Her words did much more than comfort me, they moved me. In this moment, I didn't care if she was just using her words to manipulate me like my father, I needed a mother right now. I threw myself into her arms and buried my face in her warm chest.

"I'm so sorry, mom."

She stroked my hair while she held me in her arms. I couldn't help but trace the scars on her collarbone with my fingertips. My poor mother! This was all my fault! If I hadn't of been so scared, if I hadn't of listened to Mrs. Rundle, if I hadn't of ran from them, then this could have all been avoided. The unnecessary freezing cold days in the mountains, all the fighting in our misfit group, all the stress from the confusion of not knowing what we were up against, the tranquilizers, the scars on my mother's neck… All of this could have been easily averted if I had only listened to my parents.

My mother put her finger under my chin and lifted my face up to hers. Her eyes appeared warm and soft, not as warm as normal, but it was good enough for me.

"Teslin, I am so glad that we have you back. Now you need to sleep. Tomorrow is a big day for you. You will join our Movement, and begin your new task to bring peace, equality and intelligence to this broken world. Good night, my angel."

She kissed the top of my head and then turned around to leave my room. My father followed her, without even glancing back at me or saying goodbye. Suddenly I was all alone. This was the last thing I wanted, to be alone with my thoughts. Then a sharp yelp from below reminded me that I wasn't entirely alone. Nikita was still here. So I forced my mind to focus only on her as I got ready for the rest I desperately needed.

****

About an hour later I finally found myself in bed, impatiently waiting for sleep to come and shut down the swirling cyclone of thoughts inside my mind. Bored from waiting, my eyes began to wander the small room. Although it was rather tiny, it had everything I needed, and it even had a unique charm to it. That was until I noticed a small camera in the left corner of the room. Apparently this private room was not so private after all. They were watching. Of course they were watching. I don't know why I would expect anything less. My eyes moved away from the camera and came to rest on my white uniform, hanging on the closet door. There was something on the bottom of the right side of the shirt which I hadn't noticed before, some kind of large dark spot. I squinted my eyes to see better, but to no avail. Since I had nothing better to do, and I was obviously not going to sleep any time soon, I crawled across my bed so I could inspect it further (almost waking up Nikita as she lay asleep on the mat beneath my bed).

When I was close enough, I pulled the fabric of the shirt towards me, brushing my fingers across the dark spot which I realized was actually an emblem; a pretty design of blue swirling lines inside of a dark blue triangle. As I looked closer, I saw that the dainty lines were actually letters overlapping each other. I traced out two Cs and an M with my finger. 'Cold Cognition Movement', my mind instantly solved the puzzle. But why a triangle? Why not another shape? Then I recalled the three things that my father and everyone else kept repeating to me. The three things that the Movement was supposed to bring: Peace, Equality and Intelligence. Reality finally sunk in. I was about to have a big part in this Movement tomorrow, and I still wasn't even sure how I felt about it. I lay back down in bed, more restless than I had ever been before. My mind was a constant tornado of thoughts and questions. I didn't think I would ever be able to fall asleep. Yet my exhausted body eventually overpowered my frantic brain, and a deep, dark, and nightmare-filled sleep overtook me.

Chapter Seven

The silence was deafening. I had never heard such a cruel sound before in my life. The air was filled with tension and dread. Fear hung over the room like a heavy blanket, smothering us all. I could see it on their faces, and feel it on their bodies when their skin brushed up against mine. We were all afraid. Them more so than I, as I already knew exactly what was going to happen. They had no idea what was to come of them.

I scanned the crowd of haunted faces. One of the faces especially caught my eye. A young boy, no more than five or six years old, who was looking right up at me from behind a woman who I assumed to be his mother. He gripped on tightly to his mother's pant leg as he stared up at me with his big brown eyes. I felt a pang of sadness in my heart for the little brown-eyed boy. He stood so quietly and calmly, unaware of the fact that a drill was about to penetrate his skull and lacerate an important connection in his still developing brain.

'What a shame. He is so young that he probably won't even remember what life was like with emotions. I suppose that is a good thing. Then he won't know what he is missing,' I thought, while still looking into his innocent eyes.

Suddenly a loud siren went off, and the red light above the main double doors turned green. Not a second passed before all the doors of the room flew open, and in came a legion of doctors accompanied by White Soldiers. They began taking people one by one from the large waiting room that we were currently packed into like a herd of cattle. In a quick and orderly fashion, the room of at least two hundred people dwindled down to none. As a result of being at the back of the room, I would be one of the last people to be taken. I watched as the little boy was separated from his mother. Both of them protested with screams and tears. But not to worry, the doctors had a quick solution to this predicament. They covered the mouth and nose of the boy and the mother with an oxygen mask that released blue-coloured smoke. The two became calm instantaneously. It was almost like a puff of calming blue magic. Then it was my turn. A doctor and a White Soldier came for me. The last one in the room. I felt like I was having an out-of-body experience as I watched myself being taken out of the room. I noticed my reflection on the helmet of the White Soldier. My face appeared both sad and afraid, and my eyes reflected defeat. Truth be told, that's exactly what I was in this moment, defeated. Consequently, I made no trouble for the White Soldier and surgeon, but simply let them lead me to wherever I was supposed to go. The doctor led the way and the soldier pushed me from behind so I did not attempt to escape. Together the three of us entered the room beyond the doors.

Hundreds of large metal tables flooded the colossal white operating room. Patients, or rather kidnapped victims, of all ages were restrained to the tables, and any unwanted screams were quickly subdued by a dose of the blue smoke. However, what was even more unsettling was not the screams of the petrified victims, but the sounds of the ear-piercing drills. The drilling changed its pitch depending on what it was drilling through. Whether it was through the skin, the skull, or the brain, the sounds were all different. It was a symphony of high and low toned perforating drills, accented by the bloodcurdling screams of the innocent.

Although it was the largest operating room I had ever seen, I was not impressed by this room like I was with the others in the facility. Instead, I was terrified. Absolutely terrified. My body began to rattle with fear as I was strapped down onto the raised operating table. If they hadn't of tied me down, I would have surely fallen off due to my incessant shaking. But at the sound of a drill being turned on so close to my ear, my body abruptly froze in horror. I could feel the blood draining from my face as it went completely white, almost perfectly matching my white uniform. I told myself to calm down but my body had a mind of its own. It began to move again, this time with the purpose of trying to escape my cold metal restraints. Unfortunately, they were so impossibly tight that my efforts were hardly noticed. The sound of the drill came closer and closer, and my heart responded by beating faster and faster. Not one to give up, my body continued to fight against its bonds. Pulling, pushing and shaking with all my strength. I felt the surgeon cutting away some of my hair where the drill would enter, and then, I felt the drill touch my bare skin.

My body gave one last blow against the restraints, and my right arm came free with such a momentum that I managed to completely flip over the operating table so that it was upside down. I lay face down on the cold ground, with the metal table on top of me, in incredulous shock. I felt no pain from hitting the hard ground, as I was overcome with the adrenaline rushing through my veins. The room became absolutely silent. Even the drills stopped. And then just as suddenly as it stopped, yelling and screaming began all around me. I started a frenzy.

I tried to move out from under the table, however, the three other restraints holding back my wrist and ankles made this task very difficult. Without warning, I felt myself being lifted right side up, so that I was once again facing the ceiling. The second the table stopped moving, I began throwing punches with my free arm at whatever I could get my hands on. The surgeon and the White Soldier were facing quite the dilemma trying to calm me down.

I heard the White Soldier telling the doctor to back away, and that he would handle the situation - meaning me. The soldier then lifted the restraints off my remaining extremities. Before I could even register that I was free from my bonds, the soldier pulled me from the tilted-up table, and put me in an extremely tight arm lock. He had my arm in a hold so painful, that any pressure I exerted from trying to escape resulted in excruciating pain.

"If you continue to fight, you will only break your arm."

I froze at the sound of the soldier's deep voice. For some reason it sounded familiar to me. The soldier, who was obviously a male by the sound of his voice, took my frozenness as compliance and began to walk me out of the room at such a fast pace that I had to run to keep up with him for fear of breaking my arm. He dragged me out of the operating room, through the waiting room, and into a small room full of medical supplies. Then he threw me into the room and locked the door behind us. I prepared myself for the absolute worst, and ran to the back of the room, rapidly scouting out anything I could use as a weapon. I zeroed in on a clear box full of razor-sharp drill bits. The box was sitting on the end of a knee-high shelf. I ran to it and kicked it off the shelf, spilling thousands of drill bits onto the floor. I grabbed two of the drills (one for each hand) and turned to face the White Soldier, who was currently creating a makeshift barricade at the door. He whipped around at the sound of all the commotion from the mess I made. I saw my reflection in his helmet once again. This time I wasn't afraid. I looked both fierce and crazed. Holding both of the drill bits in the air ready to strike, I looked like a deranged killer.

"Holy crap, Teslin! Calm down! It's just me. I'm not going to hurt you!"

The White Soldier removed his helmet and a mess of black curls fell out. It was Calmar. I dropped the drills from my hands and fell to my knees, clutching my heart and gasping. From all the stress my poor heart had to take these past few days, I am positive it had taken off at least twenty years from my lifespan.

"Oh my god, Calmar! Why didn't you say anything before! I was going to… I don't know what I was going to do!"

Calmar shook his head in disbelief, "I left you alone for literally three seconds! I didn't think you were going to go all psycho killer on me! Geez! I don't think you've even been here for 24 hours and you've already gone mad!" he laughed in amazement.

Still clutching my heart, I half-heartedly yelled at him, "That's not funny! After all we've been through it's a miracle I haven't gone completely crazy!"

He chuckled, "Well maybe not completely crazy. But I'd reckon you'll get there by the end of the day."

I picked up one of the drill bits from on the floor and threw one at him. He dodged it easily.

"C'mon now. I was only joking! If I really thought you were a lost cause, I wouldn't have risked my life to save you." He said this while lending me a hand, and lifting me up from the ground. I finally felt somewhat calm, enough to begin thinking logically, and a flood of questions assaulted my brain.

"How are you the same? Didn't you get the Cold Surgery?" I asked.

"I did. But the surgery didn't work on me."

"What do you mean 'the surgery didn't work'?"

"It's exactly what it sounds like. The surgery doesn't work on everyone, Teslin. Everyone's brain is different, and so sometimes the surgery doesn't work like it's supposed to."

"What? So then what happens if the surgery doesn't work? You follow along like everyone else, but you get to keep your emotions?"

"No, Teslin. I've had to pretend that the surgery worked, like I don't have any emotions. If I didn't, then I would be dead like the rest of them."

"Dead?! What are you talking about, Calmar?!"

He took a deep breath, "If the surgery doesn't remove your emotions like it should, then you get harvested."

"Harvested?"

"Yeah. They harvest your blood, your organs, your bones... really anything that is salvageable they will take and store for later or for experiments."

"So basically if you still have your emotions you die."

"I always knew you were a quick learner." He smirked at his own bad joke.

"You're hilarious," I remarked back in the most sarcastic way possible.

"But seriously, Teslin, they are forcefully taking people's emotions. We have to stop this before it's too late. Before we all become their brainwashed robots."

Now it was my turn to take a deep breath. This new information did change things, but I also still couldn't shake off what my mother and Devon had told me: that this was our chance at peace.

"Wait a second, Calmar. I know it sounds crazy, but this Movement may actually have a point. I mean, don't you think it would be a peaceful world if there was no emotion? I'm pretty sure every war has started because of some underlying emotional cause, like hate or greed. Without emotions people wouldn't argue and kill over cultural and religious beliefs anymore. We would all believe in one God, or maybe no God at all... whichever is most logical. There wouldn't be sexism or racism of any kind. Doesn't that sound like a good world to you?"

Calmar looked down at me in disgust. "Wow, have they already messed with your head?" he said angrily.

"I am just trying to see things logically here, ok! Do you know what I see in this place? Equality. I saw an older boy treat a small girl like his equal, and respected that she knew more than him.

I saw people of all races and ages working together to better the current state of the world. This Movement is making people smarter, filling their brains with so much knowledge. It's also making people logical, and taking away their hate and selfishness. How is that bad?" I threw my hands up, exasperated.

He sighed loudly, and replied in a slow and low tone of voice, "Teslin, do you know what kind of people don't have emotions? Psychopaths. This Movement is creating intelligent psychopaths. Does that sound like a good idea? You know a lot about psychology. What do you know about psychopaths?'

I paused to think about it for a second.

"Well, I know that not all psychopaths are violent killers, but I do know that they will do anything necessary to get what they want. They manipulate people, and have absolutely no concern or empathy toward the people they hurt. Also, they usually have brain abnormalities in the frontal lobe. The place in our brain which is considered to be responsible for our personalities, our abilities to empathize with others, and our decision-making and planning skills. It's the same area which the Cold Surgery is affecting. The surgery cuts the connection responsible for distributing emotional information from other parts of the brain onto the prefrontal cortex of the frontal lobe. Basically creating subjects into high-functioning psychopaths." I looked up at Calmar. He wore a face of incredulity.

"And if you are still doubting whether or not this Movement is a good idea, do you know what they are planning to do to the majority of the world's population? Well let me tell you. Some of them are going to be harvested. We'll take their blood and organs so we can sustain the lives of the chosen people as long as we can. But for the large majority, we are going to eradicate them without any warning."

I didn't want to believe him.

"My father didn't mention anything like that to me! He was open with almost everything else, so if that were true he would have told me about it too. And how do you know all of this anyways? You've only been here for over a day!"

Calmar paused for a second before he replied, "Look, I am sure your father would have told you about it, after you got the surgery. Because if he told you now, in your emotional state of mind, you would never have agreed to join the Movement. Once you get the surgery they tell you everything. They are not afraid of an uprising amongst their own people, because everything they are doing is the most logical thing to do. And when everyone thinks logical there are no arguments.

But, Teslin, they are only taking the smartest and healthiest people and annihilating the rest. You can't have a peaceful and safe world with the people on it right now, which is why most of them are going to be wiped out. They are going to start out fresh, make a whole new race of people. Maybe they will succeed, maybe they will have a world of logic, peace and equality; but it will be built on the blood of billions of innocent people. Teslin, I saw some of the plans in the military wing. They are only planning on keeping two billion people. What's going to happen to the other six billion? They can't harvest them all.

I also saw the kinds of weapons they were working on. Some of them can easily take out a city of five million people. Then they have ways to contaminate food and water supplies with deadly viruses that will kill off large populations in less than a week. They are serious about the Movement. It's going to happen unless someone can stop it.

I know that there are some crappy people in this world, but I don't think we're a complete lost cause. We still have so much good in this world, and I am going to fight for it and for our emotions. They really aren't that bad. Yeah they make you do stupid things like stand up for what is right even if it might get you killed. Or give your life up to protect someone you love. Or make you get mad at injustice and find a way to change it, to help those less fortunate than you, to give a helping hand to a stranger. An emotionless person would never do these things, because they aren't logical. Love is not logical. Can you imagine a world without love? We would be like empty robots, only doing what we needed to survive and strengthen our population. And what if they have a minimum IQ requirement to survive in the New World? Or you can't have any disabilities, diseases or deformities? They just want the strongest and smartest, Teslin. They won't let anyone else live. You think that taking emotion out of people is going to bring peace? It's only going to bring death to the human population, and change humans into something that is not at all human."

I looked deep into his dark eyes and wished fervently that he was wrong. I wished to believe that my father's Movement would change the world for the better. But I knew deep down that this wasn't true. I knew that Calmar was right. What would even be the point of living in an emotionless world? A world without passion, without music or art, without movies to watch and escape to another fantastical world. A world with no smiles, no laughter, no compassion, no love. In all honesty, I did not want to live in such a world.

"You're right. We wouldn't be human at all. My parents and friends aren't human anymore."

Speaking the words aloud that I had been avoiding even thinking about, brought tears to my eyes. Strong muscular arms surrounded my body and held me tight.

'If I didn't have emotions this hug wouldn't make me feel so comforted and loved.' I realized, enjoying being held in Calmar's arms a little too much. Calmar then took my face in his hands and pulled me close to him. My stupid heart went mad like a raving lunatic.

"We are going to get out of here, Teslin. And then we are going to put a stop to this. As long as we are breathing we will fight against this Movement."

His intense stare slowly dropped from my eyes, down to my lips. All logic and self-control vanished from my brain. He pulled me in closer until our lips were but centimetres apart. I could feel his hot breath on my lips, and his perfect black curls brushing up against my skin. My eyes closed as the indescribable desire proliferating inside of me overrode my senses. But our lips never did touch. Wicked reality made sure of that.

A loud bang made us both jump and jerk our heads toward the door. Someone was trying to get in. We had run out of time. And we didn't even have a hint of a plan of what we were going to do next. The door handle was violently shaking now. Whoever was on the other side of the door, wanted to get inside of this room desperately. I don't think I wanted to meet them, whoever they were. Calmar ran to the back right corner of the room and began climbing up one of the tall shelving units.

"What are you doing?!" I called after him in alarm. Did he really think he would be safe if he climbed up a shelf?

"Pass me one of those drill bits down there. If I can get this vent open, I think I know a way out." He, of course, was talking about the silver air vent on the ceiling.

I didn't know much about air vents, however, I had seen my fair share of action movies so I did know you could crawl in vents for a concealed route through any top secret building. I grabbed the closest drill bit and threw it up to him. He managed to pry open most of the vent with the bit, and then rip open the rest with his hands. Then he waved me over.

"C'mon, Teslin! Hurry up! We don't have much time!"

I turned back to look at the door. The shaking of the door handle had stopped, but now there was a crowd of voices outside the door, and the sound of a gun cocking. As I began climbing the metal shelf, a bullet went straight through the door lock and into the wall beside me. A wave of dread came over me as I realized they had unlocked the door. It would only be a matter of seconds before they got past our makeshift barricade. I finally made it to the top of the shelf and Calmar boosted me up into the air vent. He came up quickly behind me.

"Now don't move or speak," he was whispering now.

I looked ahead of me and was met with total darkness. Also I think he was joking when he said "don't move", because I couldn't move if I wanted to. The vent was so tight around my body that I was surprised my chest had enough room to expand and breathe properly. Then again maybe I didn't want to be breathing in all the dust and dirt around me. Hollywood had lied to me once again, crawling in air vents was not a realistic option. I felt this same disappointment when I discovered that clicking your heels together three times does not take you home.

The horrible screeching sound of metal scraping the ground resulted in my entire body going numb. I fell perfectly silent, even my thoughts came out as whispers. I could no longer hear the steady beat of Calmar breathing. We became statues as the room below us was filled with unimpassioned voices.

"What happened here?" said one of the voices.

"Someone was obviously in here who wasn't supposed to be. And they made quite a mess of things."

"They couldn't have gone far. Search this room and all the other rooms in this corridor."

"Yes, ma'am."

There was quite a lot of ruckus after this. The moving of boxes and shelving could be heard from below. But they wouldn't find us down there. I hoped to God that they wouldn't think of looking up in the air vents, because if they did, there would be nowhere for us to run.

Moments later another voice rose up, "It's all clear. There is no one here anymore."

I let out a silent sigh of relief at hearing that we were safe, for now.

"What about up there?" A voice asked.

"In the air vents?"

I stopped breathing entirely at the mention of our current hiding spot. I wasn't a regular Sunday church-goer, however, in this moment I found myself praying to God. We would surely be killed and harvested if we were captured. Second chances are only given in a world of forgiveness, not of logic.

To my surprise, I heard the other voice balk at the thought of the air vents:

"Only an idiot would try to use air vents as a way of escape. And if they were up there, they won't get very far. They will eventually come down and we will be waiting for them when they do. Now let's check the next room."

The small medical supplies room became quiet again. I heard Calmar start to breathe again.

"Okay, I'm going to try to get down now. I'll start pulling you out when I'm free."

"Okay," I said in response.

As Calmar struggled to get out of the vent, I thanked God for saving us by disguising us as idiots for climbing into an air vent in the first place. Calmar must have made it out alright, because I felt a pair of hands get a hold of my legs and begin to slowly pull me out. It was a fight to get out of the vent in the ceiling, but I eventually managed to get free from the dusty prison. As soon as I was back on my own two feet, I commenced dusting off my uniform which had turned a light gray from all the dust. Calmar interrupted my uniform maintenance session with a box of medical supplies.

"Here, hold these." He said as he placed the box in my arms.

"Okay, but what exactly are we going to do? We are going to get caught if we don't get out of here like right now!" I whispered loudly at him.

"Teslin, the only way we are getting out of here is if we can pretend like nothing is wrong. We are going to carry these boxes and walk through the hallways like that's what we are supposed to be doing. And if anyone asks us where we are going, we will tell them that we are delivering medical supplies to the military wing.

When you're walking look straight ahead, don't smile and don't make eye contact with anyone. Got it?"

He didn't even wait for a response, he was already walking to the broken door and peeking out. I really hoped that our lucky streak would continue to work, as we needed all the luck we could get. Once Calmar gave an indication that the hallway was clear, we quickly made our exit.

I kept my eyes focused directly ahead of me and my face as stoic as physically possible. I embodied every other emotionless and logical individual that passed by me, solely committed to doing my part in aiding the Cold Cognition Movement. The only thing that could have given me away was my quivering heart, pulsating at such an aggressive speed that I was positive I would go into cardiac arrest at any moment. Calmar walked in front of me, and I didn't dare focus on him for more than a second for fear of giving away our real mission. I simply kept my eyes fixed above his head, and marched on like a soldier. A White Soldier. Although we kept calm and walked at a normal pace, it took all my strength to stop myself from not bolting. Truth be told, we walked on a ticking time bomb. It was only a matter of time before we were found out and captured. We weren't dealing with normal people here, these new human beings would make it a point to find us, and find us fast. I tried not to think about what would happen if we got caught, mostly because it felt all too real. Quite frankly, I didn't have much hope that we would escape from this cold place. Every factor was against us, realistically our chances were quite slim. Nevertheless, I was not ready to give up yet and so I continued to trot behind the confident White Soldier in front of me. I had officially placed all my faith and my life, in the hands of a young man that I had known for three days. I don't know if that made my chance of survival better or worse. Hopefully better. Forcing positive thoughts in my head, we miraculously made it across white hallway after white hallway, until finally the walls changed to a silver metal. My stomach churned as I came to the realization that I only knew our plan of escape up to this point. I had no idea of what was to come next, and I wasn't about to ask Calmar in front of the group of White Soldiers that were passing us as we arrived at the metal door leading to the military wing. Calmar stopped in front of the door and I stopped about two feet behind him. I couldn't help but feel a surge of excitement to see what was behind such a fortified door. I observed closely as he entered a code into the pin pad and the first deadbolt slowly unlocked. He entered another code and the second one unbolted. This happened again and again and again, until all five of the deadbolts were opened. The heavily secured door was now defenceless, and he pushed open the thick metal door and walked through, into the secrets of the military wing.

It was even more impressive and terrifying than I could have ever thought possible. Every kind of weapon and military vehicle that you could imagine, and ones you could never imagine because they were possibly the only ones in the world, covered the cement walls and floor of the military wing. I swear we had walked into an alternate universe where any kind of weapon was possible, all you had to do was ask for it.

I turned my head towards Calmar. He must feel like a kid in a candy shop in here. No wonder he wanted to come here out of all the places in this facility. He walked towards a sparkling white military H1 Hummer that appeared both beautiful and deadly with spiked chains around its enormous tires, and a handful of missiles rigged to the top of it. There were very few things that this invincible beauty could not conquer. I found myself in a daze at her power as I copied Calmar's actions and placed the medical supply box into the back of the monster, and then followed him to one of the cement walls where countless weapons hung. He began handing me a variety of pistols, machine guns, and magazines filled with bullets, until my hands were full. Once his hands were also full, he nodded in the direction of the Hummer to indicate that's where we would be dumping our sweet stash of goodies.

As we walked back to the vehicle, the bright white lights overhead suddenly went black, leaving us in utter darkness. Three seconds later dark red floodlights assaulted our eyes, lighting up the room to reveal an army of White Soldiers marching straight for us, accompanied by an ear-piercing alarm that began screaming over the blood red lighting. The ticking time bomb of our chance at escape had just blown up. The White Soldiers halted about ten yards in front of us at a left angle. The Hummer was only half the distance from us, but at a right angle. One of the soldiers yelled out loudly over the alarm:

"Drop your weapons and put your hands up where I can see them. Do not try to run. We will shoot. This is your only warning."

We both let the piles of weapons in our hands fall to the ground. I felt like I was going to get sick. I turned my head to look at Calmar, but I couldn't read what he was thinking from the ray of emotions flashing on his face. I knew he knew I was waiting for his command of what to do next. Without looking in my direction he whispered under his breath, barely moving his lips:

"We have to get to that Hummer, it's our only chance."

I observed the Hummer in my peripheral vision. We had come at a crossroad. To the right of us was our possible ticket to survival, and to the left of us was certain death. In one hand was the end and in the other was a dying ember of hope.

'It's not much of a chance, but at least it's something,' I thought to myself as I looked at the deadly weapons the White Soldiers held. Then I remembered what my father told me about the uniform I currently wore, it was bulletproof!

"Calmar, we will make it! Our clothing is bulletproof!" I whispered excitedly, regaining hope of our possible escape.

He simply shook his head, "Not with those bullets they aren't. The only thing that can withstand those bullets in this room are the Hummers, and only for so long."

My heart broke as he said this. We were not invincible.

Then Calmar whispered again:

"At the count of three we are going to run with all we've got. They will start shooting at us, Teslin. But don't stop, no matter what happens. Get in that vehicle. Once we get inside we will be safe. Ready? One…two… three."

I didn't think my mind had enough time to even process what he just said, but my body seemed to understand quite clearly as it bolted forward at the sound of the word "three". It only took a second to run to the Hummer, and in that second, bullets flew through the air. I felt a hot sting cut through my left cheek, a bullet had grazed across my face, leaving a bloody mark behind. I heard a groan from Calmar but didn't stop to see what caused the noise. We made it to the vehicle and ducked behind our bulletproof saviour. She gave us a few seconds of grace as we hid on the driver's side, temporarily shielding us from the bullets coming from the other side. In those few seconds, I realized that Calmar had been shot in the ribs. I watched as a pool of red liquid soaked through his white uniform, expanding exceedingly larger with every passing second. The true colours of this Movement were now on vibrant display for the world to see; and they were not white nor blue, but red, bloody red. My body went into shock for a moment until Calmar shook me out of it.

"Open the door! Get in!"

I did as I was told. I pulled open the heavy door and helped the severely wounded man into the vehicle. I rushed in after him and reached to grab the handle of the substantially weighted door. I grunted aloud as I used all my upper body strength to close the door, but I couldn't close it fast enough. A bullet flew over the door and buried itself into the raw flesh of my left arm. Thankfully the momentum was enough to shut the door, and we were shielded from the storm of bullets. However, this did not exactly give me peace of mind, as the two of us were now a bloody mess. I instinctively locked the doors while grimacing from the pain radiating out of my left bicep. It was a wonder how I was still able to function and somewhat think properly when my left arm writhed in suffering. My shaking hand found the key in the ignition of the white monster; she was waiting and ready to be brought to life. I turned the key and she roared and growled in satisfaction (and anger I'm sure too, as I can't imagine she enjoyed being pelted with bullets either). As I revved up her powerful engine, it suddenly occurred to me that I didn't know where I was going.

"Calmar! Where do I go? How do we get out of here?"

I looked over at him in desperation. His face had grown so pale, void of any colour, and he was doubled over in pain, holding his left side. I could tell from the protruding veins on his arms that he was applying immense pressure on the wound, to the point where it was causing him physical pain. But he continued to hold on tightly, as if he would entirely fall apart if he let go. He managed to lift his head to look out the window, and observe the army of White Soldiers forming in front our guardian angel of metal and bulletproof glass. He gave a small nod forward.

"Drive straight through them."

"What?!"

"They are blocking the only way out of here. Drive through them." He spoke through gritted teeth, spewing anger and hate as he repeated the directions a second time.

Scared to ask him anything more, I released the brake and rolled the glimmering white monster forward. I forced myself not to think about what would happen if the soldiers didn't move out of the way. Although they were deadly, they were no match for this machine's knife-edged chain tires, nothing more than speed bumps as far as this beast was concerned. I drove slowly toward the sea of white before us.

"Drive faster, Teslin! Make them move! We don't have time for sympathy or we are going to be dead! Go faster, now!"

Calmar yelled so fiercely and maliciously that my startled foot slammed the gas pedal down to the floor. The both of us were jerked back into our seats as the white beast screeched ahead and sped straight for the soldiers. They must have been just as startled and surprised as we were, but the small army managed to avoid the razor-sharp teeth of the Hummer. I swear I could hear her rumbling laughter as she parted the White Sea and barreled down the long and wide cement road, that supposedly was the only way out this deadly place.

The road seemed to go on forever. It felt like the never-ending twists and turns were laughing at us, telling us we would never get out, and consequently devouring all our hopes in the process. The dark red lighting didn't help either, making it impossibly hard to see the obstacles in front of us. I almost drove into the wall a few times for not seeing a sharp turn ahead. Yet this wasn't the worst part. The ear-piercing alarm was still shrieking at such a high pitch, that it was making me nauseous and causing so much pressure on my brain I swear it would explode at any moment. On top of all these insurmountable factors, I could now see headlights coming up fast behind us in my side mirror. There was no time for mistakes. We didn't have a second to spare. Even though time implied that the world was against us, I couldn't make myself give up; and I fervently prayed that my desire to stay alive would be enough to do so. There was only one thing that I wanted in this moment… to be alive. So I focused all my energy on this dream, blocking out all the doubt, the noise, the pain, and the headlights. I concentrated only on the road ahead of me, on what I could control: driving us out of this concrete prison. I had to make another quick sharp turn to avoid hitting a wall at the cause of another hidden twist in the road. I could feel the spikes tearing up the cement as the vehicle unwillingly obeyed my command. Fortunately, we didn't lose too much momentum and continued to fly down the road. My eyes had adjusted quite well in the crimson lighting, and as I squinted up ahead I noticed that we were coming to a dead end. My heart dropped and commenced beating at an immeasurable speed. But as I drove closer I saw that it was not a dead end at all, but a huge metal garage-like door. However, this still didn't help us much, as the door was closed. As strong as our Hummer was, I doubt she could plow through a secured titanium door. Fear seeped through my voice as I asked Calmar questions that I truly hoped he had the answers to.

"Ok, where am I going now? How do we get out?! If it's through that door you better know how to open it!"

His voice came out hoarse and his breathing was laboured. The loss of blood was clearly taking a toll on him. I sincerely wished that the bullet hadn't hit any vital organs, but I couldn't think about that now.

"Flick that little switch down there," was all he said in response to our life endangering situation.

I forced myself to stay calm as I found the switch and flicked it on.

"Now, see that button there?" He pointed to a red button on the dashboard. I nodded in acknowledgment. "Okay, press it when I tell you to."

I had no idea what this button did or how it was going to help us get through that invincible garage door, but I had no time to question him further, as the end on the road was coming toward us at an alarmingly fast rate. We were now seconds away from smashing into the enormous door. At this moment in time my already quivering calm demeanour completely packed up and ran for the hills, leaving behind full-blown panic to take its place. Panic was a fast and effective worker, taking total control of my body without delay. I began to scream.

"Not yet!" he bellowed over my screams.

"Calmar!!!"

How I managed to yell his name through my uncontrollable screaming, I'll never know. However, I did know that we were going to either crash into or through the door, because that space cushion to slam on the brakes and avoid hitting the door was now gone. We were going to have impact whether we liked it or not.

"Okay! Now!" Calmar roared.

I pressed the red button. I wanted to close my eyes and go off to my happy place before I died, but couldn't, because suddenly I wasn't driving through the garage door, but into massive orange and red flames. My brain was unable to register what was happening until the scorching fire was replaced with blinding white surroundings. Snow! We had done it! We had made it outside! As our vehicle plowed through the heavy snow, I looked down at the red button. That door didn't just magically combust into flames; it was a missile that had blown it down. I had just set off a missile! I felt a huge smile plaster across my face. I turned to Calmar, who was also smiling, both of us temporarily forgetting our physical pain and enjoying our moment of hard-earned success.

"You are a real badass, Teslin Grove. Remind me never to piss you off."

I laughed at his comment, "I couldn't have done it without you. None of it."

I was about to say something more when I remembered the headlights behind me. After only taking a few seconds of vacation, panic was back, and stronger than ever. I looked in my mirrors and expected to see an army of vehicles behind me, but instead, the white cavalry had come to a complete stop just outside the charred and burning exit that used to have a door. They weren't pursuing us anymore, for whatever reason I didn't know. But right now I didn't really care. I was just happy that we finally caught a break, and joy and relief became the latest residents to occupy my body.

I let out a huge sigh of relief, my heart rate was still high, but it had come down significantly at the sight of the familiar landmarks around me. The towering mountains had always comforted me greatly. Yet I could not feel completely relieved or successful, as all we really accomplished was escaping from the Movement temporarily. What were we to do next? Where were we to look for help? Probably the most pressing question was: what were we going to do right now? We were both inhabited by bullets and currently bleeding all over the place (Calmar more so than I). We needed to deal with our wounds immediately before we could do anything else. There would be no one in the town hospital to ask for help. We would have to do it ourselves. I trembled to think of how painful it would be to have a bullet removed with no painkillers and no doctors. Calmar must have been reading my thoughts, or just saw the horrified look on my face, as he placed a blood covered hand on mine and squeezed it weakly.

"We're survivors. We'll find a way. Just like we found a way out of that godforsaken place." His voice sounded confident despite his potential bleak future.

I put on a brave face and smiled back at him.

"Of course we will."

I'm not sure how much I believed that, but I had recently learned that in dire situations it was best to focus on simple and doable tasks, instead of getting overwhelmed with the seemingly unconquerable bigger picture. Taking my own advice (something I rarely ever did), I concentrated on what we needed the most: safe shelter, food, and rest. The necessities. This I could do. So I compelled my mind to put aside all things Cold Cognition Movement, and fixated on finding us the safe place that we need so desperately. I thought of nothing else as I drove into the frozen white landscape.

****

Chapter Eight

He stared intently at the big city skyline lighting up the otherwise dark night. The bright colourful lights reflected off the black water, making the view even more impressive as it danced and swayed across the ebony liquid surface. Not only could he see the reflection of the phosphorescent city outline, but also the reflected image of himself on the floor to ceiling windows that covered an entire wall of his multi-million-dollar penthouse.

Dr. Joshua Lacombe wore his signature black fitted suit, whilst holding a half drunken crystal glass of expensive whiskey in his hand. His face was vacant. Only the very few close people to Joshua Lacombe knew that anytime he wore a look void of emotion, was when he was deep inside his mind. You see, when Dr. Lacombe went into his mind to ponder, he had no room for meddlesome emotions that only get in the way of thoughts. This is why he resembled something of a statue when he was deep in thought. A chiselled and confident statue, but a statue nonetheless. For in these moments he felt neither alive nor dead, neither human nor inanimate object. If he had to describe what he was in these moments, he would probably say he was something of a non-biased, logical, third-party onlooker: observing the facts, problems, and memories flashing before him, and then forming a solution, a conclusion to the orderly and systematic thoughts of his mind. These precious moments were the things he valued most in life, even more than family or friends. For above all, he worshipped pure logical intelligence, even more than life itself. Because from the perspective of Dr. Lacombe, humans were at their absolute best when they were rational. Logical beings solved problems quickly and created amazing inventions. It was those who were twisted and plagued by emotions that ruined the world.

Dr. Lacombe took a sip from his glass as he continued to stare intently out the window, his mind now overflowing with memories of the past. Memories that both inspired and tormented the world-renowned doctor. There was one memory in particular that he tended to recall upon on a regular basis. It was from many years ago, 21 years ago to be exact…

He was eleven years old at the time; a young, innocent version of himself who still believed adults had all the answers to life, or at least his parents did. Yet even at his young age, he knew that he was the smartest kid in his class, the smartest kid in his school, and very frequently, even more intelligent than the teachers themselves. His superiors praised his academic achievements, and his peers accepted and liked him for his clever remarks and good looks. However, he could care less about social status, and only played with the other children when he felt like it. He much preferred reading to socializing. He read anything he could get his hands on, from his parents' university textbooks to the library's selection of classic literature. Yet as much as he enjoyed having the title of most brilliant pupil in school, he knew there was one other who was smarter than him, although he would never admit this to anyone.

A girl, named Freedom Esmorte. She was not only the smartest person in the school, but quite possibly in the entire town. Unfortunately, her intelligence was lost to the fact that she was quite strange, and liked to talk about dark topics that were discouraged daily by her parents and teachers. She was deemed a disturbed young child by the whole town population, and was bullied on a day-to-day basis because of this. Joshua never understood why the people of his town avoided her like the plague. He found her absolutely fascinating. Freedom had pale white skin and long messy black hair that she always wore in low pigtails, tied up with two shiny blue ribbons. Her unruly bangs, that desperately needed to be cut, hung over her big, dark blue eyes. To Joshua, she was one of the Seven Wonders of the World, for he knew why she never paid attention in class or why she made inappropriate comments. It wasn't because she was some devil child like the rest of the town believed, but it was because she was so smart that she was insanely bored.

Instead of listening to their lectures in science and mathematics, she liked to watch people and study them, trying to guess what they would do or say next. Joshua loved to sit next to her during class and recess, as she would whisper under her breath her prediction of what a teacher or pupil was going to do next. The amazing thing was, she was usually right. Joshua, who was an expert in all things science, mathematics, history and the English language, was astonished at how easily Freedom could predict human behaviour. He had never really been interested in people at all before (since he found most of them to be quite hindering to his intelligence), but suddenly he found them so intriguing. As a result, the two clever children had many conversations about the way humans acted, almost as if they themselves were not humans at all:

"Do you ever notice how Thomas torments Susan all the time, by tugging on her hair and calling her names?" Freedom asked Joshua one day in the school yard, while they sat on their favourite bench under the willow tree.

"It's a bit hard not to notice," Joshua replied. "Susan screams so loudly in protest. If she would only stop reacting so dramatically, Thomas would get bored and eventually stop."

"Very true. But she won't stop. She likes the attention. And one day, when their hormones begin to interfere with their common sense, they are going to stop hitting each other and start kissing each other." She said in a rather matter-of-fact way.

Joshua gave her a confused look, "How can anyone like abuse? That doesn't make sense. And how can you be so certain about that? Those two hate each other! They don't like each other!"

An evil smile appeared on Freedom's face.

"Joshua Lacombe, you are a very clever boy when it comes to things like numbers and facts, but you don't understand people at all, do you?"

Joshua, who was a bit offended, replied in a harsh tone:

"I don't need to know about people to understand important things like science and mathematics."

"Yes, but think of how much more you could accomplish if you knew how people worked too. You would have the whole world in your hands. You could know it all."

"I already know it all."

Freedom let out a pretentious laugh, "Oh really? I bet you didn't know that all the girls in our school are absolutely infatuated with you. They can't talk about anything else."

Joshua tried not to look taken aback, (as of course he had no idea about this) and he managed to conjure up a quick and witty comeback that would change the subject entirely:

"Well, I didn't know you felt that way about me, Freedom."

"What did you just say?" she wore an angry look on her face (she hated being outwitted).

"You said that all the girls in this school are obsessed with me. You are a girl in this school, hence, you like me too. Don't you?"

Now it was Joshua's turn to wear the devilish smirk. Freedom pursed her lips together and was quiet for a long second before she carefully replied.

"There are things I like about you, and things that I would like to change."

She avoided eye contact as she spoke.

Joshua, who was grinning from ear-to-ear (it wasn't every day that he was able to out-clever Freedom), had to rub it in just a little further:

"So… you do like me then."

She shot him a deadly glare and then shouted out, "Oh why can't you just be stupid like all the other boys your age?!"

Both children were momentarily shocked at the intensity and loudness of Freedom's voice. The two eleven-year old children looked at each other with wide eyes, uncomfortable, not sure what to do next. So they did what anyone would have done in such an awkward position. They laughed. Then after they were done laughing, they went back to observing the other children on the playground, making predictions of their pitiful futures.

The months passed by as per usual, yet for some reason that Joshua could not understand, Freedom changed so drastically that he hardly recognized her anymore. Their daily recess talks began to dwindle to every other day, to once a week, and then to none at all. In fact, Freedom stopped talking all together, to anyone. The teachers were overjoyed at this (as they no longer had to constantly discipline the girl), but the students weren't too thrilled about the new silent Freedom as she was no longer fun to insult. She would just sit silently on the bench under the willow tree and stare off into the distance. Joshua tried on more than one occasion to talk some sense into her, but it was no use. Her big blue eyes were glazed over and empty, like she wasn't there at all. It was almost a bit eerie to look into her eyes, as if you were looking into the eyes of a living corpse. On the outside she looked alive, but on the inside she was gone. And for the life of him, Joshua didn't know why.

He was disappointed more than anything. The only person he ever liked talking to was now the only person in the town that didn't talk. Though Joshua wasn't mad at the troubled girl, instead he was mad at himself for thinking Freedom was his friend in the first place:

'It serves me right for getting close to someone. People are uncontrollable variables that always let you down,' he would think to himself. And then as a response to the unpleasant way he felt whenever he saw her in class or on the playground, he forced himself to forget about the strange girl whom he used to call his friend. It was easier than he thought it would be, mainly because Freedom was like a ghost now. Therefore, it was effortless to omit her from his thoughts. Instead of filling his recess period with human observations, he replaced the time with reading books, and thought this was a much better way of filling one's time anyways. It wasn't long before he forgot about the girl entirely, as if she never existed. That is, until one seemingly normal recess, when Freedom walked up to him and stood silently directly in front of the bench he was sitting on. He looked up from his book and stared back at the girl. Her normally vacant eyes looked as if someone was inhabiting them today. Joshua was curious to know what she wanted, so he closed up his book, put it on his lap, and gestured to the empty space beside him. Freedom stared at him for a moment longer, and then she quickly sat down beside him. Not wanting to scare her off (and also because he forgot how much he missed sitting beside her), Joshua remained silent and waited for her to make the first move. They sat there quietly for a few minutes, until suddenly Freedom had something to say.

"Have you ever thought about what you could do to the brain?"

Even Joshua, who was not the best expert on human relations, knew that this was a strange way to start up a conversation with someone that you randomly decided not to talk to for months. But not one to shy away from an intelligent chat about the brain, he obliged her with a response.

"To the human brain?"

"Yes, it is much more fascinating than any of that crap they teach us in class. The brain controls our every move and creates our very thoughts, the most important things in the world. Can you imagine if you could somehow manipulate the brain? Make it so that you could change people into something they were not? Like if there was something you could do to the brain that made everyone nice. That made everyone get along without fighting. Wouldn't that just be amazing?"

"Well, yes. I guess that would be nice. But why do you care so much about making people nice?"

She hesitated for a second before she spoke, "Joshua, you are very smart. I know that one day you'll create some scientific or mathematical invention that will bring you fame and fortune. You will enjoy a luxurious life, have the perfect job, and come home to a beautiful wife and kids that you don't really love as much as your work, but you pretend to for their sake. All will be good and how you thought it would be. But what if you could do something more than that? Something even better?" she turned to look at him.

Joshua cocked his head to the side in genuine wonder, "What could possibly be better than that?"

She responded in an urgent and serious tone, "What if you could control the way people think? Then you could get them to think anything you wanted."

"Why would I want to do that? I don't even like people all that much," he responded bluntly.

Freedom had to smile at his response, and Joshua couldn't help but think how beautiful she was when she smiled.

"I know you don't, Joshua. But if you don't do it, I don't know who else will. No one is as smart as us in this world."

"Well then, why can't you do it?"

She looked at him, really looked at him. And he swore that he could see a deep sadness in her eyes. It was a sadness that he had never seen before. It was both beautiful and horrifying at the same time, and he could tell that it was suffocating her. Whatever the cause of such sadness was, he silently prayed he would never have to find out.

She replied to his question with a weak voice that faded into a whisper:

"Let's just say, this isn't the world that I plan on saving."

He gave her a very confused look, but before Joshua could further implore what she meant by this remark, she took his hands in hers and spoke fiercely and sincerely.

"Promise me that you won't just do what people expect of you. Promise me that you won't live the same day again and again like the people of this town. You can do anything you can imagine, Joshua. You can even change the world if you really want to."

She stared at him intently, her dark blue eyes locked onto his. And then a wicked grin grew on her face as she spoke the last words she would ever speak to him.

"Promise me you'll change the world."

Joshua had no clue as to what Freedom was talking about, or why she was so intent on wanting him to change the world, but he figured that one day he would. Understand, that is. And if Freedom was so determined that it would come true, then he had no reason not to believe it too.

"I promise."

This was the last conversation that the two children ever had. The next day, Freedom didn't show up for school, or the next, or the next. Joshua questioned the teachers on her absence, but they just looked sheepish and wouldn't tell him anything. Finally, a week later the principal made an announcement to the class, saying that Freedom would no longer be attending their school anymore. Rumours instantly made their way around the class, through the school and into the town. Some said that she finally went completely crazy and ended up in the mad house where she belonged. Others said her parents shipped her off to boarding school. Joshua refused to believe any of the rumours, but he never did find out what happened to her. Whatever the truth may be, it was kept very quiet in the town and no one ever talked about the girl again. Everyone seemed to have entirely forgotten about her. Years later, if you asked anyone about a girl named Freedom, they would tell you that they had never heard of such a name. She was not even a mystery or a faded memory to the town, but simply nothing at all. Fortunately, Joshua was not like everyone else, and he never did forget about the girl. After her strange disappearance, he became obsessed with the brain and read any book about psychology that he could get his hands on. The peculiar girl with the long black hair and dark blue eyes may have been a burden to everyone else, but to Joshua, she was his only true childhood friend. A friend who also managed to spark his passion for neuropsychology. He was forever grateful to the girl, and as a result, he made it his responsibility to never forget her.

****

Lacombe took another sip from his glass and continued to analyze his thoughts. He switched from the girl, who to this day remained a mystery, and turned to the present. It was obvious that in the current state of the world, a planet of peace was nothing but a passing daydream. Humans were too hateful and selfish to ever really want peace, as much as they said they did. To have peace would require the complete acceptance of another person's beliefs and ways of life. We all know that will never happen. Especially when someone has grown up to think a certain way. How could they ever begin to try and think another way for even a second? Humans are creatures of habit, and they don't like too much change. It scares them.

Although the desire for world peace seemed like nothing more than a childish wish, Dr. Lacombe was determined to conquer this impossible challenge. And fifteen years ago, he solved the problem. He figured out what one factor needed to be removed from the equation in order for it to work. Emotion. Of course, this is not a unique idea. Many people before him had wondered what a world without emotion would be like, but none had ever done what Lacombe had done: Remove emotion from the equation. Dr. Lacombe had found a way to create the logical beings that he always dreamed of since a child. Of course you may be thinking 'the Cold Surgery', and you would be right, but only half right.

You see, the brain consists of billions and billions of neurons, and trillions upon trillions of neural connections. The chances of finding those connections that specifically affect emotion in the process of logical reasoning are slim to none. This being said, Dr. Lacombe spent fifteen years trying to find them, and he did. But not exactly. He did find a large bundle of connections that are responsible for transferring emotional information to the prefrontal cortex of the brain (where logical reasoning is said to take place), and when he cut this connection in his first test subjects, he did find that the subjects ceased to make decisions with the influence of emotion. However, his first test subjects were all animals, meaning that their brains are a lot less complex than a human being's. Think about it, if a human brain has so many trillions of neural connections, there is surely another way to bring emotional information to the frontal lobe other than the large connection that Dr. Lacombe found. And of course that is exactly what happened. This problem was discovered immediately after the first human tests began.

The Cold Surgery worked to an extent, in some subjects much more than in others, but there was always some emotional input that made it across to the frontal cortex. Sometimes the surgery hardly worked at all, on very strong minded and emotionally charged individuals. But in general, there was so much improvement in the subjects that the surgery did work on, even if it didn't work completely. As long as they were logical enough to override any emotions that slipped through to the frontal cortex, the subjects believed that they were fully rational beings. Dr. Lacombe was especially curious about this discovery, as truth be told, humans do have the ability to think logically. He did it all the time. He just needed to find a way to make them realize this, without letting them know it was happening. That's when it occurred to him, a way to convince humans of their logical potential. It would take a traumatic experience, vigorous conditioning, and a placebo effect. The mixture was tested and successful, and eventually catapulted into what became known to the secret testing facilities as the Cold Cognition Movement.

The traumatic experience was being violently kidnapped from your home and forced to stay awake while undergoing the Cold Surgery, the sound of drills forever haunting you. The vigorous training began right after the surgery. Time was crucial to mold the newly operated brain into one of logic and not of fear. Subjects were guided through an orientation-like video, conditioning the mind to think it is completely logical. Then subjects would be given scenarios of real life situations where emotional responses were strong, but patients were treated with highly painful shocks if they elicited an unwanted emotional response. After many years and thousands of patients, Dr. Lacombe and his international teams had this conditioning down to an art. They could create a completely logical being in less than a day. This was arguably the easiest part of the three steps. The third step, also the last step, was the most crucial and also the most delicate as it was a never-ending process. The last step was to get people to continue to believe they were purely logical beings, and that emotions could not affect their decision making abilities. This is why they told people that they may still feel emotions, but that they couldn't affect their logic. So that in case people realized they still had emotions, they would simply believe it was normal. This is also why they worked the people hard, and with very little interaction. Limited social interaction was the key, as once people started talking about possible emotions they were feeling, it was only a matter of time before this started to spread. Multiple daily reminders of their rational minds were a crucial part of the daily routine. After all, when someone continuously tells you something, you usually end up believing it; a tried and true method of mankind.

Needless to say, it was a delicate system, especially for those just new to the Movement, but it was extremely successful to those who had been in the program for many years. Children were the greatest success of all. They could be molded into amazing logical beings that were extremely intelligent in every type of intelligence. The only downfall with young children, was that their brains were still so plastic and still developing. This meant that their brains had to be monitored closely, as the brain actively created new strong connections for emotions to reach the prefrontal cortex. The Cold Surgery had to be repeated on children, sometimes annually, sometimes every two to three years. Either way, these children were hope to the New World.

This hope for universal peace, equality and intelligence, had been Dr. Lacombe's seemingly impossible goal for the past fifteen years. And now, over a thousand miles away in the Rocky Mountains of Canmore, Alberta, the same place where he lived as a young child, his dream had come true. Not only there, but it was also occurring in the other 64 locations he had created around the world. His dream was quickly shaping into the new reality.

Yes, billions of people would die, but sacrifices had to be made for the success of the planet. At least these people would die for a greater purpose than themselves.

Since he was a man of his word, he would honour all the lives that already were and would be lost to the Movement. Death was an important part of the life cycle. Death could be beautiful and inspiring. It was the idea of dying that made people want to do great things before they died. To make a difference in the world before their last breath. This is exactly what Dr. Lacombe was doing with his Movement.

The Cold Cognition Movement grew stronger and larger with every second. It was only a matter of time before the news and media spread panic across the globe. Lacombe took another sip of whiskey as he thought about it further:

'Very soon the world leaders will come together to decide what to do about my Movement, but they will fail. Emotions will be running high and no one will be able to come up with an agreed upon solution. By then, they will run out of time and the Movement will be too strong to stop. The end of the Old World will be because of exactly what the New World is seeking to destroy… emotions. Cold Cognition is the inevitable future of the earth. Nothing or no one can stop it.'

And as Dr. Joshua Lacombe stood in his luxurious penthouse and looked upon the city lights, he couldn't help but smile. Not a sweet smile that came out of love or compassion, but a wicked smile. The same wicked smile that Freedom wore on her face the day she made him promise to change the world.

****

Chapter Nine

"This will do for now."

Calmar's voice came out all twisted and broken. The pain was too much for him now that the adrenaline in his body had run out. I carefully helped lay him down on the couch of Mrs. Rundle's house. It was the best place we could think of to go, as I knew her house would be stock full of food and supplies (Mrs. Rundle seemed to always be prepared for an impromptu army of surprise guests).

"I'm going to start a fire and find something for us to eat," I said while I untangled myself from Calmar. I had him lying in a comfortable-as-you-can-be-with-a-bullet-in-your-side position on the white leather couch.

'I hope Mrs. Rundle doesn't mind a few blood stains on her perfectly pristine couch,' I thought to myself as I put the square logs into the red brick fireplace that was directly in front of the couch. This was another reason why we chose Mrs. Rundle's home, she had a source of heat. Since the power, heat, and water were still unavailable in the town, having a wood-burning fireplace was a necessity. We needed it to stay alive, to keep us warm, and to melt snow into water. I reached for the box of matches that Mrs. Rundle thankfully kept on a small stool next to the fireplace, on top of a pile of old newspapers.

Crinkling up a page from one of the newspapers, I stroke the match and transferred the orange flame onto the black and white paper. I held it in my hands, watching the flame magically devour every word and every letter. The flame never gave the dying parchment a second chance, it viciously ate it up without question. I suppose in some way I felt like the burning sheet of newspaper; I was being swallowed whole by a Movement that tore through towns and cities like wildfire. It was even as heartless as fire too. For fire didn't discriminate, it took from the rich and the poor, the young and the old, the good and the bad.

'I honestly don't even know why we are running. The Movement will consume us eventually. It's only a matter of time.'

These depressing thoughts ran through my mind as I watched the scorching flame get dangerously close to my fingers before I threw it into the fireplace. The flame quickly caught onto the dry wood, and after only a limited amount of pushing and prying with an iron rod, I created a significantly larger version of the tiny flame I held in my hand only moments ago.

I let the fire mesmerize me for a while longer until a loud groan from Calmar brought me back to wretched reality. There was no time to stare into a fire and feel sorry for myself. There was work to be done. I knew nothing about fixing bullet wounds, but today I would have to figure it out, because Calmar's wounds needed to be attended to immediately. Something would have to be done about mine as well. The throbbing and slow bleeding in my left arm was getting harder to ignore. My starving stomach would simply have to wait.

I quickly ran outside to fetch some snow. Then I grabbed a large pot from the kitchen, as well as the first aid kit that Mrs. Rundle kept under the kitchen sink (I knew it was there from a previous pumpkin carving incident that occurred a few years ago). Once the water was warm enough, I found a cloth that I could use to clear away the blood from around the wound and see what I was dealing with - though I had my doubts that I would know what I was dealing with whether or not there was blood in the way. But I had to try, for Calmar's sake.

I walked over to the poor young man with a cloth soaked with warm water. He looked up at me through half open eyes that reflected the same doubts that I currently felt. Not really knowing how to approach the situation, I thought it was best that I start with communication.

"So…umm… I'm going to clean the wound first… and then I can see what we're dealing with here," I said in a terribly fake confident voice.

Calmar, who obviously saw through my façade, somehow found the energy to sass me, "Now I'm certain that I'm going to die."

I couldn't help but let a smile crack through as I reprimanded him for his negativity:

"Calmar, that's not funny! Mostly because you could actually die! I have no idea what I'm doing, and I would appreciate a little positive reinforcement."

"Oh c'mon, you know I'm only joking. Just know that my life is in your hands."

"That's not helping!" I said as I sat down on a plush stool beside him, so I could be level with him as he continued to lay on the couch on his back. I observed the blood stained left side of the man, and felt a bit awkward as I told him the obvious.

"You're going to have to take your shirt off. So I can see the wound." I blurted out the last sentence rather quickly.

A seductive smirk suddenly appeared on Calmar's face.

"Admit it, you just want to see me shirtless."

"Pssssh. You wish."

I shrugged off his sexy Australian accent like it was nothing. But really my heart started to rev up like a V8 engine, and my mind was shouting out desperate pleas to stay calm as he began to remove his white – with splashes of red - long-sleeved shirt. Much grunting and groaning was apparently required to take off the shirt. He got as far as extracting his left arm out of the shirt when he stopped and looked towards me. I stared back at him intensely, trying so hard not to look at the extremely defined abs that taunted my peripheral vision. It was dark out now, and the only light came from the fire. So naturally the flames delightfully reflected off his toned yet injured body – making it even that much harder to ignore.

"You're gonna have to help me. This actually really hurts." He said through a pained but playful smile.

I couldn't help but smile back at him.

"Well, you lifted it up far enough that I can see the bullet wound just fine now. You can keep it like that for the time being."

I was proud of my voice for keeping it together, and quickly distracted my mind from his beautiful body by looking at the gruesome mess surrounding his upper ribs. Even though I was by no means a doctor, I knew that it didn't look good. As I began wiping away the blood that seemed to never cease from escaping the bullet hole, I began to realise just how deep the bullet went, and that I didn't have the tools or knowledge to pull it out. I would probably have to cut him open further to reach the bullet, that is if I could even find it. And at the same time, hope that I didn't drain him of all his blood.

My thoughts must have been portrayed on my face, because Calmar spoke up.

"It's pretty bad, isn't it?"

I couldn't bear to make eye contact with him.

"Calmar, I'm not a surgeon. I don't know how to do this. I mean what do you expect me to do, cut you open and take the bullet out!? I can't do that! I'll probably end up puncturing a vital organ, or make you bleed to death, or something! I can't do it. I'm so sorry."

My head hung low as the severity of our situation sunk in. I'm not sure how long someone could survive with a bullet deep inside their upper body, but I knew the verdict wasn't in our favour. Then I felt a warm hand caress my face.

"Hey, cheer up there, gorgeous. It's not like it's the end of the world."

I glared at him.

"Are you really going to joke about that in a time like this!? Especially when it might actually be the end of the world!"

"Well, who knew that the end of the world would start in Canada of all places?" he continued to joke.

At this point, I assumed that Calmar felt the need to lighten up the mood as a result of our impending bleak future and the apparent lack of blood flow to his brain. Either way, I decided to go along with his attempt at making a joke as I began to bandage up his rib cage (I thought I might as well try to stop the bleeding since there was no way I was extracting that bullet).

"Yeah, no one would have ever expected Canada! Not even us Canadians! Who would've thought that we would be the beginnings of a Movement that will cause such destruction? I mean, Canadians are so nice! We never destroy anything!" I said this only half-jokingly.

Calmar looked at me with cynically raised eyebrows, and I felt the need to retract my last statement.

"Alright, that's not entirely true. Canadians aren't completely innocent. We do destroy some things…" I paused for dramatic effect. "Like other countries' hockey teams!"

I said the punch line a little too loudly and proudly. Calmar let out a big belly laugh which was cut short from him wincing in pain.

"I'm sorry! I didn't mean to hurt you!" I instantly felt bad for his pain that my sharp wits inflicted on him.

"It's alright, I needed a laugh anyways. The pain was worth a good laugh." He said as he clutched his newly-bandaged side.

"Oh man, I'm really gonna have to watch what I say to you from now on. Because if I am my normal comedic self, I might just kill you."

He looked very amused at my last comment.

"No, I don't think we have to worry about that..."

"Oh but we do! Just wait until you hear some of the jokes I got. Knock, knock..."

"Now I'm positive that your humour is not going to kill me. It's more likely you'll bore me to death."

"Hey! Your survival depends on me, either way."

"Yeah, yeah. Whatever you say Doctor Grove. Now let's see that arm of yours."

He miraculously managed to push himself up into a sitting position on the couch, and gestured for me to sit down beside him. I got off my stool and plunked myself down on the gloriously commodious couch that was warmed by the fire. As I did this, I definitely noticed how Calmar took off his shirt completely, (it did look rather ridiculous hanging around his neck with one arm hanging down uselessly) and I wasn't complaining.

"We can't have that getting in the way," he said in reference to his shirt.

I chose to remain silent, and pretend that I was so enthralled in my bullet wound that I hadn't realized he had removed his shirt. Thankfully Calmar's focus quickly switched to my damaged upper left arm as well. He rolled up my sleeve and then began to clean around the grisly wound with a warm cloth. Even though I knew he was trying to be overly gentle in the process, I still couldn't help but grimace in pain. I forced myself to fixate on the flickering flames of the fire, and this helped diminish the pain, but only slightly. After most of the blood was cleared away Calmar piped up excitedly:

"Good news! I can see the bullet! That means it's close enough to the surface that I can probably pull it out. Lucky girl you are."

But I didn't think I was so lucky at the moment.

I had been avoiding thinking about what we would do with the bullet in my arm. Up until now, I had pushed away the thought of yanking out the tiny pellet from my arm. Because without pain killers this was going to hurt. A lot.

"I'll be right back," I said as I got up and walked out of the living room, and into the kitchen. I knew exactly where I was going: Mrs. Rundle's liquor cabinet. There was no way I was going to let someone take out a bullet from my arm completely sober. Not if I could do something about it. The liquor cabinet was above the fridge, so I had to stand on tip-toes to reach the bottle of vodka I was eyeing up so fiercely. With the prize in my hands, I returned to the fire-lit living room in a trance like state, where Calmar was currently heating a pair of tweezers over the fire. I'm not sure how I felt about the sudden energy he had for removing a bullet from my arm, but I guess it was better than the other option of me having to do it myself. I felt both scared and exhausted. I just wanted to get this over with before I passed out from hunger, blood loss, and the soon-to-be alcohol flowing through my veins.

Calmar turned around from the fire to find me standing silently behind him, holding a two-six of vodka in one arm, whilst new blood dripped down the other. My hair was a knotted mess, there was a black and red crusted gouge across my cheek, my white uniform was stained of blood from the both of us, and my eyes were glazed over wondering about how someone can still look so good with wounds that were most likely going to kill them. He turned his body so that he was facing me while still crouched down by the fire, paused for a moment, and put his finger to his chin as if he was pondering some great mystery of life. Finally, after a few moments of silence, he chose to speak in an educated tone.

"Well, I'm no psychologist. But if I had to guess, I would presume you are either on the verge of a violent psychotic breakdown, or you want to hit the town and party all night long. I'm going to go with the latter."

Not in the mood for games, I simply replied by twisting the cap off the bottle, taking a long swig of vodka, and in a I-mean-serious-business tone said:

"Let's do this, Australia."

He looked at me incredulously, and I could tell he was trying very hard not to burst out laughing as he quickly moved to sit down on the sofa. The same place where I also plunked down onto after removing my own shirt (extremely thankful that I wore a thin ivory tank top underneath the long sleeved uniform). I took another large gulp of the vile-tasting liquid for good measure.

"Teslin, slow down on the booze. You're going to pass out before I even start."

"That's kind of the point, Calmar." I sassed him back, already feeling the effects of the hard liquor.

"Alcohol mixed with blood loss and trauma is probably not the best thing for your body," he said as he took the bottle from my hand and took a swig for himself.

"Hey! I thought you just said it wasn't good for you!" I yelled at him, flailing my arms and seriously failing at stealing back my mind-numbing substance.

"I said it wasn't good for *you*! I, on the other hand, am about to perform a very intricate surgery that requires a bit of liquid courage."

"You put the tweezers in my arm and pull out the bullet! How intricate is that?! You are so ridiculous!" I shouted at him loudly.

He laughed and took another long gulp from the bottle.

"Okay, let's do this, Canada."

At this point I was no longer freaking out about the pain, because instead I felt pissed off and tipsy. I couldn't tell if I was angry about our whole hopeless situation, or about Calmar being an absolute butt. Fortunately for him, I had neither the energy nor the desire to psychoanalyze myself at this particular moment.

"Here, bite into these," Calmar passed me a handful of thick leather coasters from the side table beside him.

"What? Why?" I responded curiously as I took the coasters in my hands.

"You'll thank me later. Alright, here we go."

Not wanting to argue further, I put the coasters in my mouth and felt ridiculous. But as soon as the metal tweezer touched the raw skin of the inside of my arm, my jaw instantly clenched together so tightly, causing my teeth to tear into the thick leather. I silently cursed Calmar, desperately wishing that I had drunken more of that vodka, because the pain exponentially increased the further the silver apparatus pushed through my arm. My jaw clenched tighter and tighter until I thought it would surely snap from the excessive pressure.

"I've got a hold of the bullet. I'm going to try to take it out in one quick smooth movement, okay? I need you to take a deep breath, it will be over fast. Just try to stay calm so your muscles relax. If you tighten them, this is going to be much more painful and harder than it needs to be. Try to relax, Teslin. Think about things that make you happy."

He was gently rubbing my shoulder with his free hand in an attempt to calm me down. This only slightly worked. I closed my eyes and pictured my family and my friends, all together, all laughing and smiling. My jaw slightly loosened at the thought of this. I remembered the time that Devon, Dawson and I went camping in the mountains for a week when we were sixteen. It was a complete gong show; I'm surprised we even survived, but it was one of my favourite memories. I felt my arm muscles begin to release.

"That's it Teslin. Keep it up. Whatever you're doing it's working."

His voice was soft and calm, contributing to my tranquil state of mind.

Visions of my snow-covered Rocky Mountains clouded my senses. Throughout the continuous change that life brought, the mountains were the only thing that remained the same. Their constant omniscient presence made the craziness of existence bearable. No matter what chaos had overrun my life, I could always count on my silent giant friends to give me a balanced and impartial new perspective. They let me breathe when the world was trying to suffocate me. I consciously took a deep breath, and as my lungs exhaled I expected to find my body quite relaxed and tranquil, but my bicep muscles screamed at me instead. A horrible, nightmarish shriek that produced a pain that was past the point of tears. It was the type of pain that resulted in a confused body, not knowing whether it should vomit or lose consciousness in response to such agony. My body lurched forward as if I would throw up, but nothing other than the leather coasters fell out of my mouth. It was impossible to even cry out in protest to the horrendous burn tormenting my left arm; my body was too busy producing pain that it had no time to stimulate my tear ducts. And then, just as suddenly as it started, the pain drastically dropped down to a tolerable level, and my lungs could finally breathe somewhat normally again. The bullet was out.

My poor body shook with relief, and then slumped back into the plush couch, my eyes closed from exhaustion. I thoroughly enjoyed the moment of silence and low-intensity pain. I couldn't think about anything other than how relieved I was that it was all over. Taking another deep breath, I felt something cold and hard touch my fingertips. I opened my eyes to find Calmar putting the bottle of vodka in my hand.

"I think you deserve some of this," he said, smiling at me sheepishly.

I couldn't help but smile back at him. His enchanting dark eyes fixed on mine, and mine on his. Suddenly our future didn't seem so cold. As long as we had each other, we had a chance. An infinitesimal chance, yes, but a chance nonetheless. I continued to stare into his eyes as I raised the bottle up to my lips and took a sip. Then without saying a word, I handed it back to him, and he took a turn taking a drink while still never taking his eyes off mine. We said nothing, because there were no words quite sufficient enough to describe our feelings. We just continued passing the liquor back and forth for a long enough time that the bottle became half empty, or half full if you prefer. The only light and sound came from the flickering and crackling of the warm fire.

As I sat on the couch with Calmar, the two of us slowly becoming more and more intoxicated as the firewater became less and less, I realized that right now there was nothing else I'd rather be doing. This moment was perfect. I admit it was quite disturbing if you thought about how we got ourselves into this almost unbelievable situation in the first place, but still, perfect. Unfortunately, as everything must come to an end, so must this perfect moment. Calmar broke the glorious silence between us by his never ending concern over my health.

"I'd better bandage that up," he said, pointing to the hole in my arm where thick red blood currently leaked from.

"That's probably a good idea," I replied, a bit sad that the moment was over.

I noticed that he was a bit unstable as he reached for the first aid kit on the ground in front of him. He was so unstable to the extent that he just about fell off the couch completely as he leaned forward! I let out a laugh as he finally did manage to grab the small red bag, and was now trying to stop himself from swaying back and forth. I couldn't pass up this opportunity:

"What's wrong, Calmar? Can't handle your liquor?"

An evil smile found its way upon my lips as I spoke.

"Hey! You're going to regret saying that! You really shouldn't insult the person in charge of your medical needs."

His words were slurred as he pulled out gauze bandages from the first aid kit.

For some reason I found this terribly funny: the way he wore such a confused look on his face while rummaging through the medical supplies, and I began giggling uncontrollably. Apparently the alcohol had affected me more than I was aware of. Calmar looked up at me with an even more confused look on his face, causing me to laugh even harder.

"Oh my god, she is having a psychotic breakdown! She finally went mad! Everyone stay calm! I know how to handle this. I'm a professional!"

He put his hands up and looked around the room confidently and assertively as if he was calming down a room full of anxious people. He was also talking way too loud (which I'm positive he wasn't at all conscious of). By some miracle I was able to control my laughing enough to throw in my two cents.

"How am I the crazy one here?! You're the one talking to a room full of imaginary people, you psycho!"

My body jerked forward in deranged laughter, and it was now my turn to almost tumble off the couch. Calmar grabbed my sore arm and yanked it towards him. The vodka must have really been working as I felt no pain from this action, when I know I should have.

"Stay still, you crazy woman! How am I supposed to fix you up if you won't ever stay still? You are the worst patient ever!" He yelled as he began to sloppily wind the white bandage round and round my upper arm.

I don't know if it was his apparent drunkenness or his accent that made him progressively harder to comprehend. Possibly a combination of the two. Somewhat listening to his request, I did try to sit still as he covered up my wound. To make up for my lack of movement, I found myself yelling out complaints of "it's too tight" and "now it's too loose" for God only knows how long, until he finally announced "mission complete" and then proceeded to sing a horrible rendition of the Mission Impossible theme song.

I looked down to see that there was now a thick and bumpy gauze around the entire top of my arm, and nodded in approval to no one in particular. My growling stomach reminded me of how hungry I was. Feeling the need to act overly dramatic about it, I flung my arms out to my sides (almost smacking the still singing Calmar in the face as I did so) and announced to the world:

"Let it be known to all my loyal subjects, that tonight we shall feast! Food for everyone!"

Joyous applause filled the air as the only other person in the room clapped his hands together nosily, "Finally she says something that makes sense! Food! Yes, let's get some food!"

I ignored his insult (as he was only a simple serf in my kingdom of intoxication), and carried on with my very important announcement:

"If it is food you want, then it is food you shall get!" I rose to my feet a bit too quickly and wobbled from side to side. "Follow me, humble servant, to the promise land of nourishment!"

I pointed myself forward in an overly confident manner and took but one step before promptly falling on my face. Howls of laughter came from behind me as Calmar enjoyed my unexpected plummet a little too much. He clutched his bandaged side and laughed until tears rolled down his face.

"You were right! You are going to kill me with your humour!"

A bit put off, I sassed him back angrily, "It's a lot harder than it looks! You try it, you big butt!"

"Big butt?! What are you doing looking at my butt?" he said as he now stood on his feet, taking only two steps before he did a slow motion fall to join me on the ground.

I gave him a sarcastic look with raised eyebrows, "Wow. You got so much farther than I did. Congratulations."

We were now both half-sitting and half-lying on the ground in front of the fireplace.

Calmar turned to look at me with a mischievous glimmer in his eyes.

"I bet I can still beat you to the kitchen."

"You're on," I said as I propelled myself forward while simultaneously pushing him down to the ground.

"Hey! You're cheating already!"

"Not! You never made any rules!"

We raced our way towards the kitchen, half crawling, half-stumbling, uncontrollably spinning, with the occasional short bursts of powerwalking, all the while trash-talking and laughing hysterically. When we finally made our way into the kitchen (a whole thirty feet from the living room), instead of deciding who won (we were too out-of-breath to argue at this point) our exhausted bodies collapsed on the floor. This is where we stayed, sprawled out on the dark hardwood floor of Mrs. Rundle's kitchen, until we caught our breath. Our bodies threatened to lose consciousness, abused by blood loss, bullet wounds, alcohol, and the stressful events of the day. It really was a wonder how we were even alive. I turned my head to look at Calmar. He was laying on the floor next to me with a determined smile plastered across his face.

"We're almost there, Teslin. We can't give up now!"

He was of course referring to the close proximity of the pantry room that stood only a few feet away from us. I locked eyes on the red painted door blocking the way to our objective.

"You're lucky that I don't give up easily."

Steadying my spinning head, I used all my energy to push myself up from the ground. Calmar followed suit and we walked toward the food-filled room looking something similar to crazed zombies. Once I opened the door and entered inside, I found myself lost in a magical world overflowing with a vast variety of delicious edible material. There were baskets full of muffins, cookies, pastries and pies. Bags stuffed with chips, chocolates, pretzels, and crackers.

Overwhelmed by all the choices, I stood still for a moment, not knowing what to eat first. A loud crackling noise from behind me made me jump and spin around, only to discover that it was Calmar grabbing anything that he could hold in his arms. I let out a chuckle and followed his example, grabbing any delectable smelling thing that I could get my hands on. Moments later, after our arms were weighed down with a mountain of scrumptious goodies, we made our way back to the living room where the fire greeted us with its warmth. Sitting on the sofa, we stuffed out stomachs full of chips, cookies and pies.

There really wasn't any conversation between us as we munched away ravenously - unless of course you count the occasional request for something that the other had in their pile of sweets. As the menagerie of much needed sustenance digested in my stomach, I began to feel strength and energy returning to my body. My mind started to sober up as well (which is not necessarily a good thing as I was now consciously aware of the throbbing pain and our current grim situation). I turned my attention to Calmar, and observed him devouring an entire apple pie. He didn't even notice my gaze, for he was too starved to notice anything else. But I couldn't help myself from being a killjoy and asking a sobering question.

"Why did they stop?"

"What?" he said, with a mouthful of pie.

"The White Soldiers. Why didn't they come after us? Why did they let us go?"

Calmar swallowed the food in his mouth, and then gestured to his bloody midsection.

"Look at this, Teslin. They know that I'm not gonna survive these wounds. Our only options are to go back to them for medical treatment, or die out here. Letting us go was the most logical move on their part."

"That's not necessarily true. I mean we have a vehicle now. We can get out of here and find help!"

"Get help from where, Teslin? We don't even know which way to go. We don't know how far this Movement has spread. And quite honestly, I don't think they would have let us go if they knew we had a possibility of escaping. We'll probably run out of gas before we're even close to finding a way out, and I'm in no condition to walk the rest of the way."

"Calmar..." I began, but my voice drifted off because he was right.

There was no loophole here. No clever way out of this. We were standing at yet another crossroad. But this time there was no chance at freedom. Only certain death and possible death. We had a very slim time frame before Calmar's wounds became irreversible. Even if the bullet miraculously didn't hit any of his vital organs, it could easily cause an infection. However, even more concerning than the bullet itself, was the slow continuous stream of blood leaking from his side. I had no medical training, but it was pretty obvious that he would bleed out before anything else became an issue. I couldn't help him, and if we went on a treasure hunt to find outside help he would most likely die before we found it. If I wanted to save Calmar we had to go back to that wretched underground facility. And even then it wasn't guaranteed that they would save him. We would be at the mercy of cold-hearted logical beings. Would they actually consider helping us? Or would they shoot us dead the moment we were in range? The risks were high. But it was clear to me that the only way Calmar had a chance of survival, is if we returned to the facility. The choice was made.

"We have to go back." My voice clearly sounded disappointed as I spoke the words that we both knew were coming.

"I know." Calmar spoke in a quiet and sad tone that I had never heard from him before. It was almost as if he felt that it was his fault that we had to go back after we just barely made it out.

"Calmar, this isn't your fault. You're not the one who shot yourself."

"Yeah, I know that, Teslin. But I can't help feeling like this whole situation is my fault. If it wasn't for this damn bullet, we wouldn't even have to consider going back there. And now it's our only move."

He held his head so low that for a second I was scared it was going to detach from his neck and fall right off. As I was imagining his head rolling on the ground (the loss of blood and exhaustion must really be getting to me) he suddenly lifted his head up and gave me a very serious look.

"I may have to go back to the emotionless robots, but you don't have to."

My heart dropped as I instantly knew where this was headed.

"Teslin, you can go on without me. You can find help and be the one to stop this Movement. You don't need –".

"No."

I cut him off before he could finish his sentence. I moved closer to him on the couch and grasped his hand, intertwining my fingers in his.

"No. That's not even an option, Calmar. We are in this together. I am not leaving you."

"But, Teslin, you may be our only chance. You are strong and brave and smart. You can do this by yourself."

"No, I can't!"

"Yes, you can! Teslin, you can do anything you put your mind to. I've only known you for three days, and yet you've already proven yourself as a strong leader, a hell-of-a-fighter, and the most amazing woman I have ever met."

His sincere words had me momentarily stunned and speechless. No one had ever given me such a meaningful compliment in my life, and I felt overwhelmed by a swarm of emotions.

"Calmar, maybe I could do it by myself. But I don't want to. I want to be by your side when we enter into the Cold Cognition

Headquarters. And I want to be standing next to you when we face whatever they decide to throw at us. We are a team, Calmar. A team is only strong when it works together as one, not when it breaks apart."

He stared intensely into my eyes, like he was peering into my soul. I felt like he could see all my flaws, my secrets, and my insecurities. Yet for some reason, I was surprisingly alright with it.

"Okay." He spoke so flippantly that it made me a bit confused.

"Okay?" I asked.

"Yes."

"So…"

"So… I call shot gun," he said with a crooked smile.

I reached over to the side table, grabbed the keys to the bullet proof monster, and jingled them in the air. Then with a sly smile I looked at him and said:

"I call missile launcher."

****

The crowd before us whispered quietly amongst themselves. There were thousands of them packed into the underground arena. My father had failed to show me this stadium that held up to fifteen thousand spectators, but then again, there was a lot he had failed to tell me.

Calmar and I stood centre stage, handcuffed and waiting for our fate to be decided. Only minutes before, had we arrived at the back entrance of the military wing (the missile assaulted door had already been reconstructed), where a small army of White Soldiers greeted us with handcuffs. Without a word, they escorted us through the winding white halls that brought us to this theatre arena that I had never seen before. It was filled with people, as if they had been waiting for us, and then I realized, they had been. They knew we would come back. And now as we stood on a stage in front of a sea of white, we were entirely at the mercy of our captors. I could only hope that they decided quickly whether they wanted us dead or alive, for Calmar was clearly suffering to the point that I wanted to put him out of his misery myself to save him from any more pain. His eyes were half closed and sweat dripped down his face. A fresh red stain had made its way onto the new white shirt I had borrowed from Mr. Rundle's closet. I honestly didn't know how it was possible for him to still be losing blood, I thought he would have run out by now. But he was a fighter by nature, so I suppose that's the reason why he was able to hang on for so long.

I turned my gaze back to the buzzing crowd. How odd this entirely rational crowd was; they looked like any ordinary crowd from a quick glance, but closer inspection revealed a significantly different conclusion. The sounds of conversing voices were not filled with excitement, anticipation, or worry like they should be at a life or death trial. Instead, the atmosphere felt quite neutral. There were no bursts of laughter or smiles, nor tears or faces of dread. In fact, their faces looked almost disinterested. As if deciding one's fate was terribly boring and simply a waste of their precious time. I almost felt offended that my life was so evidently trivial to them. I began to wonder how exactly this trial would proceed.

'Would they give me a chance to speak and state my case? Would they bring out witnesses and have lawyers and a judge?' My questioning thoughts were interrupted, because without any warning whatsoever, the crowd fell completely silent. I desperately scanned the arena, wanting to find what had caused an entire crowd to turn mute so dramatically. A moving figure out of the corner of my left eye caught my attention. I swivelled my head round to see my father joining us upon the stage. It took a second for me to comprehend that it was his presence that had subdued the massive audience. A man who could instantly demand the attention of thousands of people was a man to be respected… or feared, or both. Though in this moment, I felt only fear towards my father.

He strolled across the stage like he was walking through a peaceful park, the direness of the situation completely lost on him. Stopping at a wooden podium to the right of centre stage, he took out a small electronic device from his pocket and pressed a few buttons. These buttons caused a large screen to appear on the wall behind him, and the lights above the audience to go dim. Only the lights above my father, Calmar, and I continued to burn bright. Once the words on the screen came into focus, my father addressed the crowd in a commanding and powerful voice:

"Good evening, my equals. You all know why we are here: to decide the future of Teslin Grove and Calmar Daysland. However, before we do so, we must go over all the facts in this case in order to make the most informed and logical choice. We shall also consider the individual talents of the two people on trial, and then proceed to vote on whether they live or die. The vote will take place in precisely two minutes from now. Let's begin."

As he turned to face the screen behind him, my mind went into a state of shock. In exactly two minutes I would either still have a pulse or become a corpse. Simple as that. I think I liked it better before when I didn't know what was going to happen to us. But I guess in a room full of rational people, there was no beating around the bush. My father began to list off the facts of our case in a cold manner, immune to the fact that he was deciding the fate of his own daughter:

"The two individuals were brought to our facility yesterday afternoon. They were captured and brought to us after they had managed to avoid our initial purge of the town of Canmore and surrounding area. Today, while Teslin was about to receive the Cold Surgery, Calmar broke into the surgery room and seized her before she was able to complete the surgery. They then proceeded to the military wing where our White Soldiers engaged in open fire. The two were wounded by bullets, but were still able to escape our forces while also stealing a vehicle, and create thousands of dollars' worth of damage to our military wing. Presently, they have returned to us after the realization that they do not have the expertise to treat their injuries, leaving the future of their lives in our hands as we had predicted they would." He paused to catch his breath before he went on.

"Now for the summary of individual specifics. Calmar is an ex-military special ops with seven years of invaluable experience. Today was just an example of his militaristic talent. Teslin, on the other hand, has a degree in psychology and has recently proven her capabilities as a strong leader and being able to make critical decisions in order to survive.

My equals, we are voting on the fact of whether or not they will be an asset to the Cold Cognition Movement. Their obvious hostile views toward the Movement are not an issue, as we all know the gift of logic will cure their irrational minds. So that being said, let us now vote. Will Teslin Grove and Calmar Daysland be a beneficial addition to the Cold Cognition Movement? Yes or no? Decide now. You have ten seconds."

Ten seconds began to count down on the large screen behind us, and the sea of white uniforms began to vote on their tiny electronic devices similar to that of my father's. I was no longer in a state of shock. To be quite honest, I was very much past the feeling of shock. Instead, there was a full-blown tornado of fear and horror wreaking havoc in my brain and in my body. My pulse was thumping against my veins so furiously that I thought they would surely burst into bloody fireworks. Seven seconds left. Calmar and I locked wide eyes, completely helpless. I was positive that we were going to die.

The crowd mentality always chose violence over forgiveness. Four seconds. They say that your life flashes before your eyes before you die. Pretty pictures of all your victories and regrets fill your mind before you take your last breath. It's the process of dying, a life coming to an end has to be remembered before it can peacefully pass away. This is not true. Because in those last three seconds of my life, I could think of nothing at all. Nothing. One second. A loud horn announced the end of the voting period and father's voice broke through the silence:

"The vote is unanimous."

I closed my eyes tight, waiting for the bullets to fly.

"Teslin Grove and Calmar Daysland will be a part of the Cold Cognition Movement. The two newcomers will now be escorted to the surgery room where the Cold Surgery will cure them. Then they will immediately commence their positions to further our Movement of bringing peace, equality and intelligence to this broken world. Thank you for your input in this important decision. You may now all return to your positions."

I opened my eyes to find the audience quickly disappearing, and White Soldiers marching towards me. Calmar's eyes were still wide with fear. I don't think he processed the good news either. They voted yes. We were saved! Or at least that's what I thought.

The White Soldiers walked behind us, but instead of removing our handcuffs like I assumed they would, they started to escort us off the stage. I was terribly confused at this. I mean I thought they had voted? Were we not free? Calmar wore a similar confused expression on his face, he didn't know why we were still being treated as prisoners either. We walked off the stage to a side door where my father was waiting for us. He was leaning on the dark wooden door in a very casual manner. You would have never known that only moments before he was the moderator of his daughter's death trial.

"Dad!" I called out. "They voted. We are a part of the Movement. Why are we still in handcuffs?" I searched my father's face for any signs of relief that I was still alive, for a smidge of empathy directed towards me, but found none.

"Yes, it's true. We voted yes, but that does not mean you are free. We can't take any chances with the two of you. Those handcuffs aren't going anywhere until after you possess a rational mind."

He was referring to the Cold Surgery of course. It really was going to happen. I could only avoid fate for so long, it was time to pay up. All our luck and slim getaways were over. Sooner than later there would be a drill cutting through my skin, past my skull, and into my cerebrum. My brain will be altered and I will no longer have the same thoughts, the same personality, the same emotions. I will be an entirely different person. A person of pure logic, without compassion, and without love. The horror of what was about to happen must have seeped onto my face, for my father cocked his head in curiosity. He walked right up to me so that our faces were only inches apart, and then he smiled. Not his familiar smile where his eyes crinkled in love and the corners of his mouth lifted in compassion, but a strange smile that I couldn't put my finger on exactly. It was dark and twisted, almost evil, yet with a touch of playfulness. It was… wicked.

"Welcome to the Cold Cognition Movement, Teslin."

****

Once again I found myself feeling utterly alone in the room before the surgery room. Back in the holding tank as it were. I swear it was packed with even more people than before if that was possible. It was relatively quiet other than the low fearful whispers swirling around me. 'Although something was different about this time,' I thought as I stood with my back to a corner wall, my hands still tied behind my back. It was different because last time I still had a hint of hope that things would turn out okay. Last time I felt like it was all a dream, that it couldn't actually be reality. But not this time. This time I knew it was real, and this time I had no hope of freedom. My fate was sealed. There was not going to be a miraculous escape. The sequence of absolute events was not complicated: I would get the Cold Surgery, and then I would work in the position I was placed, to contribute to and to ultimately complete the Cold Cognition Movement. There was nothing confusing about it.

'I wonder for how long I will have to do it? How long does it take to modify the brains of a couple billion people and then eradicate the rest? Will I eventually get bored of it all?' I thought, before I quickly realized that boredom was an emotion, and since I will soon be unable to process emotions then the answer was no. No, I would never get bored. I would continue at my designated task until the mission was complete, and then God only knows what would happen to me after that. While my mind went on another rant about what life would be like if the Movement succeeded, my eyes focussed on the red light atop of the door across the room from where I stood. It would eventually turn green and my old life would be over. I had never feared the colour green so much as I did now.

An abrupt noise made me tear my gaze away from the crimson light, and direct it to the entrance of the waiting room where the door had violently swung open. Two White Soldiers entered, pushing a young man into the room and then promptly leaving, shutting the doors swiftly behind them. The crowd made room for the sickly looking newcomer, who fell to the ground in weakness, clutching his side in pain. Curious about the young man, I inched forward from my corner to get a better look. As I moved closer, I was unexpectedly hit with recognition of the man. I knew him! It was Calmar. Before I could even think, my feet lurched forward and ran to him. Pushing past the frightened people, I knelt down beside him, hating the handcuffs for denying me the ability to use my hands and arms to comfort and help him.

"Calmar! What happened to you? What did they do to you?" I asked in a hushed but angered voice.

He looked up from the ground, "Teslin," he said with a weak smile. He put his free hand lightly on my cheek while his other hand continued to hold onto his side.

"What happened?" I repeated my question, trying to ignore how good it felt when he touched my skin. His voice came out so fragile like it would break if he spoke any louder.

"After they separated us, they took me into a dark room and operated on me. They took out the bullet, then they stitched me back up and threw me in here. I'm fine, Teslin. Just a bit weak from the operation that's all."

I felt my heart wrench as I looked in his eyes and saw the torturous pain he was truly feeling. His words may be able to lie to me, but if you look deep into the eyes of someone you care for, you will always find the truth. The eyes never lie. His eyes especially, held a power that made me honest. I suddenly became overwhelmed by all the sadness, suffering, and anger that I had bottled up from the past three days (and the third day wasn't even over yet). Tears overflowed from my eyes and rolled down my cheeks.

"Teslin," he said again in a soft and sympathetic voice as he wiped away the tiny liquid sorrows from my face. I couldn't stop the tears. Normally I hated crying, it made me feel weak. But right now I didn't really care. It was all over. I couldn't do anything to stop the Movement, nor the drill about to be piercing through my vulnerable brain. We were no longer at a crossroad of choice, but at a total dead end. A literal dead end. Or the death of emotions at the very least.

"It's okay, Teslin. It's going to be okay." Calmar whispered, unable to keep up with wiping away the never ending stream from my eyes.

It's funny how people think that in every terrible situation, saying "It's okay" is going to magically make it all better. That it's going to bring back a loved one, mend a broken heart, or bring back a missed opportunity. Yet as illogical as it sounds, it really does help. Not the words themselves, but the fact that someone cares for you enough to say them. That there is someone in the world who wants to ease your pain, not create more. So I couldn't help but smile when Calmar said these words to me. I closed my eyes to stop them from leaking, and became pleasantly aware of his warm hand on my cheek. A change in the pressure of his hand caused me to open my eyes to find that he had stood up from the ground and was looking down at me. His hand that had previously been pressed against his wound was now around my arm; it lifted me up from the ground and then slowly made its way up my neck. As his hand moved upwards, he gently pushed me backwards until my back came in contact with a hard wall. With his body tightly pressed up against mine, he held my face in his hands and pulled it towards his. This was the closest I had ever been to him.

My heartbeat was in a frenzy, and I found it hard to breathe. Our eyes locked together, and in this moment, I could no longer see pain or sadness or fear in his eyes. In this moment, all of it was replaced with a burning desire, with a fiery passion. I felt it too. My body ached with a relentless longing to be even closer to him than I already was, to press my lips against his. He now had one hand at the back of my head, holding a fistful of my hair, and the other grasping the top of my neck. With his thumb pressed on the jawline under my chin, he firmly tilted my head upwards, closer to him. Torturous butterflies fluttered to every sensitive part of my worn body. I lost all self-control and the instinctive animal within me took control. I forced my lips onto his. He kissed me back so fiercely that all my senses were overpowered. I was no longer in a crowded room of frightened people, but in a world created only for the two of us. I kissed him back with every fibre of my being, and silently cursed the bloody handcuffs for preventing me from hooking my claws into his gorgeous, thick hair. Thus, having to improvise, I wrapped my leg around him and pulled him even closer to me. He responded by running his hands up and down my body, caressing ever inch, kissing my lips, my cheeks, my neck. There was more than a spark between us, there was a blazing fire. We were so completely wrapped up in our world of fantastical eroticism that we did not see the red light turn green. We failed to notice the entrance of the surgeons and White Soldiers, escorting the crowd to their horrible fates, one-by-one. We were oblivious to the rapidly diminishing crowd behind us, until we were violently ripped apart.

I tried to fight off the cold, rough hands that pulled me away from him. I yelled out his name and he yelled out mine. We tried to fight off the White Soldiers. One last hoorah for old times' sake, just so we could say we didn't go down without a fight. Unfortunately, there was too many hands and arms to break free. I found myself pinned down to the ground, a plastic mask was forced over my mouth and nose. Suddenly everything became significantly blurry, and I felt as if I was in a dreamlike state. I floated off the ground and out of the dreadful waiting room, into a place where a chair and a drill were waiting just for me. How nice of them. My hands were freed from the handcuffs, only to be restrained in the familiar cold shackles of the operating table. Even through my hazy vision, I could tell that there was a significant amount of more White Soldiers around me than last time.

Through the fogginess and through the openings of all the legs and arms, I could see Calmar, sitting across from me in his own specially reserved place. Although I wasn't certain, I thought he could see me as well. I held onto this thought as hands pushed my head back onto the cold metal surface, and kept it secure with tight leather straps. No amount of luck or adrenaline would help me out of this one. My eyes, the only thing that I could move, searched desperately to get another glimpse of Calmar's face amongst the crowd of surgeons and soldiers. I used my last drop of luck to find him, and I did. But when my eyes rested on his handsome face, it wasn't the face that I was expecting to see. It wasn't a face of fear or anger like that of mine, but a face of acceptance. He finally gave up; he accepted the horrible truth. We lost. We couldn't stop the Movement, and now we would be a part of it. The very thing we risked our lives to stop, is what we would become. There was no going back. This was our future now. Our cold future. The sounds of the drills didn't scare me anymore, nor did the piercing of the drill through my flesh induce pain. I could tell when the drill moved onto my skull because the noise changed, and the surgeon had to apply more pressure to move the drill past the skull. Finally, the drill entered the posterior of my prefrontal cortex. I felt no pain as the drill cut away at my neural connections, as in fact, the brain has no pain receptors. I kept getting glimpses of Calmar in between the surgeons. My feelings of desire, passion, and love (the strongest they had ever been only moments ago) now became less and less, until I could hardly feel anything at all. I could see the expression on his face was changing as well, from one of longing to one of indifference. More and more connections were being severed in my brain. Then suddenly, the drill stopped. The drill slowly exited my head, taking along my emotions with it. Fear, anger, love, hate, compassion, joy, sadness, disgust, excitement… they all exited out the hole in my head.

****

"There may still be some emotions able to reach your prefrontal cortex. Fortunately, we can easily get rid of them through shock therapy. Meaning that we will try to get you to react emotionally to a stimulus, and if in fact you do react emotionally, we will then deliver a painful electric shock to your body."

The surgeon in front of me spoke in a detached tone of voice. She was busy writing notes on her clipboard, and thus never actually made eye contact with me as she explained my current situation.

"Normally we use very vivid, violent, and emotionally evoking videos for this procedure, as visual imagery through moving pictures is usually enough to illicit a response. But for you, Teslin, we have something special planned..."

The young surgeon then abruptly walked out of the peculiar small room, leaving me alone with four White Soldiers who stood at each corner of the room in silence. I looked around the curious tiny square. The walls, floors, and ceilings were all white, giving the room an illusion that it was larger than it really was. I looked down at the plush leather chair that I was sitting in. It was a lot more welcoming than the metal operating table I sat in moments ago; however, the leather restraints around my arms, legs, and torso gave the impression that I was not completely trusted just yet. So I simply sat back in my chair and waited. Normally in this kind of situation, my mind would be racing with questions. My emotions would be in an uproar, and I would be fighting to escape. Yet since there was no longer a hurricane of emotions tearing up my mind, I felt rather calm in the absence of such a storm.

'I wonder, if in the absence of emotions one feels calm and peacefulness. Or does one only feel calm because after having so many emotions, the phenomenon of no emotions can only be described as calm? But is it actually calm, or is it simply nothing at all? If someone was born with no emotions, would they then describe themselves in an endless state of calmness, or in a state of nothingness? They might not know what calm feels like if they had never felt stress, panic, fear or anger.'

As I sat quietly in the silent room, I began to understand the Cold Cognition Movement. I began to understand why ridding people of their emotions was so crucial in order to obtain world peace. The reason was simple. You can't have peace without peaceful people. And the current people of the world, of every country, of every race, of every culture, of every religion, were not peaceful people. In fact, we were quite the opposite. It was an interesting notion to think about.

Turning my thoughts back to the present, I speculated over what the surgeon meant when she said they had something "special" planned for me. I had been quite a troublemaker for them, so it only made sense that they would take the necessary precautions to be positive I was with them and not against them. Before I could pursue the matter anymore, the door to the small room flew open, and in entered the same youthful surgeon (still holding tightly onto her clipboard). Another two people followed behind her, pushing a machine with many different coloured electrical lines attached to it. 'This must be for the electric shock therapy', I thought to myself indifferently. Behind them came another individual carrying a black plastic storage box. He placed the black box not too far in front of where I was sitting, and then joined the others that were huddled around the machine that was placed next to me. They immediately began attaching the colourful electric wires to specific areas on my body: on my head, my chest, and even some on my arms and legs. I knew right away that this was not the controversial Electroconvulsive Therapy that I had learned about in my psychology textbooks. This machine was not used to aid individuals suffering with mental illness. No, it was used to torture individuals. To condition them to behave in a desired way. These people in white uniforms were going to condition the emotion out of my thoughts. After they were done with me, I would not dare to react to a stimulus with any kind of emotion ever again.

Once the wires were placed in all their appropriate places, the surgeon took out a small mobile-like device (like the ones I saw in the stadium), pressed a single button, and spoke into it:

"She's ready."

Barely a second went by before the white doors opened again. My mother entered the room with my father closely behind her, and trailing behind my father at the end of a chain leash, was an overly rambunctious bundle of black and white fur. Nikita! My heart instantly gave a jolt of excitement at the sight of my darling husky. I opened my mouth to say her name but a shocked scream escaped my mouth instead. For an electric current shot through my body, leaving behind an excruciatingly painful sensation.

Unable to completely recover, my body went numb in response to the torturous shock and my vision went blurry. I couldn't even begin to describe the level of pain I currently felt, because I had never felt anything like it before. I just knew that it was more piercing than getting shot with a bullet, and more overpowering than a broken heart.

With my eyes still useless, I relied on my ears to let me know what was going on. I could hear the shuffling of feet, the clanging of chains, and the howling and barking of a dog. I squinted my eyes at the scene before me until it finally became clear. Nikita was standing in front of me, chained to the ground. The silver chains were attached to the four metal clasps around her legs, and the metal collar around her neck. Her striking blue eyes were filled with confusion and fear, as she looked at me for help. I couldn't help but feel a bit sorry for her. Another jolt of electricity immediately cut short my sympathetic thoughts.

"She's just a dog, Teslin. You no longer have any emotional connection to this creature. It's just a dog. Nothing more."

I heard my father before I could see him. When I was able to see again, I observed my father opening up the big black box and pulling out a narrow, needlelike knife. My mother, who stood next to my father, seemed perfectly indifferent to my father holding the knife in his hands. The surgeon and her three helpers, who all stood around the machine I was attached to, all appeared entirely calm. The four White Soldiers, who still remained at their corner posts, wore emotionless faces under their white helmets (although I could not physically see their faces, I would have bet my life on it). My father began walking closer to Nikita with the knife, but I couldn't decipher what he was going to do next, and the faces of the people around me didn't help at all. They were altogether disinterested in the scene unfolding before them, and they stayed that way as my father drove the knife deep into the hind leg of my beloved dog.

Not in my darkest of nightmares had I ever imagined my father would do something like this. Nikita's screams in response to the sharp object slashing through her flesh made me want to vomit in horror. But my gag reflex was curtailed due to the jarring electric current flowing through my body. It was longer this time, so long that it almost rendered me unconscious.

"Remember it's just an animal, Teslin. You don't feel anything," my father said calmly as I slowly recovered.

This was not true. She was not just an animal. She was my Nikita. My best friend. I did not want to feel nothing, to think of her as an insignificant animal. I wanted to take that razor-sharp knife my father was holding, slice through his carotid artery, and watch him bleed to death. But instead, he used the knife to penetrate through the skin of Nikita's stomach. She let out another bloodcurdling screech, and I received another mind numbing shock.

This went on for a while. My mother would pass my father a knife, he would stab it into Nikita, and I would get electrocuted. A stab, a scream, and a shock. A stab. A scream. A shock. I began to slowly die, for I could no longer take the pain. Not the pain of being electrocuted, but the pain from watching the blood spill out of my precious Nikita. For this was far more painful than the shocks themselves. What made matters even worse, was the realization that she was the most innocent one of us all, and yet she was paying for the sins of us all. Nikita did nothing to deserve any of this. It wasn't her idea to run from the White Soldiers. It wasn't her plan to attack my mother in order to defend me. She had nothing to do with the escape and the damage that Calmar and I caused. Her only mistake was trusting me, fighting for me. I was the reason that she was getting stabbed to death, and I could do absolutely nothing to save her.

Now the knives staked into her body became too many to count, and the inevitable outcome of so many wounds took its toll. Nikita could take no more. Her body collapsed to the ground, the metal chains making an atrocious sound of rattling death as she slumped to the floor. She lay there, on the cold ground, bleeding out and softly whining in agonizing pain. Yet no mercy was given. The knives did not stop. However, I did notice that the shocks became less and less as my heart died more and more. A stab, a whine, no shock. A stab. A whimper. No shock. There was no shock because I didn't feel anything anymore. Not an ounce of horror, or a spec of sympathy. I watched in an unconcerned manner as my father stood overtop Nikita, grabbed the back of her neck, and roughly lifted up her head. Her persecuted blue eyes were now looking directly into my dying soul. Then with one swift movement, my father sliced her neck wide open, and I watched the remaining blood spill onto the cold, hard ground. As it ran down her neck onto the floor, it changed her black and white fur into a vibrant crimson colour. I observed the red waterfall until only drips remained. And then it stopped. As did my heart. It stopped beating. And what was left of it turned black and shrivelled away, breaking off into tiny little pieces until ultimately bursting into dust, and falling out of its cavity entirely.

My father let go of the dog's head and it dropped lifelessly to the ground. Her lovely blue eyes were still bright, but they were now just an empty set of glazed-over optical organs. They no longer housed the soul of an energetic, loving Siberian husky. I stared intently at the bloody, knife-covered corpse of Nikita, and felt nothing. No sadness, no remorse, no anger, no broken heart at the death of a loved one. For there was no love left inside of me. Every last drop of my emotions had withered away and died along with her. I was no more.

Chapter Ten

The rest of the week went by quite smoothly. I worked under Armena in the Communications Headquarters, giving out orders to the White Soldiers on the ground. Since the Movement had been very successful in the other 64 locations around the globe, we could now be more selective on the individuals that we brought in to join the Movement.

We collected the facts on individuals and decided if they would benefit us or not. Looking at their IQ scores, valuable talents, experience, potential, and their general health, we chose who lived and who perished in the New World. A few days ago even the idea of this would have made my stomach turn in disgust. A few days ago I would have never agreed to do this, because it wasn't right. However, now it wasn't about what was wrong or right, but about what was necessary to achieve our goal. Once this became my focus, I quickly realized that there was no other way to create peace in this twisted world. People will never have peace on their own, the way they are. The desire to better mankind is smothered amongst the greed, the fear, the hate, and the selfishness of the world. In the past, many have tried to resuscitate the idea of universal peace, but unfortunately, repeated words of love eventually lose their significance, leading by example quickly loses its appeal, and ultimately something radical has to be done if change is to happen.

This has been seen throughout history: the extremists always make more headway than the pacifists, simply because extremists will not stop until they are forced to, either by death or by superior fire power. Words mean nothing to someone who already has their mind made up. Extremists can only be stopped when pacifists take a short leave of absence from their nonviolent stance. Then peace is made, but only temporarily. And although this has happened again and again throughout history, what people cannot seem to understand, is that this is proof world peace is attainable. Not through loving words, compassionate deeds, or leading by example, but through force. Peace has to be forced upon the world. People have to believe that it is the only way of survival in order to embrace it. And finally, peaceful people have to be created, because they are not natural to this earth.

Our Movement, was not like any other before us. Although I am sure that some will put us under the label of extremists at first, this is not the case. You see, we are not killing because of disputes over religion, beliefs, or power. We are only killing because it is necessary to create a perfect world of peace, equality and intelligence. In the current state of the world, peace is not yet attainable as not everyone wants peace. Even those who live around you, saying they long for a peaceful world, in reality, do not - and sometimes they don't even realize this themselves. Too many people live for chaos. Simple things like stirring up trouble, creating rumours, cutting down the self-esteem of others for your own pleasure, and turning brothers against brothers, are just a few examples of how people enjoy disturbing the peace. Not only this, but it's usually the smallest, and silliest of things that end up tearing families apart, constituting illogical grudges that last for decades. So if we cannot even play nice with our own flesh and blood, how are we ever supposed to get along with people of different cultures, religions, and ideology? How can a world create peace with people like this? Well, the answer to that rhetorical question is… it can't.

But the Cold Surgery changed all this, it provided a solution to the thousands-of-years-old problem: It confirmed that although peaceful people are not native to Earth, they can be created. The Cold Surgery, the cure for humanity, was the only way to save our race. Every citizen of the world would be required to take the cure if the Movement was to be successful. And if anyone refused to become a logical being who believed in universal peace, equality, and intelligence, they would perish. It may sound harsh, but it was the rational thing to do. Disorder could never be allowed in the New World. Peace and chaos never co-exist, it's either one or the other. This is how it was, and would continue to be.

The Cold Cognition Movement was not a complex one. We had no secret agenda or plans to rule the world. What we wanted was simple: peace, equality, and intelligence. That is all. We did not desire money, resources, or political power. And for this reason, our Movement would be successful, as we did not lust for any of the bargaining tools that would be thrown at us to stop. We only wanted to create a world of peaceful people, and we would not rest until we achieved this goal. Quite frankly, even though we would be met with considerable resistance, no one would be able to stop us. Because we weren't the irrational extremists who lusted for blood and power. We were the pacifists who finally decided to take a stand and do what was necessary to have our peaceful, nonviolent world. Once the citizens of the globe realized the truth, they would not fight us, they would join us. The Earth would no longer be the home of unthinkable violence, bloodshed, chaos, and ignorance, but the residence of an entirely rational human race. No more would the ground be covered in the blood from senseless wars. No more would rivers of tears flow because of unspeakable injustice. No more would ignorance rule the minds of us all. For the Cold Surgery would fix the major flaw of human beings, and the Cold Cognition Movement would ensure the Old World was destroyed and the New World take its place.

The New World was so close that I could almost taste it. It wouldn't be long until world peace was a real entity and no longer a foolish fantasy. I was honoured to be a part of the very Movement that would make this impossible dream a reality. I played a big role in selecting the citizens of the New World. I was helping create a world where women would be seen as equals to men, where skin colour and ethnicity would be insignificant, where education was universal, and where crime was a thing of the past. The Cold Cognition Movement was the answer to the world's current state of affairs, and I would not rest until our mission was complete.

Peace. Equality. Intelligence.

****

One Month Later

At exactly 6:15 a.m., I walked into the large white cafeteria. I entered at the exact same time every day, after getting my required five to six hours of sleep. The other 18 to 19 hours of the day were dedicated to working at my designated position, seven days a week.

The cafeteria was busy. There was always a constant flow as the kitchen operated 24/7 along with every other room in the facility. I suppose one of the benefits of not being burdened with emotions, is that we were never mentally exhausted. I never became bored or tired of my task, I simply did it because it needed to be done. However, I did eventually become physically exhausted, hence the five to six hours of sleep. Today as I carried my tray filled with nutritious food, I scanned the dark blue chairs and tables, trying to find a place to sit. I found an empty seat near the back of the cafeteria where Devon and Dawson were sitting. As I began walking towards the back table, I passed Sylvan and Mrs. Rundle who were sitting together. We made eye contact and the two of them nodded their heads in acknowledgement, I nodded back without stopping to chat. We had nothing to chat about anyways, we all had jobs to get to and small talk was a waste of precious time. I then walked past a table filled with White Soldiers. Although they didn't have their helmets on, you could tell they were part of our armed forces due to the uniforms they wore: which were noticeably thicker and padded with indestructible material more so than mine and the other non-soldiers. Calmar was sitting amongst the soldiers, and he noticed me as well. I instantly remembered our kiss, as it was the last clear memory I had of us. For some reason I expected to feel my heart skip a beat and my pulse start to quicken, but of course, nothing happened. I simply looked at him and he looked at me, nothing more. So I looked away and continued directly towards the table ahead of me. I sat down in the empty chair in between Devon and Dawson. Devon was the first to speak:

"Good morning, Teslin."

She spoke in a polite tone of voice.

"Good morning," I replied, making eye contact.

It wasn't weird anymore to see her long blonde hair slicked back into a plain pony tail, or her face without make-up. I think mainly because she didn't matter to me as much. Now that my memories of her were not accompanied by nostalgia and fondness, they were simply facts of my past life.

"Good morning," the voice came from Dawson.

I gave him a nod and began to eat my breakfast, digging into the pile of fresh fruit.

We continued to eat for some time in silence, until Devon broke the silence as she finished her meal and got up to leave the table.

"Have a good day everyone."

"You too." I said in a forced friendly manner.

Then Dawson stood up, having finished his breakfast as well.

"See you later, Teslin."

"Later," I replied.

Then the two of them left the table and walked out of the cafeteria, leaving me to finish my breakfast alone at a table full of white uniforms.

After my breakfast, I made my way through the now-familiar winding white hallways in the direction of the Communications Headquarters. I passed many faces on my route, and I knew most of them by now. I memorized their faces, their names, and their position, but I had never actually talked to the large majority of them. As you only interacted with people when it was necessary to complete your given task, all other reasons for conversation were not permitted at this time. Our main focus was the global success of the Cold Cognition Movement, and everything we did was to promote our cause, which is why interaction for the sole purpose of socialization was deemed illogical and therefore, not allowed.

To be quite honest, I didn't miss the pointless niceties and gossip, but then again, 'I was a completely different person,' I thought as I pushed through the doors of the Communications Headquarters.

Commander Armena stood in the middle of the room as she always did, shouting orders into her headset. She held her slender yet muscular body in a perfectly erect posture, making herself appear even taller than she already was. I remembered the first time I met Armena, I felt so intimidated and frightened. Yet now, without my emotions hindering my better judgment, I saw her as a strong, ruthless leader, who was excellently qualified for her position. She had an impressive background as an officer of the Special Forces, as well as experience in government intelligence agencies. Armena was also a great mentor, and as a result, she let me take the lead on many cases, coaching me as we went along so that if one day something happened to her, I would be ready to take over her role as Commander.

Although I did not have nearly as much experience as Armena, apparently I had an innate talent for this sort of thing. Which was considered a great asset, as I did not need years of experience if I was a natural and could be easily coached. Today was going to be another exceptionally busy day. I could tell by the numbers and codes flashing up on the multiple screens that made up the enormous screen on the front wall of the room. This technical language used to be gibberish to me, but now it was like reading words from a book. The numbers and letters symbolized the different situations in which we were currently faced with. They could be concerning civil unrest all the way up to military retaliation. Lately we had been dealing with many attempted government military attacks, mainly because we had taken over all the major airports in the world.

Our Movement was advancing at such a rapid pace that we were presently the centre of every nation's attention. Countries were forced to take military action in their attempts to stop us. Unfortunately for them, we had insiders in every government of every powerful nation in the world, and received critical intel on planned attacks before they could even give the command to their own soldiers. The world was quickly realizing that they were losing; every second they took trying to decide what to do next, was another second that the Cold Cognition Movement grew stronger.

Our growth was incredibly fast, gaining hundreds of thousands of new followers every day. Hundreds of hospitals and laboratories around the world were being converted into satellite facilities for our Movement on the daily. There were few places in the world that we had no eyes or ears. And although our main goal was to continue to create an intelligent race of beings, we also had an intense focus on destroying the world's defense systems. Once we conquered the world's military resources, it would be an effortless task to gather the scared and helpless civilians that were chosen to join our Movement. The rest of the earth's population would, of course, be terminated. This would be the easiest part to carry out. An almost anticlimactic ending to the Old World and beginning of the New World. This ending would happen. We would have our New World. For even a small population of rational, highly-educated beings, was proving to be too much for the current illogical humans of the earth. The world was trying to play a game of checkers with advanced human beings who were experts at the game of chess. It wasn't a fair game, I admit. But we weren't playing to be fair, we were playing to win.

"What is the status of the latest incoming attack?" I asked Armena loudly.

"A convoy of ten military vehicles two minutes away from the town border, seven minutes away from our facility." She answered me while entering data into the computer and speaking orders into the mic of her headset.

I looked ahead to the big screen that had now expanded one of its smaller centre screens into a considerably larger one, projecting live feed of the heavily armed convoy headed towards us. I manipulated the holographic computer in front of me to zoom in on the picture. There had to be about fifty soldiers in total, all sitting snugly inside the ten massively armoured M1 tanks. They obviously meant business, and yet they obviously did not know what we were capable of.

"How would you handle this situation, Teslin?"

She was testing me of course, something she did quite a lot.

I glanced over at the live feed before I replied. The tanks were now 90 seconds away from crossing the town border, and only minutes away from us, their targets. But they would never make it over the border, I would make sure of this.

"Send the drone. Configure the destruction radius of the nuclear missile to encompass only the area of all ten tanks. I want this missile to be as concentrated and exact as possible."

I turned my attention to Armena and she gave me the nod of approval. I instantly repeated my recommendation into the mic on my own headset. Seconds after I spoke, the new configurations of the missile's target range popped up on my screen, waiting for my approval before sending the drone. I approved them, and the information was sent to a drone that was just seconds away from the tanks (we had at least six to twenty drones flying around the town border at all times for visual and defence purposes). Moments later the drone was hovering over the military convoy, focusing on its target. The target was locked in and a red screen immediately appeared on Armena's screen. She entered in the four-digit authorization code, and the missile was released. They were six seconds away from the border.

"May your souls be at peace," Armena said.

The screen that used to show a group of ten deadly M1 tanks was now replaced with a mushroom cloud of fire and smoke from the nuclear explosion, wiping out the entire tactical team that attempted to cross into the town of Canmore.

The rest of the day went on with not as much excitement. In general, most days consisted of collecting data on individuals and directing White Soldiers on who to bring in for the Cold Surgery, who to harvest, and who to dispose of completely. Our facility directed the operations within Western Canada, including the provinces of British Columbia, Alberta, Saskatchewan and Manitoba. However, because we were not dealing with an extremely large population, we frequently lent our services to the most North-West states of the United States. In special cases, we also provided input to the Commanders in every continent of the world (since our facility was the first of its kind, any questions about management were directed to us). As I was checking the statistics of a fifteen-year-old boy and deemed him appropriate for organ harvesting, I remembered what Armena had said earlier this morning when we obliterated the small army: "May your souls be at peace." Her comment made me wonder whether it was simply just a saying or if it meant something more. If she really did believe in souls, then did that mean she believed in an afterlife? In a heaven or a hell? Does that mean she believes in a God?

'Do I believe in a God?' I asked myself.

I was surprised that I didn't have an immediate answer to this question. Curious about why I couldn't come up with a verdict, I questioned Armena on the topic.

"Armena, do we believe in a God?" I asked bluntly.

She stopped typing on her holographic keyboard and turned to look at me, something she rarely ever did. Something about this question must have really caught her attention, but only for a second, as her focus switched back to her glowing screen as she replied:

"We believe in the most logical choice. With any predicament we look at the facts before making the most rational decision. The argument of whether or not there is a God is no different. On one side, there is the belief that our world and its inhabitants were created by an omnipotent Creator, someone or something more powerful than the universe itself. On the other hand, there is the theory that our world was created out of pure chance and life was conceived due to evolution. There is obvious proof in evolution. For example, natural selection, and the genetic commonalities of all living things. Just the fact that domesticated dogs evolved from wolves, proves that the process of evolution is undisputable. Many people, who consider themselves intelligent and educated, completely embrace the Theory of Evolution and dismiss those that believe in God as uneducated, and ignorant to the facts of science.

However, one interesting fact about scientific experiments in the laboratory, is that while we can clone and genetically modify cells, we cannot create something out of nothing. Therefore, we cannot dismiss the belief of creation altogether, since we cannot create ourselves. Also there has been many unexplainable and miraculous healings in the medical field which cannot just be regarded as inconclusive. Nothing is ever inconclusive, there is always an explanation. Therefore, because of this uncertainty, there is a possibility that spiritual healing took place. A small chance, but a chance nonetheless. Although our current stance leans toward the findings of science, what people tend to overlook is that man made this theory, and that they are choosing to put their faith in the findings of scientists, who are no better than anyone else. May I remind you that they also have feelings and skew results to get what they want. Scientists are not completely logical and pure of mind as we are. Sometimes they simply wanted to make up an answer to a question. This is where emotions get in the way, and the truth is blurred. Once a human takes a stance on which side they believe in, there seems to be little you can do to change their mind, emotions are too strong. Therefore, what irrational humans do not understand, is that it takes just as much faith to believe in a God as it does to believe in no God."

She paused for a second to catch her breath after her long speech.

I took advantage of the silence to question her further, "So with the current facts that we have, what is our stance? Do we believe in God or not?"

"We do not have a definite stance, as we do not currently know the full truth. If we are able to one day create something out of nothing then there is no God, as we have the power of creation. But until then, it does not directly affect our Movement and what we stand for, so it is not an issue. We are focused on bringing peace, equality and intelligence to this world. With total intelligence will come the truth about how this world began. So if you want to find out the truth about God, Teslin Grove, then it is pertinent that you focus on the task at hand. Because you'll never know the answer if the Movement does not succeed."

And with that, are conversation came to an abrupt end. I took the hint. It was not the time nor the place to be taking about such things we did not have the answers to; I should be concentrating all my energy on the expansion of the Movement. All my other questions would work themselves out after we had universal intellect. Of course they would. So I took Armena's advice and went back to determining the status of every resident in the City of Edmonton.

As my team and I quickly plowed through hundreds of thousands of residents, almost completing every file of the one million residents of the city, Armena received a phone call from the creator of the

Cold Cognition Movement himself, Dr. Joshua Lacombe. I could tell it was him from the small flashing white box that appeared on the bottom corner of Armena's screen. It only flashed white when he called. I had never spoken with him personally, only people with the highest of ranks were contacted by Dr. Lacombe, such as Armena, my father, and anyone with the title of Commander attached to their name. All I knew, is that whenever he phoned it was for something important (which Armena would tell me as soon as the call was over). It was a waste of time just waiting for her to end the call, so I continued on with my work while I waited. My team was just establishing a video conference with the White Soldiers on the ground in Edmonton, when Armena stole my attention.

"I have been transferred to London, England. They are in need of my expertise. The transfer is effective immediately. The chopper is waiting for me outside as we speak, ready to take me to the airport."

I stared back at her in silence, the realization of what this meant slowly washing over me: 'If Armena was leaving that meant…'

"You're in charge now, Teslin. You will be taking over my position as Commander of the Communications Headquarters. I would wish you good luck, but you don't need it. You have been trained by the best, and you are more than capable of succeeding in this position. Good bye, Teslin." She extended her open hand towards me. I grasped it tightly.

"Good bye, Armena."

It was all I could think of to say, but there was really nothing more to say. She was my mentor, my advisor, but I had no emotional connection with this woman. Truth be told, I was quite indifferent to her leaving. Our communications department would continue prosperously with or without Armena. I wasn't happy nor sad she was leaving us. It was a fact, and nothing more. I let go of her hand and she turned to leave. I didn't even feel the need to watch her walk away. My attention was directed elsewhere, at the small flashing white box at the bottom corner of my screen. I swore I felt a shiver of fear run down my spine, but that was impossible. It must have just been a ghost emotion, something that I would have normally felt in this situation was now just playing tricks on my mind. I quickly shook off this strange feeling and pressed the tiny white button. The second I lifted my finger off the holographic screen, a cold and low voice whispered into my ears:

"Hello, Teslin. It's a pleasure to finally meet you. I've heard such wonderful things about you."

It took me a moment to compose myself before I could respond.

'How strange,' I thought to myself. Calming down my heart rate wasn't a usual thing for me anymore, not after the Cold Surgery. I chalked it up to my prefrontal cortex not being able to override the significant rush of fear and anxiety that came from getting a personal call from the man in charge.

"Thank you. It's nice to finally meet you too, Sir. What can I do for you?" I asked.

"Well, Teslin, I just wanted you to hear my voice, and to know that I will now be contacting you due to your recent job advancement. However, before the title of Commander is yours, I have something of a test for you… Right now you have a video conference on hold from the White Soldiers on-site in the City of Edmonton, don't you? Well the outcome of what they are about to tell you is what I will be testing you on. If you are qualified for the role of Commander, you will know what to do. Remember what we strive to create, Teslin. A world of peace, equality, and intelligence."

The line went dead. The cold whisper in my ear had vanished. And I couldn't stop my hands from shaking as I pressed the button to activate the call with the White Soldiers.

****

"There's about 100 children in this hospital. Most are terminally ill with cancer or other diseases, and some have major brain or heart defects. Either way, none of these children are in good enough condition to transport to our nearest facility. We would have to treat them on-site before we can move them. What are your orders, Commander?"

The White Soldier who spoke, was standing in the main waiting room of a children's hospital. Observing the scene from a camera that one of the soldiers held, I could see scared parents holding onto each other as they huddled up against the walls of the hospital behind the White Soldiers. They had no idea of what was to come of them or their dying children. Amongst the small crowd, I noticed quite a beautiful bouquet of white roses that one of the mothers held in her trembling hands. I zoomed in on the roses to find a small card that read: *You can win this, Peter. You are strong!*

"Show me the children." I ordered the soldier in a strong and confident voice.

"Yes, ma'am."

He immediately took the camera from whoever was holding it, and began to walk through the white hallways where I could see many doors that led to patients' rooms. The soldier picked a room, opened the door and walked in. Inside the room were two beds inhabited by two small children attached to a variety of machines. The young kids were asleep, possibly in comas, and did not notice the soldier.

"Show me more." I commanded.

He did as he was told. Going from room to room and showing me the sick children. Most of them were sleeping, and if they were awake they were hardly at all conscious of the strange man dressed all in white standing in their room. Finally, we reached a room where a child, about five or six years old, appeared to be cognizant enough to converse.

"I want to speak to the child."

The camera went closer to the little boy's face. His sky blue eyes were wide with terror, and he clutched the teddy bear in his arms as he pushed himself as far back as he could in his hospital bed. For some reason his eyes reminded me of someone, but this wasn't the time to think of who.

"What is your name?" I asked the boy.

The boy looked so frightened that I didn't expect him to reply, but he did, in such a soft voice that I could hardly hear him.

"Peter. My name's Peter."

"Peter, what is your diagnoses?"

The child looked at me questioningly, as if he didn't understand the question. I tried again.

"Peter, why are you sick?"

This seemed to create some recognition in his light blue eyes.

"I am sick because I have a brain tumour."

"How long did the doctors say you have to live?"

"The doctors told me two months."

I could see in the child's eyes that he did not comprehend the brevity of two months.

"Thank you, Peter."

"You're welcome."

I was just about to tell the soldier to exit the room when the curious child asked me a question.

"What is your name?"

"My name is Teslin."

The child smiled at this, probably because it was not a common name.

"I have to go now, Peter."

As I spoke, the camera began to move farther away from the boy.

"Goodbye, Teslin."

"Goodbye, Peter."

Once the soldier left Peter's room he turned the camera onto his own face. He wasn't wearing his helmet so I could see his face. I think I had seen him before. I'm not sure where, but I think he might have been one of my brother's friends. 'I wonder what has become of my brother,' I asked myself. I hadn't even thought about him since the Movement began. I guess one day I'd find out, but it wasn't important now.

"What's the verdict, Commander?"

I knew the verdict before he even showed me the kids. These children were extremely sick with all kinds of conditions, some of them could even be contagious. The data currently on my computer screen told me that most of the children were diagnosed with cancer. However, even with the cure for cancer (which we did possess) it would take time to completely cure these children. This was valuable time that we did not possess. It wasn't rational to thin out our resources trying to save these children when we had plenty of healthy children to choose from. It was a cold-hearted decision, but it was in our best interest not to keep the sick children. They would only be a hindrance to our Movement. Only the strongest and the smartest survived in the New World, there was no room for the weak. So I spoke the words that I knew I had to. The words that Dr. Lacombe would have wanted me to say:

"Kill them all."

The White Soldier looked temporarily taken aback. His eyes went wide with shock, but he quickly recovered to his normal stoic state.

"Yes, Commander. And what about the parents? I imagine they will try to stop us."

"Kill. Them. All." I repeated. My voice even colder than before.

"Yes, Commander."

The soldier walked back into the waiting area where the rest of the White Soldiers stood, anticipating my orders. Our soldier's camera view of the hospital was temporarily shut off as we hacked into the main cameras of the hospital to get a better overall picture of the scene. The commanding White Soldier stood in front of his team and the trembling parents. He put on his white helmet that covered his entire face, took out the gun from the holster on his hips, and released the command from his lips:

"Kill them all."

An orchestra of bullets rang through the air, accompanied by shrill screams and gut-wrenching bellows of suffering. The bullets found their way throughout the entire hospital, adorning the white walls and floors with splashes of crimson as they acquired their targets. It was the most terrifying art that you could possibly imagine. The precious lives of the most innocent were sacrificed for the noblest of causes: peace, equality, and intelligence. As I watched the bloody images, I felt the words that Armena had spoken only hours before caress my lips: "May your souls be at peace." I hoped for the sake of the children that there was a heaven, that there was a God. For there was no place for these souls in the New World.

The White Soldiers were nearly done their mission, and I began to scan the cameras to look for any survivors. That's when I came across the live image of the waiting room. A place that no longer possessed any waiting people, for their fate had already been decided. Once again the bouquet of roses caught my eye, it lay by the body of the mother who had clasped them so tightly. The roses weren't white anymore. They were red: completely covered in blood - in her blood. The note that accompanied the flowers was now smudged to the point of illegibility. But I remember what it said.

"Check on the boy named Peter." I yelled into the mic.

The Commander of the team immediately marched into the room of the little boy, and switched the camera so I could see from his own perspective. The bed where the child lay before was now empty.

"Find him," I ordered.

It did not take long for the soldier to discover the hiding place of young Peter, which was behind the long curtains that hung around his bed. He was curled up in a ball with his back pressed up against the wall, rhythmically rocking himself back and forth. Remembering the words written on the small card, I thought how foolish and illogical it was to promise something so unattainable to a child of Peter's condition. He couldn't win this. He was not strong enough. Only the strongest survived in the New World. The bullet was released from the gun and buried itself deep into Peter's chest.

As I looked into the child's icy blue eyes, suddenly a flash of pain shot through my mind and I saw an image of Nikita's eyes. It caught me off guard and I staggered forward, grasping the edge of my desk so I did not fall over. I looked into the closing eyes of Peter again, and another agonizing stab of pain paralyzed my mind. Another image of Nikita flashed in my mind, the moment she looked into my eyes before my father slashed her throat open. I felt her pain, her suffering. Another blow made me grasp the side of my head in anguish, and the emotional memories all flooded in at once: Nikita running ecstatically to greet me at the door, my mother's laugh, my father's smile, the joy of friendship that I had with Dawson and Devon, my beautiful mountains that had watched me grow up. I remembered the fear I felt with Mrs. Rundle. I remembered the six of us fighting for our lives in the bitter cold, knowing that this was all wrong and that we had to stop it. I remembered the warm fire that Calmar and I sat together by in beautiful silence. I remembered our kiss, the drill, the stabbing, the screams, and the electric shocks. All the pain that I had been told I no longer possessed came flooding in and reeked havoc on my whole being. My body twisted and turned from the raging emotions screaming and clawing at my insides, ripping and tearing into my raw flesh as I held onto my black wooden desk for dear life. I tore my eyes from the desk and onto my screen that held the image of sweet Peter, his sky blue eyes closed forever. This was all my fault. I did this. I killed so many precious, innocent, little

Peters. My insides turned again and I felt like I was going to vomit. I wanted to die. I reached for my headset. I was just about to tear the horrid contraption off of my head and leave this heinous place forever when a terrifying, cold voice resonated in my ears…

"Well done, Commander Teslin Grove."

****

I held onto the sides of the bathroom stall to keep myself balanced as I expelled all of my food and then some into the porcelain toilet. I had excused myself quietly from the Communications Headquarters in the calmest manner possible and marched to the nearest washroom as fast as I could, throwing myself into the first open stall I could find. While I finished emptying my stomach, a new substance was released from my body.

Tears came pouring out of my eyes, splashing into the water below and creating circular ripples as if it were raining. I watched the falling teardrops for a while in admiration, mostly because I never thought I would see them again. I didn't think I was capable of making tears, because that would mean I was capable of creating emotions. The small waterfall originating from my eyes began to let up, and I believed my little episode was over when the images of blood splattered walls and crimson covered roses filled my mind. My stomach heaved again. This time I was sure there was nothing left. I tried to stand up but lost my balance and slid down the stall's metal wall. As I sat there, feeling empty and numb on the cold hard floor, I felt my old self coming back to me. The familiar mind of chaotic thoughts started a small whirlwind that grew into a deadly tornado:

This Cold Cognition Movement is not a peaceful Movement at all. The aim may be to have peace, but it certainly isn't going to be acquired in a peaceful way. The word 'Movement' shouldn't even be used to describe it, because it isn't a Movement at all! It was a mass killing. This has happened before in history, these mass killings: The Nazis slaughtered countless innocent men, women and children, the horrifying deaths in the Rwandan Genocide, the Holodomor - where Stalin created an artificial famine that killed millions of Ukrainians by starving them to death. These acts of unthinkable horror were not any different than what we were doing. We kept the strongest and brightest and terminated the rest. I was responsible for the deaths of so many innocent lives. It didn't matter if we said we had a noble cause or not. No reason was good enough to kill innocent people. Not even world peace. But it was too late.

I could never take back the things that I did, the lives that I ended. I would have to live with visions of deadly explosions, lethal bullets, and screaming children replaying in my mind over and over again. The piercing eyes of little Peter will forever burn in the back of my thoughts. What kind of Movement had I become a part of? What kind of monster had I become? And why, all of a sudden, did I have emotions clouding up my mind? I wasn't supposed to have emotions. Did the surgery not work properly, like the first time it didn't work on Calmar? Or did seeing Peter's blue eyes trigger a domino effect of emotionally charged memories that had overridden the effects of the surgery?

Then I remembered the children in the Enlightenment Program. My father had been successfully teaching these children not to use their emotions for six years. If the Movement could condition children, who have little control of their emotions and wild imaginations, then surely they could condition adults to think the same way. Suddenly it all started to make sense. The reason behind the kidnappings, the surgery, the prohibition of socializing. I understood why the Movement needed as much manpower as possible, and a way to quickly get people on their side. The Cold Surgery was the perfect answer. The fog of uncertainty in my mind began to clear away. The surgery didn't even work! Or at least, not like they told us it did.

Even if Dr. Lacombe had found the connection largely responsible for transferring emotional information onto the prefrontal cortex, there is no way that it would stop all emotions from reaching the frontal cortex. The brain was a very resourceful creature, if one path was blocked it would find or create another. Especially in a child, the brain was so plastic that if the damage wasn't too drastic, it could repair itself. But it wasn't an issue that the Cold Surgery didn't completely work, because it was the trauma and intensive conditioning that mattered.

People will believe anything if they are told something is true enough times. Constantly throughout the day the slogan of the Cold Cognition Movement was heard over the speaker system, or seen on screens: Peace. Equality. Intelligence. These three words were told over and over again to us, as well as the insistence to always make the most logical choice. Telling people to fight for universal peace, equality and intelligence was a way to keep people motivated and make their conscious feel less guilty. That way, even if people knew something was not quite right, they clung on to the idea that they were doing good. And with no social communication, there was no way to discuss our thoughts or ideas about the Movement. We simply did as we were told.

Humans were always capable of logical thinking and working together, it apparently just took a traumatic experience to convince them of that. In our new state of mind, we were conditioned to believe that we could only think logically. Even though we always had the mind power to break the spell, the conditioning was too good, too clever, for most people to even realize. And for those that did, they were probably too confused or scared to say anything. I had to admit that the whole plan was brilliant, yet so fragile. Its success rested on the fact that people were willing to believe it was real. Luckily for them, people are willing to believe in anything. It brought propaganda to a whole new level of brainwashing, and was no doubt the most successful placebo effect in history.

The 'Cold Cognition Effect' is what historians would call it one day, that is, if it ever was stopped and the world went back to normal. But how can you stop such a giant, well-oiled machine? Especially because it wasn't just a Movement, it was a war. And not a war against nations, but against every resident of the earth. There were only two sides to this war, the followers of the Cold Cognition Movement and those of the Resistance. This is why it was so different than any other war before it, because no one came out a winner. We did not fight for power or gold, but for minds. You either lost your life or your emotions. But the promise of peace that was attached to the latter made it the more appealing choice. Whether or not peace actually did happen, one thing was for certain: The world would never be the same after this war. You wouldn't be able to go back to your normal life after this. I was now questioning all of it, if it was even real or not, or just a way to cut down the human population and keep only those with the strongest and most desirable traits. Anything was possible at this point. The only thing I was sure of, was that I had to do something to stop it. Even if I failed miserably, I had to try.

A sudden sharp tapping noise of heavy heels walking across the hard floor shook me back to reality. I quickly pushed myself up off the ground, wiping my tears and trying to compose my current shaken state of mind. I took a deep breath, flushed the toilet, and walked out of the stall, walking straight towards the sink so I could splash water on my face. This was in case anyone noticed my red skin and eyes (so they would think it was because of the frigid water and not from crying). The icy water on my hot flesh felt so pleasant that I almost smiled, but I didn't, because I felt the stare of someone watching me. I instinctively looked up, and in the reflection of the mirror was a beautiful woman severely glaring straight into my green eyes. She had the same colour hair as mine and the same facial bone structure. This was no ordinary woman. This was my mother.

I turned around to face her, and she walked towards me and handed me a small towel. I took it without a word and dried my face. Her blue-green eyes were still locked onto mine; the way she always did when she wanted to scare me into confessing something I did. I couldn't control my emotions any longer, and I burst out crying uncontrollably.

"Mom, I killed all of those children. They are all dead because of me!" I said in between heavy sobs. "I can't do this anymore! I can't be a part of killing innocent people anymore! This is wrong!"

"They were already dead, Teslin. You just sped along the process. You did what had to be done." My mother's voice came out harsh and unsympathetic.

"I'm a monster! A murderer!"

"Teslin, get a hold of yourself!"

She slapped me hard across the face, and I was in such a state of shock that I instantly stopped crying.

"You're no more a monster than you were before."

"W-What do you mean?" I stuttered, holding my burning cheek.

"Remember when your friend got pregnant, and you told me that there was no way she could take care of a baby? You told me that her parents would disown her, and that the only way out of the situation was to get an abortion. I tried to convince you otherwise but you fought against me, saying that it was her body and her right. You drove her to the clinic, and you held her hand as they ripped the fetus from its life source. How is that any different from what you did today?"

"You know that's not the same thing, mom! It was a fetus! Not a person! I can't believe you are even bringing that up, it's illogical!" I was yelling now.

"Oh is it now? Because the last time I checked, a fetus is an organism made up of cells just like you and I. The only difference is that a fetus hasn't left the womb yet. It's still alive and it's still human."

"It's just a bunch of underdeveloped cells! Not a real person."

"Well in that case, if you can tell yourself that a fetus is nothing, you can tell yourself that now. Those children in the hospital were all just a bunch of cells anyways."

"That's not true! They had lives, memories and families!"

"And you think that that fetus wouldn't have had a life? The fact of the matter is you took away her chance of survival. She never got to have her own life or meet her family, you took that away from her. Exactly like the way you just took away the future from those sick kids. But at least you gave the children a bit of a chance, I mean you wouldn't even let the fetus fight for her life, because she didn't have a voice to scream at you with. Don't think for a second that if she did, she wouldn't fight for her right to live! Because she would have. But you seem to be fine with ending her life, so you can do it again now."

My mother took a step closer towards me before she spoke again.

"It's a cruel world, Teslin. It always has been. But now we have a chance to change that. We can create a world without murder or violence or hate. It won't be easy, and many sacrifices like the ones today will have to be made. But it will all be worth it, and we can finally live in a world of peace." Her face changed and she almost looked scared. She grabbed tightly onto my arms and stared forcefully into my eyes, "You have to be strong in this New World, Teslin. If you are weak, you will die."

She let go of me and stepped back, her face returning to one of familiar indifference.

"Now clean up and get back to your task."

She marched out of the washroom and left me alone with my thoughts. I looked at my reflection in the mirror. I looked scared. Taking a deep breath, I closed my eyes and calmed down my nerves. When I opened my eyes, an emotionless face stared back at me. Now I looked deadly. And appropriately so, as the next world war had begun. But this one was different; the ground knew it, the birds knew it, the wolves knew it, even the mountains knew it, because this war was not fueled by hate or greed, but by no emotion at all. By only logic. There would be no rules to this war, what needed to be done would be done in whatever means necessary. The Movement wanted to keep only the smartest and strongest, and wipe out all the rest. They wanted to start fresh, in a New World of equality, peace, and intelligence. From a logical standpoint I guess it made sense to wipe out most of the population. Our world had become more violent, hateful and greedy than ever before. I always had hoped that these people would change if they got a second chance, but this time they wouldn't even be given a chance. This time, they would only be given one option, death. Not even a humane death, but a death of necessity. It was going to be a cold world, not one of warmth, dreams, imagination or love. Unless something could be done to stop it, this would be the future of the world.

I had to try to do something. If I could somehow tell people that they have been conditioned to believe they have no emotions, maybe they would realize what they were doing was wrong and fight back. However, I couldn't just announce this over the intercom, they would be skeptical of my words (as they were taught to be) and I would no doubt be killed before I even gave my whole speech. I would have to be smart about it. I needed help from a source above my father. Someone in great power that people would listen to. I thought hard about it; Who would have that kind of pull? Then it came to me, that cold voice in my ears: Dr. Joshua Lacombe. If he had the power to create all of this, he must have the power to stop it! I had to find a way to get in contact with him! I had to convince him to end this war! I had to do it, because quite frankly, I don't know who else would.

Chapter Eleven

The next two hours were the hardest of my life. Trying to pretend that nothing was wrong, while continuously deciding the morbid fates of innocent people, was slowly killing me as much as it was killing them. To make matters worse, during those couple of hours I sentenced more people to death than to join our Movement (an emotionless future, but a future nonetheless). I could not save these people even if I wanted to, because their cruel ending happened to be the rational choice. If I had spared them, my cover, and any chance I had at stopping this war, would be gone. I had to tough it out until the end of my shift. In that thirty seconds when shift-change occurred, no one was looking at my screen. They would only be concerned with logging out of their own computers and making room for the others that took over their post. Even so, I had to be quick and I couldn't get caught. If the smallest suspicion arouse it would all be over.

In those thirty seconds, I had to search the database and send Dr. Lacombe's contact information to my personal device. It would no doubt be a blocked number, but I had learned enough about hacking in the last month that I was confident in my abilities to solve this little problem. I was almost too overqualified for the job after what our department had to deal with in the past few weeks. Due to the recent overwhelming government interest in our Movement, we had quite a few intelligence agencies attempting to hack into our computer systems. Of course they were unsuccessful, but mainly because our tech support was the best in the world. Nonetheless, we took a step further by constantly changing our passcodes every few hours, so that even if these government agents got through our first wall of defence, they would be met with a solid wall of continually changing codes. So in light of all the recent tech training I had learned, tracing a blocked number was not an issue. The possible issue, was the fact that my plan rested on the hope that this was still the doctor's current number, and that he hadn't switch it yet. If this was the case, then I would have to wait until the next time he contacted me and try it all again. I prayed that this would not be the case, as with every lost second the Movement grew more indestructible.

To be honest, I didn't even know if it was possible to put a stop to it after only a month since its international birth. 'How on earth am I supposed to make a difference if even trained military soldiers and intelligence agents can't make a dent?' I thought to myself in despair. A glance up to the large digital clock on the main screen resulted in me pushing these doubtful thoughts to the back of mind, and focusing on my task of the present moment. It was a minute to shift-change, and I was ready. Normally when I watched a clock tick down, the seconds seemed to stretch into minutes, but now they seemed to melt into milliseconds. My hands began to sweat and my blood pressure rose. This might be my only chance. There was no room for mistakes or getting caught. I wiped my hands on the pant legs of my uniform as the last five seconds counted down. Five. Four. Three. Two. One.

Typing as fast as I could, I brought up the call log and rapidly searched through the list. The people around me were now standing up and starting to leave their desks. Scrolling, scrolling, and then finally I found a blocked number. Dammit. The time didn't match up, it wasn't his call. I could see Christian, my Second-in-command, in my peripheral vision walking towards me. Every muscle in my body tensed up and I could hardly force my fingers to keep scrolling. It had to be around here, it was around this time that he called. Then finally I saw it. A blocked number that called around two hours ago, right after the massacre in the children's hospital. Without hesitation, I sent the data to my personal device and logged out of my computer almost simultaneously. Just as I pressed the last key that logged out of my session, Christian was standing behind me.

"What are you working on that requires such attention and brings you till the last second of your shift?" he asked in a deep throaty voice.

I turned around to face the man who was twice my age and double my size.

"Furthering the Movement, of course. Every second counts. I wouldn't want even one of those to go to waste." I looked him straight in the eyes, praying that my answer was sufficient enough. There was something about this man that suggested he had been a gentle giant before all this, when he still had his emotions. But now, as he stared back at me with empty eyes, I saw a terrifying monster capable of ending lives with the sound of his voice and the tap of his finger. I felt myself begin to perspire. Finally, the tall man nodded in approval, my answer was sufficient enough. I returned his nod, and then quickly moved out of his way and walked at a fast pace out the doors of the Communications Headquarters, thanking my guardian angel for not letting him see through my lie or notice the sweat on my forehead.

Keeping my legs moving at a normal pace was difficult, as every fibre in my body wanted to run through the winding hallways. All I wanted to do was lock myself in my room and wait in solitude for 3am to arrive, then I could contact him. Unfortunately, what I wanted to do and what I needed to do were two very different things. If I simply walked to my room without getting any food from the cafeteria, they would know something was wrong. I'm sure they would just think I was sick at first and send a medic, but once I checked out alright they would look for other possible answers to my unordinary behaviour. They would check my computer activity and that's when they would find what I had done. I honestly can't say what they would do next, but I imagined it wouldn't be in my favour. Needless to say, I couldn't let it get to this point. It was crucial that I remained under the radar. I was not a patient person by nature, but today I would have to be out of necessity. I had to wait until 3am. That's when I could make the call.

The reason why it had to be exactly 3am, was because there were eyes everywhere in the facility, even in my own room. The large majority of the residents in this facility believed that there was never a time nor a place where they could not be seen. Only select people knew that the cameras of every department were shut down for maintenance every day for about one to five minutes. Those in power went even further and changed the times of maintenance every day, making sure that no one could get away with anything. Fortunately, I was one of these lucky people who knew of this secret, and therefore, I knew that today at 3am, the eyes overlooking the living quarters were temporarily shut.

'This is when I would strike, when the beast was asleep,' I thought to myself as I turned down the white hallway leading to the cafeteria. As I entered the ginormous room, I walked straight towards the kitchen where I was handed a tray of food. My stomach turned as I looked down at the perfectly cooked chicken and steamed vegetables on my plate. Eating was the last thing I wanted to do, but I had to do it. I couldn't risk making even the slightest error. People would notice if I didn't eat, and that would right away cause suspicion. I was surrounded by rational minds, and could make no mistakes. So I found Dawson and Devon in the crowd and went to go sit beside them like I usually did. They barely said anything like they usually did. It was almost natural acting like I had no emotions. I suppose it was because I recently had a lot of practice. Unfortunately, this little act of mine did not last for long. As the three of us walked out of the cafeteria together, I couldn't help myself. I had to say something, they were my best friends after all. Under all the psychological conditioning they were still the same loving people, I just had to remind them of this.

So as we walked down the hallway leading to our sleeping quarters, I whispered under my breath, "Do you guys really believe in what we are doing here? I mean, we say that our cause is honourable, but I've killed more innocent people than I have saved. I guess, I just find it ironic how we want peace yet we are doing the opposite to achieve it."

Devon, who was walking slightly in front of me, stopped abruptly and turned around to face me. Dawson, who was walking on my right side, ceased walking as well. Devon glared at me with fierce eyes and her cold voice turned to ice as she spoke:

"This is the only way to create peace in a chaotic world, and you know it. Sacrifices have to be made. So whatever you're planning, Teslin, don't do it. I will have no choice but to turn you in. This Movement is more important than you or me or our friendship. Don't be an idiot."

I tried not to look like I was in shock, but how could she possibly know that I was planning something? I did nothing at all out of the ordinary. Could she really see through me that easily? I couldn't look in her scathing eyes any longer, so I turned to Dawson for help.

"Don't look so surprised, Teslin. We've known you all our lives. Of course we can tell what's going on in that head of yours," he said.

There was no sense in denying it, "So then you're okay with what we're doing here?"

Devon, who seemed to have all the answers, replied before Dawson could even open his mouth, "There has always been war in the world. But this time it's different. For the first time ever we are fighting for the future of humanity. And when we win, there will be peace, because this is the war to end all wars."

I didn't know what to say back. Suddenly my position against the Movement began to weaken by her manipulative words. Maybe she was right. There was nothing wrong about wanting peace. But then why did it feel so wrong? Forcing people to inhibit their emotions and using their subconscious fear to control them was not a world I wanted to live in. It didn't matter that it would create artificial harmony. It was wrong.

"Why are you so against peace? I thought this was what you always wanted?" the voice came from Dawson.

"I'm not against peace!" I retorted.

"Then continue working at your appointed task, continue being loyal to the Movement, and you shall have your peace." Devon spoke in such a menacing way that a shiver went done my spine. I stared at her with wide eyes, she had never spoken to me like this before. This young woman, who used to be my charming, loving, imaginative best friend, was now something completely different. She was not my friend anymore. She was my enemy.

"Good night, Teslin." She said before she turned around and walked towards her dormitory.

"Good night, Teslin," Dawson repeated as he walked off to his dorm.

"Good night," I replied quietly, although no one could hear me. I stood in silence for a moment not really sure what to do or feel, but the sounds of footsteps coming down the hallway behind me, gave the necessary jolt I needed to move forward in the direction of my own room.

****

I instantly collapsed onto my bed when I reached my private room. I found out why I had my own room, it was because of my high position of power. Normally I wouldn't have cared if I had to share a room or not, but today I was extremely grateful that no one else was in this room with me. Because no one else could see me laying on my bed, clutching the pillow like it was my lifeline. No one could see the silent tears rolling down my cheeks, and no one was there to witness hopelessness swallow me whole. I felt so alone in a place full of thousands. I couldn't remember the last time I laughed, or smiled.

Beginning to feel quite depressed, I forced myself to stay positive and think about my plan instead. There was a very small chance that it would work, I would most likely end up dead. But this almost-certain possibility didn't make me feel afraid, because I would rather be dead than live in a world without emotion. I didn't want to live in a world without laughter, or smiles, or love. A world where I had to pretend not to care. A place where the murder of the innocent was allowed in certain circumstances, and no remorse was allowed to be felt. A planet void of compassion. Just the thought of this made me clutch my pillow even tighter. What was the point of such a place? In this New World, humans would not be humans, as the very essence of what makes them human would be repressed to the point of *non-existence*.

My tear ducts abruptly stopped producing salty liquid, and instead went wide with fear and amazement. It suddenly hit me just how brilliant Dr. Lacombe's plan really was. I doubt he didn't even care that the Cold Surgery wasn't as effective as we were told. The important thing was to force people to think rationally, void of any emotions, by any means necessary. Because the reality was, it would be impossible to remove all emotions from such a complex organ as the human brain. This is why he only focussed on the part of the brain where decision making occurred, targeting a more direct area made the whole theory more probable. Even so, out of the trillions of neural connections residing in the brain, it would be next to impossible to locate every single connection that had a role in transferring emotional data to the prefrontal cortex. Yet this wasn't an issue for the sly doctor, because he wasn't really interested in cutting neural connections for every citizen of the New World for years to come. For what he truly wanted to do, was something much more alarming. He wanted to alter the very foundation of the brain. He wanted to force the brain to evolve. This time, without emotions. It was a bloody brilliant plan. People wouldn't even realize that it was occurring. If the Cold Cognition Movement did succeed in taking over the planet, all they had to do to continue the desired emotion-free state-of-mind, was to use strict control and fear as motivators. Then, as the generations went on supressing their emotions, the act would become so natural that people would eventually stop activating the emotional centres of their brain. Next, evolution would take over. And as the years passed by, the human brain would slowly loose its emotional capabilities, and eventually, emotion would no longer exist in the brain at all - or at least not in the parts that affected logical reasoning.

It was a horrifying thought; a human race evolved into emotionless robots. What made it all the more terrifying was that it could actually happen. However, there was one major complication that Dr. Lacombe had not accounted for… something that would put a hitch in his plans for a peaceful world. No matter how intelligent or rational these new beings may be, they would not want peace on their own. The reason being is simple, humans are not peaceful creatures, with or without emotions. People possessing empathy are capable of inconceivable horrors, yet so are those without empathy. Humans know how to survive. They know what they must do in order to feed, clothe, and shelter themselves. Yet unfortunately, when humans get together, chaos and violence easily breakout. Large groups of civilized people can quickly turn into a mob of dangerous animals in an instant. In reality, people cannot exist together as equals and in peace, there must always be an order, always someone in power to keep the peace. Order is established to create a false illusion of harmony, because peace is not natural, it is not real. In fact, peace is not a mutual state of tranquility, but a compromise of power. The majority must be willing to give up their control to a select group of people in order to avoid complete chaos.

'Oh my God, that's it!' the lightbulb in my brain lit up so bright I thought it would burst. All of a sudden everything made total sense. Of course the doctor was clever enough to know this, more than that, it was what he wanted. Dr. Joshua Lacombe was not interested in a utopian world of peace, equality, and intelligence, no, what he really wanted was much more human than that. He aspired to be the leader of the New World. The Cold Cognition Movement was nothing but a cover up for what he really desired, ultimate power.

I sat up in my bed, in response to this realization. Now I was more determined than ever to stop him. My mind was made up. I would put an end to this Movement, or die trying. Ironically it was his own fault that the concept of death didn't scare me anymore. Probably because it felt like I was already dead. He had taken everything away from me: my family, my friends, my freedom. I had nothing to lose. And those who have nothing to lose, are the ones who should be feared the most, because they are unpredictable and can rarely be controlled. So as I sat in my bed watching the hands of the clock tick round and round in a never-ending circle, I whispered to all the souls that I had taken, informing them that their deaths would not be in vain.

The minutes crawled by so painfully slow that I swore they were moving backwards. To make matters worse, I couldn't sleep. Every time I closed my eyes, visions of innocent blue eyes haunted my thoughts. It was impossible not to think about little Peter, about the thousands of lives I killed, about Nikita, Calmar, Devon, Dawson, Mrs. Rundle, Sylvan, little Nisku, my brother, my parents… I lay in my bed, watching the clock turn to its own steady beat, unaware of the anxiousness currently exuding from my skin. It was almost time. Very shortly the cameras in my room would be disconnected, and I would confront a man who was possibly the most powerful human being in the world. My stomach turned from the thought of his hair raising voice. This was not just any conversation. The fate of my future would be decided in the next few minutes, solely depending on the decision of Dr. Joshua Lacombe.

Of course just to spite me, the clock began to tick significantly faster as it neared the 3 o'clock mark. Time never was my friend; why should he start now? I pulled out my personal electronic device (which was basically an extremely advanced smartphone) from the pocket of my uniform, and held it tightly in my clammy hands. 'I'm ready as I'll ever be,' I thought to myself as I watched the last seconds tick down. Finally, it was time.

My hands were apparently more prepared than I was, they got right down to work, rapidly decoding the encrypted number. I looked up at the camera facing my bed, and hoped to God that it was turned off. Feeling paranoid, I threw my jacket overtop it so that it stopped staring at me (this also bought me some more precious time, because if the camera turned back on before I was finished, the tech department would momentarily think it was a problem on their side, not mine). I tore my attention back to the holographic screen. I did it. The number was deciphered and waiting for me to make the next move. My finger hoovered overtop the button that would connect the call. It was trembling. I didn't realize how scared I actually was until this moment. But I couldn't be scared now, I had to be strong; so I closed my eyes and took a deep breath. When I opened them I pressed the button before I could give it another thought. A bright light shone out of the small device, projecting a small screen onto the empty wall behind my bed. The pixelated image on the wall quickly developed into a clear picture of an attractive man in his thirties wearing a fitted black suit. The man's appearance caught me off guard; his penetrating blue eyes accented by his tan skin and dark hair were enough to leave me stunned. I wasn't quite sure who this man was, or whether or not he was real, until he spoke. A cold voice rose from the speakers on my device, and enveloped the small room.

"Hello, Teslin."

The man spoke in such a confident and intimidating tone, that I immediately wanted to hang up and bury myself under the safety of my bed covers. My throat was so dry; I was afraid that if I opened my mouth to speak nothing would come out. Thank goodness my subconscious determination was stronger than my doubts: 'You have made it this far, Teslin. You can't back out now,' the voice in my head forcefully encouraged.

"H-Hello, Dr. Lacombe," I stammered in a quiet and hesitant voice. I already sounded defeated, my inside voice began angrily shouting at me, 'You're never going to get anywhere showing this kind of weakness! Suck it up, and be strong!'

A crooked smile appeared on Dr. Lacombe's face; he seemed to be amused by my feebleness, "I presume you went to a lot of trouble to contact me so late. So tell me, Miss Grove, what is it that you want?"

"I want you to stop the Movement." I almost shocked myself at the abruptness of my request and the fierceness in my voice. Determination and ruthlessness were apparently very present in my mind, in spite of my fear and doubt. Yet by the calm look on the doctor's face, he wasn't surprised at all. He almost looked as if he had been expecting it.

"And why would I ever want do that? To put an end to the world's only chance at peace?" he asked.

"Well you must have a very distorted definition of peace; one that includes killing innocent men, women and children." Anger began to seep into my voice.

Dr. Lacombe tilted his head to the side in a curious sort of way, "You've been working so well for the past month, making sacrifices as we've all had to do. So why is it that you are suddenly so against us? Why were the children in the hospital so important to you, Teslin?"

My heart skipped a beat. The doctor was so direct, that it made me uncomfortable, and I started to lose my head.

"They were innocent children! They couldn't even defend themselves," I said furiously.

"Thousands of innocent children die every day from disease and starvation. Why aren't you upset about those children? Why are the ones that just died more important? Millions of children have died in the span of your lifetime, and you seemed to have lived quite a happy life despite this."

"But I never killed any of those children! I killed these ones!" I was yelling now. But despite my outburst, Dr. Lacombe kept a calm and powerful demeanour. He began to lecture me:

"Don't you realize that once our New World is complete, no child will ever die from hunger or violence again? And with our focus so heavily centered on medical advancement instead of fighting wars and killing each other, eventually children won't have to die of diseases either. What you did, Teslin, was a required sacrifice that will strengthen the Movement in the long run. You can't break down every time someone dies. You never did before, so why start now? With the rate humans are going they would have eventually bombed themselves into extinction. What we are doing is saving the human race from complete annihilation; creating a world of stability and future. Humans have no future in the current state of the Earth. There is only hate, fear, greed, destruction, and death. This is not the world I want to live in. I no longer want to live in a world where emotions are used to twist the truth, sway the votes, and encourage irrational thinking. Humans aren't evolving any more. We are starting to go backwards: repeating history and continuing the same mistakes made by the generations before us. Fortunately, we can do something about our present bleak circumstance. We can change it. We can cure the human race of their biggest downfall, and save them before they kill themselves and the planet along with them.

You're an intelligent girl, Teslin, you know deep down that there is no other way for peace to ever grace this hellish earth of ours."

Dr. Lacombe, finished with his speech, sat back in his leather chair and waited for my response. I stared at him, hating myself for being attracted to such a monster. I could not let him sway me with his cold ideology. I could not allow myself to listen to his words, because when I did, it was hard not to believe them. 'Remember what he really wants,' the determination in my body was not yet ready to roll over and die. 'Remember what the Movement has taken from you. Do not be afraid, you have nothing to lose.' And I suppose I didn't, I was just one life. There were millions of others who could easily replace me. So I might as well go down fighting. This was my resolution as I replied to Dr. Lacombe's manipulation.

"You may think that, but I don't. And please, do not play innocent with me. You're not doing all of this for the good of the world. No, you want something more than peace, don't you? Tell me, Dr. Lacombe, what happens when the Movement does succeed, who will be the leader of the New World?"

This left the doctor speechless, but only for a moment. Then a devilish smile caressed his face, and a pretentious chuckle escaped from his lips.

"You're a clever girl, almost too clever. So I will give you a choice. You can either continue to be a part of our world-changing Movement, by simply going back to the way things were and acting as you have for the past month, or… you can die. You have ten seconds to decide."

"I don't need ten seconds. I already know that I don't want anything to do with you or your Movement."

"I'm sorry you feel that way, Teslin. It will be a shame not to have you around anymore. You did such great work."

My heart began pounding against my chest. My sweat glands went into overdrive as my mind processed the consequences of my choice… I was a dead woman.

The doctor cleared his throat to assure he still had my undivided attention, "Because I am a man of fairness and principles, I will give you exactly five minutes to say goodbye to your friends, and pray to whatever god you believe in, before I send the command for your immediate termination. Good bye, Teslin."

The screen instantly went blank and then shut off. I was staring at an empty dark wall, my mind completely vacant. It was as if my body completely froze over, not a muscle flinched; static, white noise immobilized my thoughts. I was physically and mentally paralyzed with fear. A prisoner to my very own emotions, I could do nothing but sit on my bed and stare helplessly at the ivory coloured wall. And that was when I heard a noise off in the distance. It was too muffled to comprehend at first, but I knew it was there as the voice grew increasingly louder with every second. The faint whisper continued to rise until it became both audible and comprehensible. My pupils dilated, and my hands began to tremor, for I realized that the noise was my own voice, and that it said solely one word: "Run."

And I did just that.

Stumbling off my bed, I frantically grabbed the backpack that hung in my closet and stuffed it with as much clothing as I could. The clothing was pure white and proudly bore the Cold Cognition emblem, but it would be needed to combat the cold if I survived. I had little else in my room but a water bottle, and a knife; so I packed those too, placing the knife inside my boot for easy accessibility. While I stuffed everything into the backpack, my mind busied itself with escape routes. I needed the quickest exit possible, and preferably the busiest so I could have a chance at slipping away unnoticed. My brain scanned all potential escape plans: the nearest exit was the main loading dock where we received and shipped general supplies.

There was always a constant flow in the large loading bay. Not to mention heavily armed vehicles which were used to escort the fully stocked semis once they crossed the town border. At least one vehicle was kept waiting in the bay for emergency back up. This would be my ride to freedom, or to my demise if fate chose to be cruel. Either way, it was the best option I had. A quick glance up at the wall clock told me that a minute and a half had gone by since I spoke with Dr. Lacombe. Less than three and a half minutes were left to escape. There was no time for revising the plan, it would have to work.

I briskly exited my room and marched down the hallway towards my destination. Moving at the fastest acceptable speed without looking suspicious, I made no eye contact with the people passing by me in the white maze. Keeping my focus forward and my facial expression neutral, I could only hope that no one stopped to question me, as they would certainly notice the trepidation in my voice and panic in my eyes. 'Stay calm, Teslin,' my logical inside-voice repeated over and over again. There was no use worrying myself into a frenzy and consequently ruining any chance that I had of escaping; time was running out. Thankfully the main loading dock was close. I reached it in less than a minute, and pressed my thumb over the fingerprint reader that granted or denied access into the bay. One of the perks about having commander status was guaranteed entry into all areas of the facility. As I watched the red bar of lights above the finger pad change to green, I wondered how far I would have gone to support the Movement if those children hadn't affected me so strongly. Then again, I suppose I should just be thankful that I would never have to find out. There was no going back now, even if I wanted to. Demanding my mind to focus on the present, I pushed open the heavy titanium door and entered into the last phase of my potential escape plan.

An aura of orderly chaos reigned over the entire loading bay, as it overflowed with bodies dressed in white busily unloading, loading, and sorting essential goods. The ten lanes of the bay were currently all occupied with semi-trucks. This was a good thing, that meant there was more than one empty escort vehicle for the taking. The apparent hectic activity was also a good thing. Since everyone was so intently concentrated on their given tasks, my arrival went virtually unnoticed. An ember of hope began to glow on top the wicker of my eternal candle.

'I might actually do this. Luck seems to be on my side for once! Maybe she's trying to make up for all the times she has abandoned me lately,' I thought to myself while I slipped past the bustling area around the semis and towards one of the open garage doors. The White Soldiers usually parked our vehicles near the overhead doors for quick and easy accessibility in case of an emergency. If luck still felt like being kind, I would find my ticket to freedom just around this row of large pallets that I currently crawled behind. I crouched low to the ground listening for footsteps. Hearing none, I rose up and slinked around the corner into the open to find that luck was indeed still my friend. Only five yards away from me was a row of parked SUVs, all sparkling white and fully armed with missiles. A smile arose on my lips without my permission. I couldn't hide the overwhelming wave of relief and happiness I felt at the sight of freedom. Now all I had to do was take it. Careful not to make a sound on the hard cement, I leaped towards the empty vehicles on tiptoe, the way a trained dancer would silently fly across a stage. I strategically went for one of the centre vehicles so I would be temporarily shielded on both sides from unwanted eyes. Once the SUV was in arms reach of me, I clasped the handle and opened the door. I had but one foot in the door when a low voice stopped me dead in my tracks.

"Where are you going, Commander?"

Frozen in absolute shock, I stood halfway in the vehicle as the blood drained from my face. But only for a second. For that's how long it took me to remember that I wasn't going down without a fight. Once the fight response registered in the rest of my body,

I stepped down from the SUV, slowly turned around to face the White Soldier standing behind me, and spoke in a cold, emotionless tone:

"One of our drones went down by the town border. I am going to repair it."

The White Soldier removed his helmet as I finished explaining myself. It took me a second to realize that the soldier questioning me was in fact, Calmar. Yet the sight of his alluring demeanour brought me no relief. The bonds of friendship (or in our case something a bit more than friendship) had little to no significance in the rational world. I knew that I could not rely on him for help.

"You're going by yourself without backup?" he asked skeptically. I desperately wanted to believe that he only asked this question because he was concerned for my safety, but I knew it was not the truth. The reason he asked was due to the fact that we only ever sent teams of two or more out into the snowy abyss. It was a legitimate reason to be leery of my actions. But now it was imperative to put his suspicions to rest.

"We just did a surveillance of the affected area with another drone. There is no enemy close enough to be alarmed. Therefore, I am perfectly capable of doing this task myself." I sounded confident and powerful, the way a Commander should. Ironically, I could thank Armena (the woman who taught me how to rate an individual human life, and dispose of those unworthy of the Movement) for the ability of thinking so quickly on my feet. Yet despite my dominant appearance, Calmar didn't look completely convinced. I had to end this conversation before it gave him any more reasons to be concerned about the legitimacy of my words.

"Anymore questions soldier, or can I go back to my given task?" I asked abruptly.

"Of course, Commander. But may I request to accompany you on your mission? There has been an increase of enemy drones in the area, and I don't think it's safe for you to go alone. It would be a shame to unexpectedly lose someone of your talent and importance."

I was about to object his offer, when I realized there was no time to argue with him. I had, at the most, a minute left before the command to end my life was given. If that happened, any hope of evading this Movement and finding a way to stop it would be lost. I had to leave now.

"Alright soldier, get in," I said, whilst stepping into the vehicle myself. "And be quick about it. I have a strict time limit."

"Yes, Commander." He walked around the front of the vehicle and hopped into the passenger seat. I threw my backpack in the backseat, not thinking anything of it.

"Do you have the required supplies to fix the drone in there?" he asked, referring to the backpack.

"Obviously." I hoped my curtness would shut him up. Too many questions would no doubt create a tear in my already thinning plan. We drove out of the loading bay and onto the snowy road, driving as fast as possible without raising his suspicions even more. I began thinking of ways to get rid of Calmar before he became a problem: pretending we arrived at the site and then running back to the SUV and driving off without him seemed like the most plausible and humane option. Though the most pressing concern I had now, was not Calmar, but time itself. I had seconds left before Dr. Lacombe contacted the Commanders, and then only a few moments more before a plan of action was in progress. Just then, the deadly road demanded my full attention as I turned a corner too fast and hit an icy patch. We went sliding across the road at the complete whim of the unforgiving black ice. Miraculously the tires found something to grip onto, and I managed to regain control of the vehicle just before we slid into the ditch. Paying more attention to the road now, and also concentrating on trying to slow my heavy breathing, I hoped that Calmar wouldn't say anything about my almost accident. But of course, he did.

"You could have avoided that mistake if you had simply decelerated on the turn."

"Thanks for the tip," I said through gritted teeth.

"Teslin, are… are you angry?"

I instantly felt nauseous. My stomach contorted itself into a serrated knot and consequently lacerated my insides. This was it. He finally caught me off guard. My cover was blown. After all, how could I explain this irrational burst of emotion when I wasn't supposed to have any? I hectically tried to think of something to say that would explain it, but I never got the chance as my father's voice suddenly filled the frigid air. His voice originated from the radio attached to Calmar's shoulder:

"This is a Code 11. We are requesting the immediate termination of Commander Teslin Grove. All members of the Movement are in critical danger of this individual. Therefore, you are authorized to shoot on sight. As of now, the Commander is classified as a deadly rogue citizen. Do not show her mercy, for she will show you none. I repeat, we are requesting the immediate termination of Commander Teslin Grove. This is a Code 11."

Before I even had time to fully register the words over the radio, there was a gun pointed at my head. I can't say I was surprised, but that didn't lessen the pain of betrayal that I felt in my heart. Calmar's past feelings for me were obviously not even a passing thought in his decision to follow orders without question. Our struggle for survival in the mountains, our fight against the Movement, the horrible-turned-wonderful night in front of the fire at Mrs. Rundle's, the way he kissed me before the Cold Surgery, all of that meant nothing to him. And I suppose it was best if it meant nothing to me as well. But I couldn't bring myself to forget him. Even now, as he held a gun to my head, I couldn't help but get lost in his mesmerizing brown eyes, wishing to taste his lips once more and to get the chance to finally run my fingers through his thick dark hair. The very man who wanted to protect me from the horrors of the Cold Cognition Movement, was now the man who wanted to kill me in order to help the Movement. This previously kind and righteous man who had become so meaningful to me, was now my enemy. 'What a twisted world we lived in,' I thought as Calmar pressed the gun hard against my skull.

"Pull over," he said in a voice without even an inkling of emotion.

Unfortunately, I didn't react fast enough because he then moved the gun down to my temple and pressed even harder.

"Now," he commanded.

The painful pressure on the side of my head was becoming unbearable to the point where it began affecting my vision. I had no choice but to do as he said. I slowly pulled over to the side of the empty mountain road and stopped the vehicle. The gun moved from the side to the middle of my forehead as I turned to look directly at Calmar. I wanted to face my killer head on. There was also a small part of me that hoped he would change his mind once he got the chance to stare into my eyes; that he would suddenly be reminded of our past together and join me in the fight against the Movement. But of course, luck chose to abandon me as she usually did, and Calmar calmly pulled back on the trigger. A shot was fired. Yet for some reason I didn't feel the sensation of death overtaking my senses. Instead, I heard a yell from Calmar as if he was in some kind of pain. And he was, because in that split second before he pulled the trigger, the fighter in me took control and slammed his arm down on the dashboard with such a force, that it caused him to drop the gun onto the floor. I didn't even give him a second to recover before I was punching and kicking in his direction.

There was no way I could overpower him with physical strength, I had to rely on the element of surprise and thinking strategically if I was to survive. It didn't take him long to fully rebound from my attacks and retaliate with deadly intentions. A warm fluid began to spill from my nose and mouth as his fists connected with my face. I was momentarily in shock as I had never been hit so violently in my life. He took advantage of my lapse in aggression and lifted me right up over the arm rest that separated the both of us. I was now sitting on his lap with our bodies pressed close together (which may sound romantic, except the excessively tight headlock that was cutting off my supply of oxygen sort of wrecked the mood). I knew I would not last long in such a comprising position. I had to act quickly, so I used my legs to push off the dashboard and angle myself in a way that squished Calmar up against the passenger door. During this maneuver I was able to temporarily loosen his grip around my neck, giving myself a breath of critical air before he could tighten his grasp again. My oxygen levels were dangerously low and I was on the verge of unconsciousness. 'Don't let him win so easily, Teslin! Fight for your life!' the voice in my head screamed. This was the motivational boost that I needed. The fading adrenaline in my body started to rise, and I was now determined to try one last time to break the lethal hold Calmar had on my neck. In one swift movement, I placed my feet onto the dashboard a second time and used all my strength to force him further into the door. Then I grabbed hold of the door handle and pulled it open. The door flew wide open from the pressure of our body weight pressed against it, and the two of us went tumbling out of the vehicle and into the snow covered ditch.

In the middle of our fall to the ground, I was able to escape the death grip around my sore neck and roll in the opposite direction of Calmar. Coughing and gasping for breath, I crawled as fast as I could away from him without looking back. Thankfully the adrenaline pumping through my veins made me numb to the pain of the freezing cold snow on my bare hands, and the biting air swirling inside my lungs. Nonetheless, I did not get very far when I heard the crunching sound of footsteps on the frozen ground coming from close behind me. It finally dawned on me that I could not run away this time. Running wasn't an option anymore. This time I had to face my fears. Gathering what courage and strength I had left in me, I just barely managed to stand up and face Calmar (who was standing menacingly only a few feet away from me). He barely had a scratch on him, and I was a bloody mess.

"You can't win, Teslin. Surrender now and I will make sure your death is painless."

I couldn't even stand up properly; my body shook violently from the overdose of adrenaline and shock. I was truly horrified that Calmar had just attempted to murder me, and still intended to do so. But after taking a few moments to steady my aching body, I eventually found my voice.

"I won't ever give up, Calmar! You know that. After all, you're the one who told me I should fight against this. And now you're fighting for it? How could you?!" I spit blood onto the ground in disgust. He didn't seem to be the least bit fazed by my words.

"People change their minds, Teslin. Especially when they accept the errors of their old ways. I have always let suppressed emotions steer my life instead of taking control of it myself. But now that I am cured of my faults and possess a rational mind, I have the chance to create a better world. And that is exactly what I will do. I will not let you or anyone else ruin our chance at peace while I'm still breathing."

"You're willing to kill me for lies, Calmar. You're conditioned to think the way you do. Because if you were thinking clearly, you would know that there is nothing peaceful about this Movement!" I was yelling now, because I was so indescribably frustrated of that fact that I would not convince him of the blatant truth. He was brainwashed in the most effective way possible. I was not going to change his mind, but that didn't mean I wasn't going to try.

"This is not a Movement of peace, but of power! We aren't helping people! We are controlling them! Can't you see that?!" I screamed.

At this point I was so blinded by rage that I hardly even cared about the blood dripping from my nose and into my mouth. Then

I realized how quiet Calmar was, and for a second I thought that I actually got through to him. My heart gave a start, all too hopeful that everything would be okay and he could still be mine. It beat faster as he stared back at me with a curious look, standing silent for a while longer before he spoke.

"The only thing I see is a person ruled by their emotions."

Suddenly the dam holding back fear and despair burst open and overrun my body, drowning my last spark of hope. A new kind of horror washed over my body as Calmar began walking towards me. There was no begging for mercy now. He came towards me with the empty eyes of a cold-hearted killer. I stumbled backwards as I turned to run away, but he was too fast. Lethal arms wrapped themselves around my neck and forced me to the ground. I lay on top of his body, flailing my arms and gasping for air as he patiently waited for my heart to stop beating. The kicks and punches I threw at him were utterly futile. He was too strong. I kept fighting but the effects from lack of oxygen began to take their toll, and the world began to fade away. Darkness welcomed me in a way that it never had before. I was truly dying. And of course, luck be cruel as usual, I remembered the knife hiding in my right boot only when I had but a few breaths left. So I used up the rest of my essence to grab the knife and stab it blindly behind me before the devil claimed my soul.

****

The darkness only lasted for a few moments before I saw light again. Ironically, I felt more pain than I had in life. I had assumed that death would be peaceful, but the excruciating pain that I currently felt (especially around my throat) said otherwise. 'How odd that breathing hurts so much in death. I would have thought it to be a lot easier… but I guess I've never been dead before,' I pondered as the light grew brighter. My eyes finally fully adjusted to their surroundings, and I could register a snowy road with a parked white SUV in front of me. Memories before my death told me that this was the place I died, which I thought was a strange thing. Shouldn't I be on my way to hell by now? Or maybe the reason why I lay at the place of my death was because I was a tortured soul, a ghost, that was doomed to roam the world until I was at peace with my unfinished business. This theory would definitely describe my situation: I had quite a lot of unfinished business.

While I began to further my ghostly hypothesis, I slowly became aware of a warm sensation on the skin of my neck and around my upper body. Instinctively touching the affected area, I found that the warmth was coming from a liquid substance that was on my neck and soaked into my coat. Moving my hand in front of my face for further inspection of the mystery liquid, I discovered my fingers to be covered in dark red. Blood. The warm liquid was blood. The blood-covered hand in front of me began to shake and I shoved it into the white snow beneath me. A horrifying realization began to shake not just my hand, but my entire body. In a dream-like trance, I pushed myself up off the ground and turned around to face the cold truth. It wasn't my blood. It was his. I wasn't dead. He was. He lay peacefully in the crimson coloured snow with a knife sticking out of his neck. I dropped to my knees and looked at him for a long moment. It took me a while to realize that my blood-covered hand was no longer shaking. Instead, it moved to embrace the body, and with the help of my other hand, lifted him up and rested his head against my chest. I closed my eyes and held him in silence. Nothing but the howls of the bitter wind could be heard. I wanted to stay there holding him in the peaceful quiet forever. But reality would not allow me such happiness. Reality told me to be grateful that I was still alive, and to run once again if I wanted to stay that way. It was time to say goodbye.

So I leaned over and kissed the top of his forehead. Then I rested my cheek on his, and whispered into his blood splattered ear:

"I'm so sorry."

I gently lowered his head back onto the red snow. And then for the first time, I ran my fingers through his thick, slightly curled, dark hair. It was something I had always wanted to do since the first time I laid eyes on him. Fate was a cruel, cruel thing. Everyone that I cared about were either dead or my enemy. The very man that I could have possibly loved was now dead. And I killed him. Not out of hate, but because of a cruel twist in fate did I have to kill him. I looked down at his face one last time. How could he still be so beautiful and strong even in death? It was just added salt in my already deeply cut wound. I wanted to scream out in anger. I also wanted to cry out in utter despair, but tears wouldn't be sufficient enough for a tragedy such as this. There is only one answer to a crime as horrendous as this. Revenge. And that is exactly what I was going to do. I stood up from the icy ground and looked down at the still body of Calmar. I hoped in death he had no memories of his past life, because he would be absolutely devastated to know that he died for something he did not believe in. He may have not stopped the Movement like he wanted, but I still could. I could save others from this cold, cruel fate. I didn't know how, of course, but that didn't matter. What mattered now was that I felt more determined than I had ever been in my life. If the past month had proven anything, it was that I was a force to be reckoned with.

'You can lead an army. You can make tactical and logical decisions. You don't give up. You are a fighter,' these thoughts overwhelmed my senses, because they were true. A chill went down my spine as I comprehended the truth. I could really do this. It only took one person to start a revolution. Why couldn't that one person be me? So with one last look at the brave man laying in the snow, I made him a promise that I intended to keep:

"I will end this."

With the listening Rocky Mountains as my witness, I would have to keep my promise now, or die trying to attain it. There was no going back. No giving up. I knew my decision was made as I got into the white SUV and started driving down the winding road. It was almost dawn, and the sky and snow-covered mountains radiated an eerie, dark blue colour. Even though I had no idea where I was going, the beauty of the mountainous landscape distracted my troubled thoughts about the unknown future. I felt strangely calm as I crossed the town border, like there was no one else in the world at this moment. Only me, the road, and the mountains. I breathed in deeply and felt grateful for these few seconds of peace. For the calmness of my surroundings did last merely seconds. As I could see the reflection of a drone coming in fast behind me in the rear-view mirror. The nuclear missiles that it carried on each of its sides told me that it wasn't a simple surveillance drone. This drone had one sole purpose. To seek and destroy. I had used these exact drones many times before to do my own dirty work. They were efficient and exact, a perfect weapon to use on your enemy. Unfortunately for me, this time I was not using the weapon. This time, I was the enemy. I was the target this drone was seeking to destroy, and these drones rarely missed. The only hope I had of surviving was to outrun it.

So I slammed the gas pedal down to the floor, and repeated to myself the promise I made only moments ago:

"I will end this."

CPSIA information can be obtained
at www.ICGtesting.com
Printed in the USA
LVOW12s0543240616
493964LV00002B/11/P